PAMELA BRITTON

on the
edge

HQN™

ISBN-13: 978-0-373-77103-5
ISBN-10: 0-373-77103-7

ON THE EDGE

www.HQNBooks.com

Printed in U.S.A.

AUTHOR'S NOTE/ACKNOWLEDGMENTS

I started writing my NASCAR books convinced that I could tackle such a project because I thought I knew all there was to know about racing.

Hah!

Since I try so hard to make my books feel "real," the tiniest little detail will ofttimes hang me up, such as: Exactly what gear would you be in when rounding turn four at Lowe's Motor Speedway? And how many gears does a race car have, anyway? What does a "spring rubber" look like?

For answering these questions and more, I wish to thank my darling Doombah Farkleface, who never minded my numerous e-mails. And also to her husband for never getting mad when I bugged him while he was working beneath race cars (I swear I thought I called the shop:)). You two are the best and I truly couldn't do this without you!

The number 16 Roush Racing team for putting up with me while in the garage, especially Jack Roush, who's never failed to greet me with anything but kindness, and Nicole Lunders, whose e-mails always make me laugh.

My friends at NASCAR, who've been so wonderful throughout the writing of my NASCAR books. Thanks for all the great catches, guys.

To my wonderful editor, Abby Zidle, for agreeing to work with me even though she knew nothing about NASCAR. Abby, I hope I've converted you into a fan. If not, at least you now know that "wedge" can be something other than underwear riding up your...well, *you know*.

Thanks also to Cherry Adair, Kelsey Roberts and Leanne Banks for sparking the idea for this book, and for all the help with its prequel, *In the Groove*. You guys are miracle workers.

Lastly, to my readers. I can now say with absolute certainty that NASCAR fans are the best in the world. Your letters and e-mails keep me going whenever I feel like black-flagging my NASCAR projects. THANK YOU!

Pamela Britton

on the
edge

If At First You Don't Succeed...
By: Rick Stevenson, Sports Editor

Not many race teams can claim a fan base the size of Newman Motorsports, founded by five-time NASCAR NEXTEL Cup champion Randy Newman, and carried on by his widow after Randy's tragic death four years ago. There isn't a NASCAR lover out there who doesn't wish the plucky Rebecca Newman well. So I'll have to admit it's been painful to watch her various teams struggle in the years since Randy's death. Her best finish was twelfth in last year's NASCAR NEXTEL Cup Series, and that was only because a major wreck took out half the field. Her NASCAR Busch Series team hasn't performed up to par, although they managed to post a top-ten finish a few months back. And her NASCAR Craftsman Truck Series team? Well, suffice it to say none of her drivers is making headlines this year.

And now she's hooked up with Sanders' Racing to hold what insiders have now dubbed *The Variety Show*—a spinoff of Roush Racing's *The Gong Show*.

I just want to tell the Variety Show folks one thing: don't forget the good old days.

Don't get me wrong. I understand that racing being what it is today, team owners are looking for more than just a good driver. And, heck, no one can dispute that Roush's Gong Show has produced some outstanding talent. I don't blame Sanders and Newman Motorsports for holding their own version of the talent search. And I'm all for it as long as the reality show can find the real thing—a wheel man, someone who can drive the wheels off a stock car. Who can pilot a vehicle nearly two hundred miles per hour and make it look easy. Who will draft, bump or nudge in order to win a race. Because the best part of any racing TV show—heck, the best part of racing—is drivers being…drivers.

But, hey. What do I know? I was never any good at anything but hockey.

PART ONE

The Child is father of the Man.
                    —William Wordsworth

PROLOGUE

TEN-YEAR-OLD Lindsey Drake stood before the glass entrance of Newman Motorsports and tried not to pee her pants.

Okay, so maybe this wasn't one of her better ideas. But what choice did she have? She couldn't just stay home in Kentucky and watch her father waste his life driving around some little dirt track. He was better than that. *Someone* had to point that out to him.

She just wished she wasn't so darn scared right now.

One of the glass doors swung open and Lindsey jumped back a foot. Cool air ruffled the hair beneath her baseball cap, her ponytail touching her back as she peered up at the man who exited. *Newman Motorsports* and the name *Sam* were embroidered on his denim-blue shirt instead of a name badge.

Uh-oh. Had he come to chase her away?

"You comin' in?" he asked.

Lindsey gulped. "Y-yes, sir."

"Well, then come on in here. We're letting all the cool air out and on a hot day like today that's not good."

It was hot, North Carolina's partly cloudy skies doing nothing to keep the heat at bay. "Uh. Okay," she said, ducking beneath the man's arm, the backpack she wore catching the edge of the metal door. "Sam" gave her a curious glance, then let the door swing closed behind him and headed toward one of the many cars parked in front of the two-story glass building, fluffy gray clouds reflected in their front windshields.

She was in. The whole way down from Kentucky she'd wondered how she'd do that. She'd have thought there'd be security. But nope. The big old chrome-and-marble lobby was all but deserted. Course, now it was on to the next step: Rebecca Newman.

"Can I help you?" a woman asked when Lindsey stopped before a reception desk. Rebecca Newman? Lindsey wondered, glancing up. Nope. Just a lady sitting behind a burgundy counter, sort of like the one at her doctor's office, only without the sliding glass windows, and with big block letters that said *Newman Motorsports* written beneath the countertop.

Lindsey let her backpack slide off her left shoulder, the straps dangling from the ends of her fingers. She looked for a place to set it down only to straighten suddenly, the pack slipping from her hand to thunk on the floor.

"Holy crawdad," she murmured, her mouth dropping open, a habit her daddy said would freeze her face into a permanent cow grimace if she didn't watch it. But at the moment Lindsey didn't care about cows because what she'd just glimpsed took her breath away.

A showroom full of cars sat behind a wall of glass to her left, T-shirts and other souvenirs hanging on the walls around them. The scent of newly printed shirts mixed with the nose-twitching smell of rubber tires, a smell both familiar and comforting thanks to the repair shop where her daddy worked. Some of the cars were the same ones she'd seen on TV. And they were right there—only a few feet away. There was the blue Dino Cereal car. She loved that car, and the cereal. A couple of years ago they'd given away Hot Wheels inside the box—

"Can I help you?" the woman repeated, her tone snapping Lindsey back to the present. It was the same tone Principal Evans used when he caught her running in the halls.

"Are you lost?" the woman prompted.

"Ah, no," Lindsey answered. She straightened her shoulders, speaking the words she'd practiced the whole way down. "I'm here to see Rebecca Newman."

And Lindsey was proud that she'd sounded firm, thanks to all her practicing. Frances Pritchert, one of the school's most popular girls and her archenemy, had called her a coward recently when they'd been playing volleyball and Lindsey had ducked out of the way of the ball. But she *wasn't* a coward, and this would prove it. Nothing was going to stop her from convincing Rebecca Newman, owner of Newman Motorsports, that her daddy was the best driver in the whole wide world—and that they should hire him.

"YOU'RE NOT going to believe this."

Becca Newman glanced up from the papers she'd been studying to see her assistant, Connie, standing in the doorway with the wide-eyed look of a person who'd just found Russell Crowe stashed beneath her desk.

"What won't I believe?" Rebecca asked, rubbing her temple with her left hand. She had a headache. Probably the financials she'd been studying for the past hour. Not good.

"There's someone out in the lobby who wants to see you."

Maybe it really *was* Russell Crowe out there. "Who is he?"

"It's a she."

Damn. Not Russell. "Does *she* have a name?" Rebecca asked. It wasn't like Connie to be so secretive.

Her assistant leaned forward, her short-cropped black hair swinging over one shoulder and swaying back and forth. "It's a little girl," she said, blue eyes still wide. "She's insisting on speaking to you."

"Insisting?"

"I'm not kidding," Connie said. "Sylvia downstairs said she trotted up to the reception desk like she owned the place, and then told Sylvia that she needed to see you."

"Where are her parents?"

"That's the best part," Connie said, looking almost gleeful. "Apparently, the dad's up in Kentucky and he doesn't know she's here. He's a race car driver and the little girl thinks you should hire him."

She what? "You can't be serious."

"As a heart attack. Sylvia demanded the girl tell her the dad's name and phone number, but she refused. Not until she talks to you. Sylvia wants to know if she should call the police."

And Connie looked so completely enthralled by the situation, Rebecca knew this wasn't a joke.

"Where is she?" Rebecca asked, standing, hands resting on her cherrywood desk.

"Downstairs. Sylvia didn't know what to do with her."

"Are you sure the kid's alone?"

"Positive. We're closed to visitors today, remember? Nobody's roaming around."

Closed. Monday. Of course. She'd known that, she'd just forgotten. Easy to do what with everything that'd been going on.

And now *this*.

"What should we do?" Connie asked as Rebecca started to move past, only to pause atop the checkered flag rug that stretched from desk to door.

"Bring her up— No, wait. I'll go downstairs and get her. Tell Sylvia once I've got her out of the lobby to call the police. The dad's probably looking for her."

Connie nodded, some of the amusement fading from her face. "Should she call 911?"

"No," Rebecca said, getting up. "At least I don't think so. Just call the police."

REBECCA DIDN'T KNOW what she'd been expecting. No. That wasn't true. She'd been expecting a teenager, one with piercings and tight-fitting clothes. She was *not* expecting a precocious-looking ten-year-old with hair as red as her own and freckles to match.

"Hi," Rebecca said with a smile. "Can I help you?"

The girl's blue eyes lit up, her mouth dropping open for a second before she appeared to swallow. Rebecca resisted the urge to glance behind her and see if maybe Hillary Duff stood there. "You're Rebecca Newman," the little girl gasped.

"That's me," she said, taking in the little girl's khaki shorts and the overlarge backpack she clutched. Then she caught sight of the shirt she wore and her stomach flipped over like a broken fan belt. Randy's smiling face stared out at her.

Rebecca had to force herself not to look away.

"I never thought—I mean, I was hoping you would, but I never thought I'd actually get to *see* you."

"Well, here I am," Rebecca said, forcing herself to focus on the problem at hand. "What can I do for you?"

"I… Well, I…" The little girl straightened. "May I please speak with you privately?" she asked, flicking her chin up and shouldering her backpack as if facing Mount Everest.

Rebecca tilted her head, silently impressed. Obviously the girl was scared to death, and yet she faced her as if nothing short of an atomic bomb would deter her.

What else could she say but "Sure"?

But it obviously wasn't the answer the child had been expecting. "Really?"

"Really," Rebecca said, fighting back an unexpected smile. "Follow me." She led the girl behind the reception desk and down a short hall. Rebecca peeked curiously at her when she thought the girl wasn't looking. Nothing out of the ordinary. She might be any young girl from American suburbia with her battered tennis shoes and equally battered black-and-pink backpack. She wore socks that slid down her ankles, socks the dull brown of cotton that hadn't been bleached in awhile. Red hair so bright it looked almost fake spilled out of the adjusting hole of her baseball cap, reaching nearly to her shoulder blades.

"You have an elevator?" the girl asked as Rebecca swiped her pass card at the double doors.

"We do. Keeps people from getting upstairs when we don't want them to," Rebecca said. The elevator doors opened instantly, fluorescent lights turning the girl's skin so pale Rebecca could see blue veins just below the surface. *The poor thing is terrified.*

"What's your name?"

"Lindsey."

"Well, Lindsey. Welcome to Newman Motorsports." She smiled again.

The little girl tried to smile back, she really did, but Rebecca could tell she wasn't up to it. It was an effort for Becca to keep from placing a reassuring hand on her head.

"This way," she said when the door slid open with a whoosh and an energetic *bing!*

Connie looked up from the second floor reception area, her blue eyes openly curious. But the little girl didn't follow; she was too busy gazing down at the showroom/souvenir shop through the windows that allowed visitors to peer into the lobby below, potted palms framing either side of the glass.

"You can see into the race shop, too, if you follow me."

"I can?"

"Yup," Rebecca said, sliding her pass card again and opening up a door to the left of Connie's gray Formica workstation. There were offices down the hall and a wall of windows to the left.

Once the showroom ended, guests could view the pristine race shop below.

"Wow," the little girl said. "My dad would go nuts."

"Is your dad a big race fan?"

Blue eyes looked up at her, and for a moment the fear faded, replaced by what could only be called derision. "He's not a fan—he's a driver."

"Oh," Rebecca said, her amusement returning. "That's right. Well then, yeah, he probably would go nuts. Nothing but state-of-the-art equipment down there."

Equipment I can't afford.

"So. What can I do for you?" Rebecca asked after she opened the last door at the end of the hall—her office. She took a seat behind the polished cherry desk, the dreaded financials she'd been studying shoved firmly aside. The truth of the matter was the little girl's appearance was a welcome diversion.

Once again, Lindsey's attention had wavered, so much so that she dropped her backpack with a thud right in the middle of the checkered flag carpet. "Ohmygosh," she said. "Is that the championship trophy?"

Rebecca didn't follow her gaze. She never looked at the oak trophy case anymore. It was just a reminder of a life she'd lived long ago. If she didn't still have sponsors to impress, she'd have long since torn the darn thing down.

"Yeah," she said. "One of them." And then she cleared her throat, trying to get her attention. "Lindsey, the receptionist downstairs told me that your dad doesn't know you're here."

"He doesn't," the little girl said, turning to face her, that stubborn chin lifting again. "And I'm not going to call him, either. Not until I tell you all about him."

"You mean convince me to hire him."

"Exactly." And Lindsey's gaze was so direct, so serious, Rebecca had a hard time thinking of her as a little girl. Such maturity. And a wealth of determination. Before Rebecca could think better of it she found herself saying, "Okay, then tell me about him."

Blue eyes went wide, disbelief taking the place of determination as for the second time that day she said, "Really?"

And here at last was evidence of her youth, for the high-pitched squeak sounded all too girlish. "Really," Rebecca repeated, biting back a smile as she leaned into her black leather and chrome chair.

"Well, he's only one of the *best* drivers in the whole wide world."

Weren't they all?

"He wins races every weekend."

That didn't mean much. There were tracks all over the country, tracks that a lot of drivers could dominate. "What does he race?"

"Oh, all kinds of stuff, but mostly late-model stock cars. Right now he's running a modified."

Just as she thought. Small-time.

"But before he started driving locally he did the Silver Crown Series."

That made Rebecca's brows lift in surprise. "Was he any good?"

To her absolute shock, the little girl said, "He almost won the year-end championship. Everyone said he probably would've if my mom hadn't gone and messed things up."

"Really," Rebecca said because despite telling herself it didn't really matter, by now her curiosity had been piqued.

"My mom left my dad for John Garreth."

"You're *kidding*."

"Nope."

"Wait a minute, wait a minute. The year your mom left your dad was the year John Garreth won the Silver Crown championship?"

"Yup. The same championship that got him hired by the Unsers. And the moment he went big-time, he ditched my *mom* big-time. Serves her right, too." There was bitterness in her voice, too much for one so young.

Becca leaned forward in her chair, completely thrown. She'd heard of Garreth. Who hadn't? The man was renowned in open wheel. Had been a major name for—what? Five, six years now?

"How old were you when all this happened?"

"Four. But I remember," she added quickly. "Daddy was never the same after that."

No one ever was when they'd been left behind. "I bet not."

"But he's still a good driver," Lindsey said. "When the NASCAR Elite Division came to town, Daddy kicked their butts even though he hadn't driven a car like that in ages. One of the guys in the series said he should run the Southeast Tour Series full-time, but my dad said it was too late. Only it's *not* too late. I read about a driver who didn't go big-time until he was thirty-two. That's the same age as my dad. All he needs is for someone to give him a chance."

"And you want me to do that?"

"Aren't you looking for someone to drive your cars?"

"I am, Lindsey, but I have to be honest. The drivers we're considering have a lot more experience—"

"So does my dad—"

"*Recent* experience," Rebecca added.

"So does my dad." And the little girl lifted her chin, her jaw thrust out so far, it was like she pushed against the world with it.

At Rebecca's raised eyebrows Lindsey said, "He drives me to school every day."

Which made Rebecca smile. "Okay. Well, while driving on the street can certainly be dangerous, I'm afraid it's still not the same."

Lindsey's chin began to sag. "Please, ma'am. Give him a chance—"

"Ms. Newman," Connie interrupted, the door swinging wide before Rebecca could stop her. "The police are here."

The little girl gasped, turning toward the door so fast her ponytail whipped her in the face. She took a step back when she saw the two officers, nearly tripping over her discarded backpack. Bratz, Rebecca noticed on the nylon flap.

"Lindsey," Rebecca said gently.

"You called the police?" the little girl asked, whirling back to face her, ponytail a step behind once again.

"Your parents need to know you're all right."

"Haven't you been listening?" Lindsey said, sudden tears causing her eyes to glisten. "I don't *have* parents. I have a dad. That's *it*. My mom left us and she hasn't been in touch since. And because of that my dad had to give up racing in the big leagues. He tells me that that's not true, but I know it is. When that man said my dad should go back to drive the Elite Division my dad told him he couldn't because his number one priority was me."

"Your daddy's right," Rebecca said softly, holding up her hand when one of the officers stepped forward. "You *should* be his number one priority."

"But that's not fair," Lindsey said, tears breaking free. "He's a good driver, ma'am. If you watched him you'd see that in a heartbeat. I know. I've watched stock car racing all my life. Ain't nothin' I don't know about the sport. I know your daddy was a big-time racer and that you met your husband in high school."

The little girl's face suddenly fell. "I'm sorry. I promised myself I wouldn't mention him and like an idiot I went and did it. I'm so sorry about your loss."

Rebecca's stomach kicked up a boulder that lodged right in her throat. "That's okay."

"He seemed like a nice man."

"He was."

"Just like my dad," the little girl said.

Becca felt her breath catch, the child's words

like a kick to the gut. Still… "But if that man at the track offered your dad a job, and he turned it down, what makes you think my offering him a job will be any different?"

"Are you kidding?" Lindsey said. "My dad thinks Newman Motorsports is one of the best in the business. We used to watch your husband win races all the time back when he drove for Sanders' Racing." The little girl's eyes had brightened again. "And I know from TV that you're holding some kind of open audition for drivers next month. I heard someone talking about it on the radio, too. They said you're doing it with Sanders' Racing, and so I figured if you don't want to give my dad a look, I'll go over to Sanders' next."

One of the officers cleared his throat; Rebecca glanced up for a second before she looked into Lindsey's eyes.

Don't, Rebecca. Don't do it.

But Rebecca knew only too well what it was like to want something for someone so bad you'd practically sell your soul to get it. It'd been like that with Randy. She'd given up so much of herself to help him with his racing career, even put off having kids.

And now it was too late.

"Pleeeease," Lindsey drawled, as if sensing Rebecca's weakness.

"All right," Rebecca said softly. "Tell you what. Give me your daddy's number and I'll ask him if he's interested in coming down and talking to me—but only *talk*. That the best I can offer."

"I'll take it," the little girl said, the smile that burst across her face so bright and full of hope and joy, Rebecca couldn't help but feel her own soul lighten.

It'd been a long time since that had happened.

CHAPTER ONE

"WHERE IS SHE?" Adam Drake asked the minute Rebecca opened her front door.

She'd been expecting him for the past half hour. Heck, Becca had even raced to meet him at the front door of her home when she'd heard his car pull into the driveway. What she wasn't expecting—oh, no, what she absolutely did *not* expect—was what he looked like.

Holy crawdad, she thought, using Lindsey Drake's favorite expression, one she'd heard time and time again since the moment she'd offered to bring the little girl to her home rather than have the police take her to a shelter when they couldn't reach her father right away. She'd been expecting someone pudgy, maybe even short a few strands of hair. Someone who spent the weekends stroking his ego by lording it over other drivers whenever he won a race, maybe even someone who made a play for the trophy girls. But this man…this man looked like someone the *trophy girls* made a play for.

"Mr. Drake. Hi. I'm Rebecca—"

"Where is she?" he asked again, looking like he just might push past her if she didn't invite him in soon. Good heavens, her head didn't even reach his shoulders. He was the Incredible Hulk, Mr. Clean come to life (but with a full head of hair), his small, flat nose set between brilliant green eyes.

Rebecca, really!

He was staring. No, waiting. Impatiently.

"She's, ah, she's in the back," she said. "Swimming," she added when he brushed by her the moment she stepped back from the door.

"Lindsey," his big voice boomed, echoing off her twelve-foot ceiling. "Lindsey Samantha Drake, answer me right now!"

"Lindsey Samantha Drake can't hear you," Rebecca said, tapping him on the shoulder. "Insulated glass," she offered by way of explanation. And there he went staring at her again. "She's through here," she said.

He followed her, Rebecca feeling—what?—as she walked in front of him. Maybe self-conscious, she thought as she led him past the living room and through a double-wide arch that led to the kitchen and ultimately the back patio. Yeah. That was it, she admitted. Self-conscious. She felt awkward in a way that reminded her of when she was a teenager and the local hunk had come into the McDonald's where she'd worked. She'd been so flummoxed she'd put his food in a Happy Meal box.

"Daddy," Lindsey called out the minute she spotted her father standing beneath the veranda, the two-by-two planks above their heads painting shadowy prison stripes on his light blue shirt.

"Lindsey Samantha Drake, get out of that pool *now*."

Rebecca jumped. The word *now* sounded like the crack of an uncorked motor.

Lindsey, who'd been in the midst of pushing herself out of the water, paused, droplets dripping down her face and arms and onto the faux stones that surrounded the kidney-shaped pool, the look in her eyes reminiscent of a squirrel caught in the KC lights of a truck.

"Now," he yelled again when she sunk back down in the pool.

"Mr. Drake," Rebecca said. "Is it really necessary to yell?"

"Is it necessary?" he asked, turning back to her. "Is it *necessary?*" he repeated and Rebecca thought for a second that his eyes might start bulging like a Chihuahua's. "Perhaps it's not necessary to *you,* but *I* just spent a full day scared out of my wits that someone had kidnapped my daughter, and so she ought to be grateful I'm just yelling instead of hauling her sorry butt out of the pool and paddling it with that pool net over there."

"You were supposed to think I was going to Brandy's house after school," Lindsey offered in a tiny little voice. "Just like I always do when it's an early release day."

Adam turned back to the pool. "Maybe," he said in a dead-calm voice, "you should have told Brandy that."

"I left a message on her cell."

Mr. Drake smacked his head. "Oh, well, that was good thinking, especially since Brandy's cell phone was taken away from her last night. And so no wonder she looked confused when she showed up on our doorstep right after I read your note about going home with her after school."

"Oops."

"Oops?" he repeated softly, taking a step toward his daughter. Lindsey sunk even farther into the pool like a hippo hiding from a predator. A guilty hippo. "Oops," he said again, glaring down at the pool. "I spent hours talking to every law enforcement agency in Kentucky, every miss-

ing persons bureau and every troubled teen counseling center alerting them that my daughter might be a runaway or might have been kidnapped or might have who knows what. They were this close to issuing an alert." He touched his thumb to his index finger. "Only suddenly I get this phone call from the world-famous Rebecca Newman—"

"I'm not really world famous," Becca said quickly.

"The world-famous Rebecca Newman explaining that, no, my daughter's not missing. Oh, no, she's in Mooresville, North Carolina, begging for a job." He drew his shoulders back, which made them look even more impressive, Becca noted. "For me," he said, stabbing at his chest with such force Becca winced.

"I'm sorry, Daddy," Lindsey said, peering up at him between thick red lashes, freckles looking more pronounced against her pale skin. "I was going to call you after I was done talking to Ms. Newman."

"Do you have any idea what you've put me through?"

"Uh…no?"

"You could have been mugged or raped or worse on that damn bus."

"But I wasn't—"

"You think that makes me feel better?" he asked,

leaning toward her. "You *could* have been. You *could* have been abducted. You could have been taken away from me, and if that had happened…"

Rebecca saw him lean back, saw him swallow, saw his hands clench. Then, like leaves suddenly too tired to hang onto an autumn branch, his anger just fell away. All at once he looked like he wanted to pull his daughter to him. And probably never let her go.

Rebecca felt her throat tighten.

"Go get your clothes," he said quietly.

Lindsey looked down, the crystal blue water stirring around her neck and lapping at her ears. Then she slipped from the pool, settling at her father's feet. She paused for a moment, as if waiting for him to do something—maybe pat her on the head, or hug her—and when he didn't, her shoulders slumped. Blue eyes that had looked so brave this morning looked perfectly miserable when they met hers. Rebecca resisted the urge to reach out and comfort her as she walked by leaving wet footprints in her wake. As much as she hated to see Lindsey's misery, she knew it was earned. From the sound of things, she'd put her father through hell.

The moment the door closed behind Lindsey, Mr. Drake turned to her. "Ms. Newman, I'm sorry for being so short with you. Obviously, I was anxious to see my daughter. I swear, since her mother left, sometimes she seems like ten going on thirty. But she's not just my daughter...she's my best friend, too. And if I'd lost her..."

He'd have felt as if his world were ending, and she knew the feeling well. "It's okay," she said, feeling suddenly tongue-tied.

It was then, as he faced her fully, that Rebecca felt it again, that same frisson of awkward awareness she'd noticed when she opened up her front door.

Adam Drake was a hunk.

And for a woman who'd seen every size and shape of race car driver—not to mention quite a few good-looking men—that was saying quite a lot. His black hair matched black lashes that lined his eyes in such a way it almost looked like they were rimmed with eyeliner. The irises between those lashes were the exact same color as the pool tiles that rimmed the water—a green so crystalline they looked almost translucent.

"No, it's not okay. After all you've done, the least I could do was hold on to my temper."

"It was understandable," she said, having a hard time maintaining eye contact—and yet unable to look away. "You've had a tough day."

He took a step toward her. "But offering to bring her home with you," he said. "To let her stay here with you while I drove down this afternoon, that was above and beyond. I still can't believe she took off like that—spent the whole morning riding a bus just to meet you—but I'm grateful for your help."

Why had she greeted him at the door wearing nothing more than a white bathing suit top and an after-pool skirt?

"I couldn't let the police take her to a shelter," she said, resisting the urge to go to her lounge chair and don the matching thigh-length top. "Not after talking to her. She's something else, your daughter."

"That's for sure," he said, swiping a hand over his face. "And she's also going to be grounded for the rest of her life when we get back home."

Rebecca smiled. "I have a basement that might double as a dungeon in the meantime."

"Does it have shackles?"

"No, but it might have a chastity belt. Never know when that might come in handy."

"Are you kidding? She's been wearing a chastity belt since she was two."

They both chuckled, Becca stepping forward and extending her hand. "Hi. I'm the not-so-world-famous Rebecca Newman."

"Adam Drake," he said.

And it was funny because Rebecca had expected his hands to be hard, perhaps even rough. They weren't.

She blushed.

"Nice to meet you," he said softly.

"Nice to meet you, too," she said, pasting a bright smile on her face before meeting his gaze again because, horrors upon horrors, she was certain he could see the color staining her cheeks.

"You're not what I expected," she said, her blush spreading down to her cleavage upon realizing she'd spoken the words aloud. Drat her fair skin.

"And you're not what I expected," he said.

"Is that good or bad?"

Now she was fishing for compliments? Golly, what was *wrong* with her?

"Good. Definitely good. The TV doesn't do you justice."

"Thanks," she said, finally looking away. She was never comfortable with comments about her looks. She usually felt like such a fraud when people called her pretty.

They lapsed into silence, the only sound the hum of the pool pump and the slurp of the gutter. Rebecca fished for something to say.

"Nice view."

PAMELA BRITTON 39

He'd beaten her to it, but that was good. "Thanks," she said again.

The house was situated at the end of a cove shaped like a comma so you could just barely glimpse Lake Norman through the trees. On a partly cloudy day like today, the water in the lagoon looked as smooth as unpoured paint. Becca loved the privacy the pine and oak provided. So had Randy.

Randy.

The name evoked the usual amount of sorrow. It also reminded her that she had no business gawking at Adam Drake.

"Don't be too hard on her," Rebecca said, trying for another change of subject.

"Well, she's lucky you agreed to take her in. I have a feeling any other team owner would have handed her over to the police."

"Oh, I don't know about that," she said, wondering what this man knew of her—and if he realized none of it was true, she thought with a wry smile. "We're all human when it comes right down to it, no matter what the press might say."

"I'll take your word on that. But in the meantime, I'm sorry to have bothered you. Lindsey has always been headstrong, but this takes the cake. I'll be sure to make her apologize and then I'm going to get her back to Kentucky and lock her in her room for the rest of her life."

She smiled. "Actually, I was impressed by her resourcefulness."

"This wasn't resourcefulness. This was stupidity."

"Oh, I don't know about that. She managed to get what she wanted out of me."

"And what was that?"

The smile on her face widened. "I made a deal with your daughter, Mr. Drake. In exchange for your name and phone number I agreed to sit down and talk to you about driving for Newman Motorsports."

ADAM THOUGHT he'd misheard her.

"She's pretty persuasive, your daughter," Rebecca Newman added.

So he *hadn't* misheard her. "You agreed to do *what?*"

Her smile widened, deepening the lines between her cheekbones and her nose, tiny dimples appearing near the corners of her mouth. It was a crooked smile, he noticed, the right side of her mouth lifting higher than the other.

"Talk to you about a job," she said, tipping her head sideways, the red hair he'd always admired on TV looking even prettier in person.

"Now why'd you go and do that?" he asked, though he did so more to distract himself from her toned and tan stomach than anything else. That stomach was perfectly accentuated by an off-white swimsuit, a matching skirt hugging her waist. And just at the waistline—was that a belly button ring?

Rebecca Newman, widow of NASCAR legend Randy Newman, wore a *belly button ring?* He didn't know whether to be shocked or intrigued.

"Look, Ms. Newman." He stopped himself from running his fingers over his face a second time. "There's no need to adhere to any bargain. I didn't raise her to bribe people into doing what she wanted, and I don't think it'd set a good example if you do what she asks."

"Don't you want to drive for me?"

Actually, what he wanted to do was quit stealing glances at her damn belly button ring. "I think you and I both know I'm not exactly qualified for the job."

"Why don't you let me be the judge of that?"

"You're kidding, right?" he asked again because he just couldn't believe he was having this conversation with her.

"Nope. Let's sit down over there beneath the umbrella while we chat."

"Ms. Newman, really, you don't have to do this," he said, a breeze kicking up and bringing with it the smell of water and pine. "You can tell Lindsey that you and I talked while she was gathering her things. Speaking of which, how much do I owe you for the swimsuit, 'cause I'm certain she didn't pack one for her trip down here."

"Call me Becca," she said, tipping her head in the opposite direction. "And you're right, she didn't pack a bathing suit, I bought it for her on the way home from the shop, but you're not reimbursing me and you're not slipping away, either. I promised your daughter we'd chat and so we'll chat."

"This is ridiculous."

"Not really," she said, taking a seat beneath a square umbrella, the water refracting light onto the underside and looking like a miniature Aurora Borealis. "Didn't you used to drive the Silver Crown circuit?"

"Yeah. But only for a couple years."

"A year and a half," she corrected, and at the raised eyebrows he shot her she said, "I checked up on you."

"Then you know how messed up that year and a half was."

"No. What I know is that you almost won the championship your first full season doing the circuit. And that you almost won a Southeast Tour race last month, despite having limited time in the driver's seat of a heavier car."

"But I didn't pull it off."

"Because you lack experience. But you almost won that championship. Probably would have, too, if not for your ex-wife."

He just about shot up from his chair. "Where the heck did you hear about *that?*"

"Relax," she said with another smile. "Your daughter told me the story. Tough break," she said. "Or should I say dirty pool on John Garreth's part? I've heard he does whatever it takes to win."

"No one forced my wife to sleep with him."

"No, but if another driver had come on to me while Randy was alive, I'd have decked him."

And there it was again—that brief hint of loss he saw lingering in her eyes.

You shouldn't be checking out Randy Newman's widow.

"Yeah, but you have class. My ex-wife didn't."

She seemed surprised, and then maybe flattered because he could have sworn she blushed. "Thanks," she said. And then her eyes narrowed. "I think."

"No. You do," he said. "I could tell the moment I first saw you."

"So why don't you want to drive for me?"

"I never said I *didn't* want to drive for you."

"So…talk to me. Tell me why I should give you a shot."

She was serious. "Look, Ms. Newman—"

"Becca," she quickly corrected again.

"Becca," he said, although it felt weird to call her that. "I would love a shot at driving for you, but the fact is, I can't."

"Because of Lindsey?"

"She's my first priority."

"She wants this for you."

"She has no idea what being a professional race car driver entails."

"She wants to find out."

"It's a pipe dream."

"Maybe," she said with another tilt of her head, red hair falling in thick waves over her right shoulder. "Maybe not."

"If you're about to offer me a job, save your breath."

"Actually," she said, "I'm not. What I'm about to offer you is seat time at next month's time trials."

He went speechless.

"They're in Charlotte and Martinsville, so you'd have to travel a bit. And you'd have to compete with other drivers." She smiled dryly.

"Insiders call it *The Variety Show,* but if you're any good, you might get a chance at making a team, and not just *my* team but a Sanders race team, as well."

Funny, as he sat there listening to her he could think of a thousand reasons why this was a bad idea—his job back home, Lindsey's schooling, his age—and yet the main reason he didn't want to do it had nothing to do with *any* of that.

He didn't want to do it because if he failed, he'd end up looking like a fool in front of Rebecca Newman, and suddenly that just wouldn't do.

CHAPTER TWO

HER DAD THOUGHT Rebecca Newman was hot.

Lindsey watched from the other side of the kitchen's sliding glass door, staring at her dad in amazement as he said something to Rebecca Newman and then looked away, just like Tim Roseburg looked away from *her* whenever they made eye contact.

Brandy, her best friend, said Tim Roseburg had a crush on her.

Lindsey felt her brows lift so high it tugged at her hairline.

Ohmygosh, she thought, bouncing up on her toes. If her dad thought Becca was hot, that would be so cool. Maybe he would ask her out. Maybe Becca would fall in love with him. Maybe they'd get married and they'd move to Mooresville and her dad would become a famous race car driver.

Or maybe not, watching as her dad shook his head, his expression grim.

It looked like they were arguing. Was he refusing to try out for Becca? She crossed her arms and tapped her foot, thinking, *Yup, that's exactly what he was doing.* He'd used the same expression last year when she'd asked him for a cell phone.

Darn it. Now what?

She just knew her dad would kick butt at the tryouts. And she knew Becca would really like her dad if given half a chance. Brandy's mom thought he was a hunk. Frankly, that grossed her out, but she had a feeling Brandy's mom was right. Women always gawked at her dad. But her dad didn't look at Brandy's mom like he was looking at Becca now. Not even close.

He shook his head again and Lindsey realized she better do something quick. "I'm back," she called after opening the door so fast, it banged against the dividing pane with a clunk. She winced and pulled the thing closed more slowly. When she turned back, both adults were staring at her.

Uh-oh.

"Hey, Dad, did Becca tell you she likes to fish? I couldn't believe that when I heard it because I didn't think there was a woman in the world who liked to fish. I know I sure don't, and so when I heard that I thought you two should go out fishing together."

Her dad's frown turned into a glower.

"Or not," she added.

"Are you ready to go?" he asked.

"Um, yeah. I suppose. But I thought maybe we could all sit down and have dinner…."

"I ate on the way here," he said gruffly.

"Yeah, but I didn't, and Becca told me her housekeeper makes these really great burritos—"

"We'll get something on the way," her dad said, standing, but he was so tall, he had to duck until he was away from the shelter of the umbrella.

"Ms. Newman, it was a pleasure meeting you. I'm just sorry it was under these circumstances."

"But, Dad, Becca was going to talk to you about trying out for her team."

"She did. I said no."

She wanted to run to her dad and shake him. She wanted to grab him by the arms and make his teeth chatter. She wanted to…she wanted to give him a time out.

"But, Dad—"

"No buts. I said no and that's that. Now, say goodbye to Ms. Newman."

Lindsey couldn't speak. She stood there for a full five seconds, waiting for her dad to change his mind. He didn't and she knew better than to argue.

She sighed, saying, "Goodbye, Ms. Newman.

Thank you for everything. I won't *ever* forget seeing the shop. Or looking through your photos. Or eating lunch with—"

"Enough," her dad said. "Time to go."

Becca ignored Adam's frown, stepping forward to say, "You're welcome, Lindsey," and then giving her a hair-nuzzling hug—wet, red strands and all. Lindsey wanted to cry. Becca Newman was so darn *nice*.

"If you ever need anything, don't hesitate to call. Your dad has my home number."

"Thank you," she said over the lump in her throat.

Becca stared down at her for a moment longer, kind eyes looking sad. Then she flicked her hair over her shoulder and turned to Lindsey's dad.

"Mr. Drake," she said, "I really wish you'd reconsider about next month."

"Sorry. We've imposed enough. C'mon," he said to Lindsey.

"Maybe we can come back and watch the try-outs?" Lindsey said, bouncing up on her toes in excitement at *that* excellent suggestion. And maybe she could get her dad to change his mind before then....

"Sure," Becca said at the same time her dad said, "No."

Drat it all. Why couldn't he make this easy? But

even her next suggestion—that they should stay the night and go and tour Newman Motorsports tomorrow before they left—was met with a firm, "No." Lindsey figured she better give up. Her dad had the same look on his face as he had when she'd tried backing his truck out of the driveway, crushing a few garbage cans along the way.

"Goodbye, Ms. Newman," she said.

"Bye," she replied softly.

But it wasn't until they were out and into his battered truck that he let her have it. He didn't yell. All he said was, "If you ever do something like this again, I swear, Lindsey, I'm sending you off to boarding school."

"I'm sorry, Daddy."

"And don't try that 'daddy' stuff with me."

"Okay, Daddy," she said.

"And don't, not for a minute, think that I'm interested in Becca Newman."

Okay, that shocked her enough that she felt her mouth drop open.

"Close your mouth," he said. "I saw right through you. You were trying to matchmake."

"But, Dad, she's really great."

"She's not my type."

"Yes, she is. She likes to fish. And she owns a race team—"

"And that's the most obvious reason why she and I would never work out. She's rich. And famous. And I'm not, repeat, *not* going to *The Talent Show,* or whatever they call it. Becca Newman is in a class by herself, and I'm not. The two of us getting together would be about as likely as Spock falling for a human."

"Who's Spock?"

Her dad stared at her for a second, blinked once, then said, "That's sad."

"Why?"

"You don't know who—?" Her dad shook his head. "Never mind," he said, starting up the car.

Lindsey crossed her arms in front of her, mentally saying goodbye to Becca's fancy house, mumbling under her breath, "Everything I went through, and he went and said no."

"I heard that."

"So?" she said in exasperation, sitting up again. "You've always taught me to never walk away from a challenge, and yet here you are doing it. What kind of example is that?"

He stared at her for another second before saying, "Clever."

Lindsey felt hope spark within her.

"But it won't work."

She released a huff of irritation as she faced the

windshield again, slamming her back against the battered leather seat so hard the springs squeaked.

"You're not being fair," she said.

"Not another word," he warned.

"But—"

"Not. One. More. Word," he warned. "We've got a long trip ahead of us and I want peace and quiet the whole way."

THEY MADE IT back to Kentucky in one piece, but Lindsey's boring life in Louisville seemed to be even grimmer after the excitement of her trip to North Carolina. Not even telling her best friend Brandy all about her trip to Newman Motorsports—and watching her eyes bug out when she told her she'd gotten to meet Becca Newman—had helped ease her disappointment.

When she heard her dad answer the phone nearly two weeks later she'd been thinking about calling Becca Newman herself. She had her phone number. And Becca had said she could call anytime. Maybe if her dad talked to her—

"Ms. Newman, really, thanks again for everything…"

Ms. Newman?

"…but I really can't."

"Can't?" Lindsey cried. "Can't what? Is it

really her?" she asked, hand outstretched toward the phone. "Can I talk to her?"

He frowned, shook his head, waved her away and said, "I appreciate the offer, however."

Lindsey gasped. Becca Newman was trying to get him to North Carolina again. She was sure of it.

"I can stay with Brandy," she hissed, bouncing up and down again. Her friend's mom would only be too happy to do her dad a favor.

He shushed her with his hand again, shaking his head.

"I can't, Ms. Newman. I really can't," he said. "But, again, I really thank you for the offer."

Yes, he could. All he had to do was say yes. "Let me talk to her," Lindsey said.

He shook his head again, but not at her, at something Becca must have said. "I'm sure Lindsey understands that sometimes adults have to put other priorities first."

"No, I don't," Lindsey said, bouncing so hard on the linoleum floor that her father moved with her.

"Lindsey," he hissed after covering the phone, giving her a stern look.

"But I *don't* understand, Dad," she said. "I don't understand why you're saying no to an opportunity that might end up changing our lives." She grabbed his free hand, squeezing tight. "That might have a huge impact on our future. On *my* future. How can you turn your back on that? How can you just walk away from something that might end up allowing me to go to college?"

His eyebrow changed from slashes to straight lines. He looked like he might say something, but then he said, "What?"

Becca must have repeated what she said.

"That's absurd." And then, "*A thousand dollars?* Just to go down there?"

What was this? Lindsey thought. Was Becca Newman offering to pay her dad? Oooh, smart move on Ms. Newman's part. Lindsey *knew* she liked that woman.

"Look, I appreciate the offer—"

Lindsey dove for the pile of bills her dad stashed near the phone. It didn't take her but two seconds to find the one she was looking for, waving the Final Notice bill from ConEdison in front of her dad's face.

"A thousand dollars," she hissed.

Her dad closed his eyes. "The most I can do is promise to think about it."

Holy crawdad! Promising to think about it was almost like saying yes, at least in her dad's world. They couldn't afford to say no, and her dad knew it.

Maybe her life wasn't over after all.

CHAPTER THREE

TWO WEEKS LATER Adam found himself parked outside the Concord, North Carolina, racetrack, the Speedway's grandstands stretching above him, intimidating even when viewed from the outside, their jagged edges framed by a partly cloudy sky.

Adam rested his hands against his truck's steering wheel and stared up at those grandstands as if they might collapse should he be so bold as to approach.

He didn't move.

From the other side of the twelve-story structure came the sound of a race truck roaring around the track. They'd already started.

He'd known they would have. Hell, the other drivers had all been bused here earlier in the day. Adam hadn't wanted to leave Lindsey alone for any longer than necessary, so Becca had excused him from the pretest tour of the race shops and the briefings—those he'd received via mail. Frankly, she'd probably excused him because she really didn't want him to show up. And why would she? They had plenty of qualified drivers to see that day. Rebecca Newman probably hadn't even noticed his absence.

You're a fool for wondering if she thought of you at all.

But he couldn't deny the fact that she was part of the reason why he was here.

Face it, Adam—you're plumb terrified.

His cell phone rang, causing him to jump. He glanced down at the caller ID, recognizing Lindsey's best friend's cell phone. He didn't know why she'd asked for a cell phone when she always used her friend's. But Lindsey was the other reason why he was here and so he answered.

Silence greeted his *hello* and then, "You don't sound like you're at the track."

That little observation was undoubtedly the result of too many Saturdays spent out at the local speedway. "Actually, I'm sitting outside of the track," Adam admitted. He felt like a kid caught sneaking out of school.

"Da-ad. It's eleven o'clock. You should have been there three hours ago!"

"And you should be at school."

"I'm at lunch."

"And talking on the cell phone at school isn't allowed."

"I'm in the bathroom. Nobody can see me."

"You still shouldn't be—"

"Da-ad. Don't change the subject. Why aren't you at the track?"

"I got lost."

"Sure you did," she said, and in the background he heard the sound of a toilet flush.

"You really are in a bathroom."

"You're trying to change the subject."

"I got lost," he repeated, suddenly feeling like the child in the relationship. The truth was he *had* gotten lost, but not enough to make him three hours late. He'd been driving around—thinking.

"You should have brought me along," Lindsey said. "I'd have made sure you got there on time."

"Lindsey, don't start," he said, his hand clutching the black steering wheel, the thing warming beneath the hot North Carolina sun. "I told you there was no way you were missing another day of school, not after your last trip down here. Consider this part of your punishment."

"You just don't want me there," she said.

He didn't. He couldn't stand the thought of his little girl, the one who stared at him with hero worship in her eyes—most of the time, anyway—watching her dear old dad fall flat on his face.

"It's better this way."

She sighed. One of those you're-so-wrong-even-if-you-don't-know-it sighs. Adam realized he'd better stop her before this conversation spiraled into a complete role reversal.

"Lindsey, I've got to go. Obviously, I'm late."

"Then why are you sitting outside the track?"

Because I've got stage fright.

"I'm waiting to go through security." And now he was lying to his little girl.

"Oh," she said. And when she spoke again Adam could hear the longing in her voice. "Good luck, Dad," she said.

"Thanks, Lin."

He started his truck again, his foot hovering over the accelerator. But in the end he realized he had no choice. He had to go through with it. As humiliating as it would be, if he didn't try taking a lap or two Lindsey would be devastated. Plus, what kind of an example would it set if he chickened out? This was the opportunity of a lifetime—as she'd so aptly reminded him—and the fact that Lindsey had somehow managed to orchestrate it only made it all the more important.

He had to do it. *Dammit.*

"WHERE IS HE?"

"Where's who?" Cece Sanders asked, tipping her head back to peer up at Rebecca.

They sat on top of pit road wall, a clipboard with two built-in stopwatches across the top resting in Cece's lap, a pen in her right hand. Becca thought Cece looked like part of the race team with her Sanders' Racing baseball cap and white shirt, her blond hair pulled back in a ponytail. Out on the track, last year's runner up for the ARCA title did his best to impress Blain Sanders, Cece's husband. And, of course, Becca herself, but much to Rebecca's chagrin, she hardly paid attention.

"You're waiting for *him*, aren't you?"

Becca shrugged, wishing she had a clipboard and stopwatch so she could pretend interest in something else. Alas, she'd decided to let Cece keep the records that day.

"You are, aren't you?"

"Yes," Rebecca admitted with a sigh.

Becca saw Cece bite back a smile before she turned away, her eyes kept in shadow thanks to the bill of her cap. A second later a blurry streak of red, white and blue crossed the start/finish line— a race truck Sanders' Racing had built just for this tryout roaring around the track. She should be listening to the conversation between driver and crew: seeing how well the kid who drove articulated his truck's performance, or if he sounded flustered or laid-back. Heck, seeing if he could talk and drive at all. Some drivers couldn't, or just didn't, and that was okay—but only to a point, because in the end it was a team effort that won you races, and you couldn't have a team if there was no communication. So at the very least she should have a receiver plugged into one ear like Cece did. She *should,* but she didn't. Instead she glanced toward the infield, scanning the cars that were parked between the garage and a nearby outbuilding, all the while wondering for the umpteenth time where he was.

"That was a good lap," Cece said as the truck raced toward turn one. "Good enough to qualify fifth or so at last year's Craftsman Truck race. Not that you care." When Cece looked back the teasing smile was still in place.

Rebecca looked away, her gaze lighting on the crew members who stood a little farther down the wall. A square, green canopy over the tops of their head cast a Martian-like glow over their faces. Behind them, a bit farther down pit road, a tent had been erected, the ten or so drivers left to go stand around pretending to ignore the others. A few of them had family members with them, but for the most part it was a solemn group.

Becca's gaze moved back to the pit crew. Blain Sanders pressed down on his headset, his lips moving as he spoke into the mic.

"What's Blain saying?" Rebecca asked, trying to change the subject.

Cece huffed, the sound part snort, part chuckle. "Wouldn't you like to know?"

"Cece—"

"Admit it. You have the hots for that little girl's daddy."

"I do not," Rebecca said. "Now stop. You're stressing me out."

"Well here's something to add to that stress then. I just saw a truck exit the infield tunnel—"

"What? Where?" she asked, turning and peering through the twelve-foot-high, black, wrought iron fence that Becca always thought looked a bit out of place at a racetrack.

"Right there," Cece said, pointing.

Becca turned. Sure enough, a truck headed toward the garage, the familiar white pickup looking as beaten and battered as the first day she'd seen it sitting in front of her house.

Adam. Tingles spread through her body causing the ends of her fingers to vibrate. *He was here.*

"You want to go greet him?" Cece asked with a teasing grin.

"No," Rebecca said, looking away.

"Fine. I will."

"Cece—"

"Here," Cece said, shoving the clipboard and pen in her direction, the cord that dangled from her ear swinging around. "I'm dying to meet the man, anyway."

"But, Cece—"

"See you in a few." And then her smile turned positively wicked. "With your boyfriend in tow."

"He's not—"

But Cece was already gone, trotting off with a quick wave and a smile. Rebecca flatly refused to watch her walk away.

"Drat that woman." She should have never told her about her encounter with Adam Drake and his daughter. She should have told her friend that she'd heard about his driving through the grapevine. She should have just added his name to her list without any fanfare. But, no, she'd shot off her mouth and—

The race truck roared around turn three.

"Crap," Rebecca said, fumbling with the clipboard in time to record the elapsed seconds on one digital clock and then immediately starting up the second. They had electronic timers on all the cars, but Cece liked to do it the old-fashioned way, too, just in case.

Concentrate, Rebecca. Don't glance behind you. Don't. Just focus on what you're here to do.

So when she was done recording the lap time she forced herself to study the pages beneath the top score card. Of the drivers set to drive today, eight had already gone, leaving twelve to go, one of them Adam Drake. Four of the drivers had been pretty dismal, at least judging by their lap times and Cece's scrawled notes. Three had been average. Only one looked good and that was the driver currently out on the track, one Sam Kennison, Rebecca saw, flipping back to the top page and studying the kid's stats. Twenty. Blond hair and blue eyes. Cute, judging by the photos they'd taken earlier. And personable, judging by the Q&A they'd had him fill out. Gone were the days when all that mattered was a driver's ability. Now you had to consider marketability and sex appeal, too.

Adam Drake had sex appeal in spades.

"Hello, Ms. Newman."

The clipboard slipped from her hand. Rebecca lurched and caught it, the metal back jamming against one of her long fingernails and causing her to gasp. When she straightened, she knew her face glowed as brightly as an overheated brake pad.

"You okay?"

"I'm fine," she said. It didn't help matters that Cece stood behind Adam, her hand covering her mouth, her eyes laughing loudly even if her mouth did not. "And I'm glad to see you made it."

"I did," he said, giving her a smile that exposed wonderfully masculine teeth.

Masculine teeth? What the heck was that?

"Sorry I was late. I got a little lost on the way out."

"Where's Lindsey?"

"Still grounded after that little stunt last month."

"Oh, too bad. I was looking forward to seeing her." She sounded too fake. Too chipper. Too…

Okay, just admit it. Too smitten.

It didn't help that Cece had stopped laughing. She began to move her hands, mimicking sign language from *Austin Powers. You complete me,* she pantomimed.

Stop it, Becca warned with her eyes.

But Cece didn't stop anything and so after a glance at Adam—who was busy watching the truck on the track, thank God—Becca lifted a fist and narrowed her eyes for good measure. She managed to drop her hand just in time for Adam not to notice—she hoped.

"Here," Rebecca said, shoving the timing board and pen back at Cece. "You can have this back. I'll go introduce Adam to Blain."

"Oh, great. I'll go with you," Cece said, having to shout over the sudden roar of the truck as it came down pit road. All three of them paused as Cece prepared to record the lap time, but the truck was coasting.

"I guess he's done," Cece said as the engine abruptly shut off. He rolled down pit road and into his pit stall.

"Who is that?" Adam asked.

"Sam Kennison," Cece answered, falling into step with them, Adam in the middle. Adam didn't see it, but Cece leaned back, lifting her eyebrows in a "He's cute" kind of way.

"Kennison. Kennison. Is that Carl Kennison's kid?"

"It is," Cece said. "Do you know him?" she asked as the truck finally came to a stop.

"I've bumped into him on a track or two."

"Well, that's him waiting to help Sammy out of the truck," Cece said.

Becca followed Cece's and Adam's gaze, watching an older man with gray hair and a middle as big as a Bridgestone tire rush forward to lower the net, taking the steering wheel, the driver's helmet and then the HANS device a second later.

"Outstanding," he was saying to his son as they walked up, placing the helmet and HANS on the roof, his face flushed with pride. When the driver emerged, Becca ran her eyes over him, thinking the kid didn't look a thing like his old man. And he really did look like a kid, Rebecca noted. No five o'clock shadow in sight.

Holy crawdad, she felt old.

"You kicked ass out there, son," Carl said, clapping Sam on the back of his beige firesuit with *Addeco Insurance* sewn onto the front.

Carl turned back to Blain Sanders, who stood nearby. "Told you the kid could drive. He's a chip off the old block. Give him a couple years and he'll be vying for a Cup championship." Carl's eyes swept the group of people surrounding Blain, passing by Adam only to return again with such swiftness it looked like magnets had drawn them back.

"Holy shit," he said to Adam. "What the hell are *you* doing here?"

Adam's shoulders were suddenly stiff with tension. Not surprising. It wasn't so much what Kennison had said, but the way he'd said it. As if Adam had no business being in Concord.

"Actually, Mr. Kennison, Adam's here to test," Becca said.

Silence. Nobody spoke. "You're kidding, right?" the man asked, his eyes going from hers to Adam's. "I didn't see his name on the list."

"A late addition," Cece said. "We've heard some great things about his driving."

"We have?" Blain asked.

Cece gave her husband a look perfected by years of marriage. It said: *Don't contradict me, oaf.*

Blain said, "Oh, yeah. We have."

Becca would have laughed if she wasn't too tense to do more than nod in agreement.

Carl glanced back at his son, motioning him forward. "Sammy, come here and meet the man who cost me the Kentucky Speedway year-end championship."

Ah. That explained it.

Adam stepped forward, a pleasant smile on his face. "Aw, now, Carl. You're not still grumbling about that, are you?"

Carl's eyes narrowed, his ruddy cheeks turning redder. He was definitely still grumbling, Becca thought. Grumbling like Mt. St. Helens before it erupted. But a glance at his son must have reminded him this was neither the time nor the place to rehash the past.

"Nah," the older man said. "I figured we were even when I introduced your wife to John Garreth."

Out of the corner of her eye, Becca saw his son and Adam stiffen, the son warning, "Dad…"

"They sure hit it off, didn't they?" Carl added.

Okay, that does it, Becca thought.

She stepped forward and with as pleasant a smile as she could muster, said, "Thanks for coming today, Sam. Mr. Kennison," she said, giving the older man a look that was as cold as nitrous oxide, "it was a pleasure to meet you. We'll be in touch with Sam as to whether or not he's made the cut for tomorrow's testing."

Blain and Cece exchanged glances. They usually sat down and chatted with the drivers after their session, letting them know if they might have a shot at day two's test—a full day of media training, photo shoots and television taping.

It was apparent Carl Kennison expected that very thing because he looked as if he'd just been insulted. "Don't you want to talk to my boy?"

"No," Becca answered, cutting off whatever Blain had been about to say. "We have a lot of other drivers to see today, including Mr. Drake here. We'll call you."

Which was not the norm, but she didn't care.

She turned her back on the man, saying to Adam, "If you want to suit up, the bathrooms are open at the end of the garage. You're in the last group to go, so you have a bit of a wait."

But Adam still stared at Sam's father, and Becca could tell he wanted to say something more—probably something insulting.

She stopped him by turning and then pretending to almost collide with Mr. Kennison. "Oh, Mr. Kennison," she said pointedly. "You're still here. I'm sorry. I thought you'd left." She turned to the crew members standing near the wall. "Boys, put a fresh set of tires on it and take her back to stock. We need to get a move on or else we'll be here all night."

Finally Mr. Kennison seemed to get the message, though she could tell his son knew exactly what had caused their abrupt expulsion from pit road. She could hear the kid all but growling in his father's ears as they walked away, Sam shrugging out of the top portion of his firesuit and tying it around his waist. Becca smiled to herself.

"You mind telling me what that was all about?" came a low, slightly irritated voice.

Becca glanced up, Adam having leaned so close to her head that their lips almost touched when she turned.

She stopped breathing for a moment.

"What do you mean?" she managed to gasp, catching Cece's amused eyes behind him.

Adam must have followed her gaze because he turned to Cece and Blain and said, "Excuse us a second," before hooking his arm with hers and marching—yes, marching—her away.

Uh-oh.

CHAPTER FOUR

"I DON'T EXPECT favoritism, Ms. Newman," Adam said.

Rebecca Newman's eyes widened in surprise. "Favoritism? Mr. Drake, I assure you, you'll be receiving no preferential treatment here."

"That's not what it sounded like," he said as they stopped near an opening in the black fence that separated pit road from the garage, heat radiating up from the asphalt. How could she look so calm and cool in her sparkling designer jeans and frilly white top?

Her lips had parted, her face turning pale and then pink and then bright red. And all at once Adam felt amused. No. He felt flattered, because judging by the guilt that poured into her green eyes, she *had* been defending him.

"I don't need you to fight my battles for me," he said softly, admiring the way her red hair fell past her shoulders, the ends curling near her breasts. "I appreciate that you've taken such a shine to my daughter that you feel a certain measure of loyalty to me, but it's not necessary. We both know I'm probably going to make a fool of myself today. Heck, I didn't even make a hotel reservation for tonight 'cause I know I'm not going to be around."

The blush had started to fade, her pretty mouth clamping together before her face softened. Oddly enough, she appeared to look relieved. "Loyal to your daughter. Yeah. I guess that's what this is."

What *what* was?

"But Carl Kennison is an ass," she added, her cultured accent making the word *ass* sound high-falutin. She tilted her head saying, "And you're not going to make a fool of yourself."

He scratched the back of his neck, his nervous habit. He wondered if tilting her head was hers. "Thanks for the vote of confidence, Ms. Newman, but we both know it's a crapshoot."

"I told you to call me Becca. And I'm not in the habit of saying things I don't mean. You're more than qualified to run a few laps around here. Heck, Adam, you could hardly do worse than some of the other drivers we've seen."

"Oh, yeah?"

"Yeah," she said, lifting her hands to her throat and pretending to choke.

He smiled. From behind them came the sound of the race truck's engine, both of them turning in time to see a crew member snap the window net in place. Smoke drifted out of the tailpipe for a second, momentarily obscuring the yellow and red grandstand seats in a gray haze.

"I don't know why I came." He hadn't meant to say the words out loud.

"You'll do fine," she said, placing a hand against his arm, only to draw it away quickly. But the image of her manicured nails and smooth, white skin against his own tan arm imprinted on his mind. She didn't have the hands of a woman who worked around race cars. Heck, she didn't look like a woman who hung around a racetrack at all.

"Would you do me a favor?" he asked, having to remind himself that they were from two different worlds, and that after today he'd never see her again.

"What's that?" she asked.

So beautiful. And way, *way* out of his league.

"Would you tell Lindsey that I did okay? No matter what happens?"

She seemed to lean back a bit, her face going momentarily slack before softening, the look in her eyes kind. "Of course," she said softly.

"Thanks," he said. Behind them, the engine revved once before the driver put it in gear and took off down pit road. Once again they turned and watched.

"You know," Adam said, watching as the red, white and blue truck headed toward the track, "I really don't mind making a fool out of myself. That I can handle. I'd just hate for Lindsey to think her dad is a total idiot."

"You're not an idiot."

He looked back at her, wondering how a celebrity such as herself had stayed so nice.

"Although I feel I should tell you that if you break it, you pay for it," she added.

He laughed, saying, "I might be washing a lot of dishes then."

"Given the size of my kitchen, that might come in handy," she said, a smile coming to her face, chuckles slipping from between her own lips.

"Wait a second. I might have to wash *your* dishes?"

"Of course."

"That does it," he said. "No deal."

She laughed when he pretended to turn away, grabbed his arm and said, "I was just kidding."

He couldn't help but take a moment to simply stare, and to think to himself how bizarre it was that he was standing on pit road with Becca Newman. "Well, I guess that makes us even because I was just kidding about being a race car driver."

"Yeah, right," she said.

"Seriously. I've never raced anything in my life. My daughter and I cooked up a scheme to see if we could get you to put me behind the wheel of one of your trucks."

Her eyes narrowed. "Liar. Not only did Carl Kennison recognize you, but I did a Google search for you the day your daughter came to visit. You've not only driven modifieds, but you've driven everything in between, too."

"Dang," he said, shaking his head. "I was hoping to freak you out."

She smiled back. But just as suddenly as his mood improved, it deteriorated again. "Guess I better go change," he said, the roar of a single engine getting louder and louder as the driver out on the track exited turn four.

"Yeah. And I need to watch him," she said, flicking her chin toward pit road.

"I'll be back."

"Adam," she said after he'd turned away.

"Yeah?"

"You really will do fine."

YOU REALLY WILL DO FINE.

Adam stared out at the windshield of the test truck, his hands clenching the steering wheel with such force the tips of his fingers started to tingle, though that might be in part because the motor revving beneath the hood felt like a jet engine.

Relax.

Yeah, right. This was the biggest moment of his life, second only to when Lindsey had been born. No chance in hell that he was going to top that, so why not just relax?

"Okay, Adam," Blain Sanders said right as Adam tried to scratch the back of his neck. "Just take it easy at first. Get a feel for how she handles. Becca tells me you've been racing modifieds and, as you know, they're way lighter than trucks. I don't think I need to tell you that it's gonna feel way different than what you're used to driving."

So what the heck was he doing here?

But he wouldn't go down that road. Nah. He owed it to Lindsey and to Becca Newman not to make a total ass of himself. So all he did was open the mic and say, "Roger."

"Go ahead and take her out when you're ready."

He didn't think he'd ever be ready. But he put the truck into gear, anyway, sinking into the padded seat that had been adjusted to fit his tall frame and

easing the vehicle forward. It was a real race car—
all right, truck. But he'd raced just about everything
there was out there. He could handle this.

Adam shifted through the gears, the two walls
that framed pit road quickly running out until he
was suddenly there, out on the track.

At a speedway.

Holy shit.

To his right the dark gray posts that held the
catch fence slipped by faster and faster. He'd seen
the sight on TV a thousand times before.

But never like this.

And even though the track's name had changed
in recent years, it would still always be Charlotte
to him—and it seemed surreal to be driving on it.

Easy, he told himself. *Just be cool. Get a feel
for it, like Sanders said.*

Sanders. From Sanders' *Racing.* One of the
most famous owners in the history of the sport.

The truck bobbled.

Concentrate!

He shifted into fourth gear. It didn't matter who
was watching him, he told himself. He wasn't
here for Blain Sanders, he was here for his
daughter.

Taking a deep breath, he let the asphalt slip
beneath him, faster and faster, bringing the truck

up to speed. Down the backstretch again. Press the accelerator. Back off near the corner. Use the brake to throw into turn three.

Damn near the same.

It felt damn near the same as driving a modified, only faster and…different. Faster and yet slower because as his vision narrowed, the world outside became a blur so that speed became hard to gauge. He headed out of turn four, the grandstands unrecognizable now because he went so fast—his left foot hovering over the brake, right foot easing off the gas, but not a lot. He didn't need to ease off because he was in control, the truck responding to his hands as if he'd driven race trucks his entire life.

Maybe in his dreams he had.

"How's she feel, driver?"

Adam headed into turn two again, the back end breaking loose. They'd have to fix that if he wanted to improve his lap times.

"She's loose out of the corner. And really, really tight going in."

"The last driver thought the truck was loose going in and tight coming out."

"Well I don't know why he thought that when it's pushing damn near into the wall."

As if to illustrate his point, the truck drifted into the rubber marbles of turn one, Adam easing the truck down and back into the groove. Close. He'd almost lost it. And when he stabbed the accelerator, it broke loose yet again.

He tried to drive the truck that way for a couple laps, his spotter rattling off lap times—times that weren't all that great.

"I'd like to come in early," he said. They were given twenty laps to feel out the truck, but Adam didn't see the point in hanging out.

"Roger that," Sanders said after a momentary silence. "You can come in early if you want."

Less than a minute later he was on pit road, the truck rolling to a stop in the makeshift pit stall.

"What kind of adjustments do you want?" Sanders asked, leaning into the window as the truck idled.

This was part of the test, Adam realized, because Sanders knew what adjustments to make. In fact, he probably knew better than Adam did—this was *his* truck.

"Loosen her up for me with a track bar adjustment, if you don't mind. That ought to fix the tight going in problem."

"Track bar? You sure you don't want to take out some wedge first?"

"Nope. I don't want to lose the forward bite. Let's do the track bar first and see how that helps."

He caught a glimpse of something in Blain's eyes then, something that looked like approval. "Roger that," Sanders said. "Loosen up that track bar," he told the crew.

It wasn't like a race day pit stop—this was a test session and so everything was more leisurely—but to Adam it felt real. No, *unreal* to be sitting on pit road, the speedway's massive grandstands—empty—stretching up to his right like a giant bowl, the angle was so steep. There weren't thousands of fans watching his every move, no TV cameras trained on his car, but Adam didn't care. If he never drove a race truck again, he'd always remember this.

And that's when he started to relax. Truly relax. He had nothing to prove to anybody, he realized. He was there by the grace of God and his daughter's strong will. He hadn't wrecked the truck and to be honest, he didn't think he would. So if he went fast, great, if not—no big deal.

"All set," Sanders said a few seconds later.

"Roger," Adam answered, putting the truck into gear.

It was better. Still not great, but better. And his lap times were good, lower than the target lap times they'd set. Course, that probably didn't mean much. He had a feeling that the target lap times were probably more like a goal and not anything else.

Two more trips to pit road and they had it the way he liked it. It felt fast, but that was only because he'd never driven a one-and-a-half-mile oval. He could have stayed out there all day.

All too quickly Sanders said, "Okay. Your twenty-lap session is over. Bring her in."

"Do I have to?" Adam felt comfortable enough to quip.

"'Fraid so, buddy."

"Shoot. And here I was hoping to stay out here until the next truck race."

"NASCAR might have a thing or two to say about that."

"You think so?" Adam asked.

"I think so." Sanders joked back.

And so he brought it in, Adam studying the crew's faces in the hopes of gauging how he did. Alas, he couldn't tell a thing. He handed the steering wheel and helmet to the crew member who released the safety net, detaching himself from the audio system and the various safety restraints until he was free to wiggle out of the car.

"That was fun," Adam said, catching the man's eye as he pulled himself out the window.

"It *looked* like fun."

"I might have to come back here and do that driving school just so I can experience it again."

And it was funny, because it was only after he said the words that he finally noticed how the other crew members were staring at him. They hovered near the wall, looks of approval on their faces. Blain's next words confirmed what he already suspected.

"Adam, you won't need to *pay* someone to drive here," Sanders said. "You drove faster than last year's race winner."

It felt as if he'd stomped on the brakes. His world came to a screeching halt, only to grind fast forward again. "Come again?"

"You were fast, Adam," Blain said. "Real fast. That target time was set by last year's race winner, and you shattered it to hell and back. We'll definitely want you back for phase two tomorrow."

He looked past Blain to the woman standing behind him—Cece Sanders, he recognized.

"Well, I'll be damned," he said.

CHAPTER FIVE

"HE LOOKS AS SHOCKED as you do," Cece said a few moments later.

"I can't believe it," Becca murmured for about the hundredth time.

"What I can't believe is that he hasn't tried out for a team before."

"He couldn't. Not while raising his little girl."

"What a waste," Cece mused.

"It wasn't a waste," Becca said. "I respect and admire his sacrifice." Her words trailed off because she'd noticed the look on Cece's face.

"Got you," her friend said with a grin.

"You know, there are moments when I truly want to throttle you."

"No, you don't," she said, her blue eyes all but twinkling. "You love me too much and you know it."

Becca sighed, looking over at Adam Drake again. "I do."

"The question is," Cece added. "What are you going to do with him?"

I know what I'd like to do with him.

Becca closed her eyes, mouthing a silent curse. She hadn't felt this kind of attraction to a man in years, and she couldn't believe it was rearing its ugly head now. When she opened her eyes again Cece was staring at her in open amusement.

"Maybe we're getting ahead of ourselves. We still have to consult with your crew chief and Blain. They might not have liked his lines or thought he was consistent enough."

"Becca, he went faster than the target lap time we set—and you know that time was set by last year's series champion. They're gonna love him."

"Okay, but even if they do love him, we don't even know how his media testing will go. And we still have to see how he does on a short track."

"He races short tracks every weekend. Dirt tracks, no less. Martinsville will suit him perfectly."

"Yeah, I know," Becca murmured, staring at Adam who was laughing at something Blain said. Golly, he was gorgeous. The dark blue firesuit that had seen better days was a bit snug on his tall frame—

Cece's face suddenly blocked her view. Becca drew back. "What?" she cried.

"You're cracking me up."

"Why?"

"You have no idea, do you?"

"No idea about what?"

"You like him—and I don't mean his driving. You're attracted to him."

"Yeah, well, so? It's not like I'm going to do anything about it."

"Why not?"

"Because I'm not ready."

"Becca, it's been four years."

"I know, and I'm still not over him."

The humor faded from Cece's eyes. "Becca, Randy's gone—"

"Don't," Becca said, holding up her hand. "Don't say it. I'm not ready, Cece, and that's all there is to it."

"So what are you going to do?"

"Treat him like I would any other driver," she said. "I can ignore how he makes me feel. It's just physical, that's all. I need a driver, damn it. And if he turns out to be good I can't afford to let him go to another team, because you know with numbers like his someone will snap him up."

"Blain will give him a job. We're looking to expand and Adam Drake is just the sort of driver Blain would love to put into our development program. To be honest, Becca, if he does well at Martinsville, I think you'd be a fool not to snap him up, too."

"I know," Becca said, tipping her head back and staring up at the partly cloudy sky. It was getting hot. Well, it was always hot in North Carolina this time of year—she could feel sweat begin to trickle down her neck—but this time it wasn't from the heat.

"Here he comes," Cece hissed. And then, louder, "Well, I'm going to go give Blain my notes. See you in a bit."

"Cece," Becca hissed, not wanting to be left alone. Too late. Her friend had already fled, giving Adam a smile and a wave and a "good job" pat on the back as they crossed paths near pit road wall.

Okay, Becca. Put your game face on.

"Congratulations," she said a few moments later. "The boys driving after you will have to work awful hard to catch up."

"I still can't believe it."

"Well," she said. "I'm pretty certain we'll want you back for media testing tomorrow. Course, we all have to weigh in on your performance, but I'm pretty sure you're a shoo-in."

"I didn't reserve a hotel room."

"Don't worry. We'll find you a room."

"Are you sure, because I can always sleep in my truck."

"Don't be silly," she said. "I'll call the shop and have them make you a reservation. Just hang out here for a bit while they get things lined up. Maybe call your daughter. I'm sure she's dying to know how you did. I'll let you know just as soon as I hear something."

ADAM WATCHED her turn, the smile she'd shot him just before she'd walked away full of professional politeness. In fact, he'd wager he'd seen that smile on TV at least a hundred times.

Cool as a cucumber, he thought. But she was right. He needed to call his daughter. She'd be over at Brandy's by now.

She answered on the first ring.

"Well?" she asked, the word almost a yelp.

"Well what?" he teased.

"Daddy," she scolded. "You know what."

"How was school today?"

"Da-ad!"

He chuckled and said, "I did fine."

Silence, and then, "Define 'fine.'"

Smart girl. She knew the questions to ask.

"I did good, Lin. I did real good."

"You did?" she squealed.

"The best of the day so far."

"I knew it," she shot out. "I *knew* you'd kick ass!"

"Lindsey," he scolded. "You know better than to use that kind of language."

"He kicked ass," he heard her scream to her friend. "I *told* you he would."

"Right on," he heard Brandy say in the background.

"Lindsey, please tell me Brandy's mom isn't standing nearby."

"She's downstairs watching *People's Court.* Sotellmewhathappened."

He bit back a smile, shaking his head as he took her through the day's events. She interrupted him about every ten seconds. By the time he'd told her all there was to know, plus a few details she didn't need to know—no, he didn't pee his pants when he heard how good he did—it'd started to sink in that he'd done it. He'd made it through the first phase. And now he had to come back for tomorrow's testing, which meant he had to ask Brandy's mother about Lindsey staying for two more nights.

"So now what?" Lindsey asked.

"I have to stay here through Wednesday."

"You think your work will mind?"

That was something Adam had wondered

himself. He'd worked for Ralph's Automotive for years. Ralph even sponsored his weekend racing. But there was a difference between an employee with a hobby and an employee who might be changing careers.

Damn. He'd really done it.

"I'll work it out."

"So I get to stay here a couple more nights?"

"Yeah. Let me talk to Brandy's mother to see if it'll be okay."

"It'll be okay. And if it's not, I'll go down to the local shelter."

"You will not," Adam said. "You'll stay right there until I can come get you."

"Does that mean you're going to come get me now?"

"No. So don't get your hopes up. You're staying in school."

"Da-ad."

"No arguments. Now. Let me talk to Brandy's mother."

But Brandy's mother sounded as excited as his daughter did—not surprising since she was a huge race fan. She even came and rooted for him during the Saturday night races sometimes. Everything was so easy to arrange, it almost seemed preordained—and maybe it was.

But Adam's smile faded when he hung up. The truth was he wished Lindsey was there with him. His daughter might be ten years old, but she was his best friend. He missed her company.

He glanced toward pit road. Cece and Becca looked to be in a heated discussion. But then Cece tipped her head back and laughed, Becca swatting her friend in the arm in obvious exasperation. He wished he was a fly on the wall because he had a feeling they were talking about *him*.

CHAPTER SIX

THEY COULDN'T FIND Adam a hotel room in all of Charlotte.

There was some kind of conference in town, and that combined with a local sporting event and concert had every hotel within thirty miles filled to the brim.

Adam had resigned himself to sleeping in his truck, but Cece Sanders suggested he stay with Becca.

"Why not?" she said. "She's got plenty of room."

"That's not necessary. I can sleep in my truck."

"You will not," Cece said. "I'd offer you our guest house, but our nanny's living there and so we don't really have the room."

"You have five *extra* rooms," he heard Becca mutter to Cece.

"And they're all being redecorated. The house is a mess," Cece said, and Adam was certain he saw amusement in her eyes. "Plus, we're expecting company. But like I said, Becca's got room—"

"Cece—"

"Unless you really want him to sleep in his truck."

He saw what was going on then. Frankly, he was surprised he hadn't put two and two together before. "Ms. Sanders, Becca, there's really no need to worry about me. I don't mind camping out here."

"Security will mind," Cece said, arching her brows in Becca's direction.

"Fine. He can stay with me," Becca said. "But you're going to have to wait until I'm through watching everyone test," she said, looking at him as if expecting him to try to back out.

He almost did exactly that, but something about the way she looked into his eyes gave him pause. There was something there, a sort of aloofness that Adam saw right through.

She *was* hiding an attraction.

He held her gaze. She blushed.

Or did she? "That's fine," he said, watching her closely.

The blush spread down her neck.

Well, I'll be...

He didn't know what stunned him more, that Becca Newman found him attractive, or that Cece Sanders appeared to be setting the two of them up.

"Okay then," Becca said. "I'll meet up with you later.

"Thanks," he said, but he was looking at Cece when he said it.

"You're welcome," she said with a secret smile.

HE HUNG OUT at the track for the rest of the day, unable to keep his eyes off Becca. And if he were being honest with himself, he could admit to secretly having fantasized about her for years. That was why he'd agreed to stay at her place—well, that and because he didn't really want to spend the night in his truck. She was racing royalty. The daughter of a five-time NASCAR NEXTEL Cup Series Champion, a man who'd been the son of a racing legend himself. He remembered seeing Rebecca on TV when he'd been younger, standing next to her dad in Victory Lane. When he'd heard who she was he'd become completely smitten, had even felt a pang or two when she'd married Randy Newman. And now here he was, talking to her, interacting with her—cripes, staying with her. It didn't seem real.

When he pulled up in front of her house a few hours later, it seemed even *less* real. Last time he'd been here, he'd been so consumed with worry for Lindsey that he hadn't even noticed his surroundings. But now he could see that Rebecca Newman lived in a home bigger than the dealership down the street from his garage. The two-story brick house looked like it was Civil War–era, but he suspected it was less than ten years old. Set amidst tall pines and lush foliage, the home belonged on the cover of *Better Homes & Gardens,* especially with a 7-UP-can-green lawn surrounding the premises. Her yard looked like a damn golf course.

"Go on in," she said after getting out of the sporty red Cobra. "I've got some files and stuff I need to grab from the back."

Adam slung his overnight bag over a shoulder. Lindsey had insisted he pack it even though Adam had been convinced he wouldn't need it. "Can I help you with anything?"

"No, no," she said, waving him toward the front door as she used her keys to pop open the trunk. "Michelle, my housekeeper, will show you to your room. Just go on in and introduce yourself."

But he went over to her, anyway, which might have been a mistake because the minute he was close to her, he smelled her and that seemed somehow wrong. Becca Newman shouldn't smell like the wildflowers that bloomed near his Kentucky home. And that smell shouldn't make him want to stand there, to close his eyes and figure out exactly which flowers they were.

He'd turned into a poetic fool.

"Here," he said, holding out his hands.

"It's okay," she said, piling another file atop the five or so she held in her arms. "I've got it."

"No, you don't," he said right as she piled some loose papers on top, except she didn't get them square and so a few of them glided to the ground with the back and forth motion of falling leaves. "See?" He bent down and scooped them up. When he straightened he realized she wouldn't look him in the eyes. "Here," he said, placing them back on top again.

"Thanks," she said, her hand holding the papers down. "Look," she said after the trunk lid slammed with an audible pop. "I'm probably going to eat up in my room, so you—"

"Don't."

"Don't what?"

"Don't eat up in your room. Eat dinner with me."

"I beg your pardon?"

He looked away for a moment, knowing he needed to get this right. He didn't want to sound unprofessional, but he didn't want her to think he was merely being polite, either. "Have dinner with me," he said, suddenly deciding that to heck with it. He *liked* Becca Newman. What would it hurt to get to know her better?

"I need company tonight," he admitted. "Usually, I have Lindsey around to calm me down whenever I'm amped up, but she's not around and I really wish she was. So do you mind standing in for her?"

"Mr. Drake—"

He lifted his brow at her relapse into formality.

"Adam," she corrected. "I have a lot of files to review. Even though we've cut the field in half, tomorrow will be just as grueling as today, and Wednesday will be even harder and so I really need to study the drivers' profiles."

"Please?"

"I don't think—"

"I promise not to make a pass at you."

Green eyes widened. "I never thought that you would."

"But you're worried about it, aren't you? Don't," he said, squirming a bit at the lie. "I admired your husband too much to ever disrespect his widow."

But instead of the relief he expected to see, what flitted through her eyes was something almost like irritation. But it was gone so quickly he might have imagined it.

"Thank you," she said, a silent "I think" tacked onto the end of that sentence—or so he suspected.

"We can go to a restaurant if you like," he said. "If that would make you feel better?"

"No," she said with a sharp shake of her head. "That's not necessary."

"Are you sure?"

"I'm sure."

BUT SHE WASN'T SURE.

In fact, as she changed into some cotton capris and a casual yellow top, she found herself thinking she'd been a fool to agree.

I admired your husband too much to ever disrespect his widow.

What the heck did that mean? Was she so dried up and dusty from lack of, well, lack of *that* that she no longer appealed to men? Or was he seriously too in awe of her husband's memory to try to touch her?

Shouldn't you be glad he doesn't want to touch you?

Don't answer that, she told herself firmly.

So she went downstairs a few minutes later, no closer to understanding why Adam Drake had her riled than she was before. He'd been a perfect gentleman every time he'd come near her.

Maybe *that* was the problem.

Maybe she wanted him to touch her, the way

Cece had teased earlier. They'd been standing near pit road right after Adam's test session and she'd hit her friend in the arm when Cece had said that. Only now she wondered if Cece had been right.

"There you are," Adam said as she slipped out of the house and onto the patio, where Michelle had set out dinner. Fajitas by the look of it, she thought, eyeing a tray of grilled veggies and meat. One of Becca's favorites. The smell of cooked onions alone made her mouth water.

"I was about to dig into this stuff without you."

"You should have," Becca said, suddenly aware of how nervous she'd become. No, not nervous. Terrified. "I wouldn't have minded." She swiped a lock of hair from her face. Why had she left it down? Why had she taken the time to curl it so that the ends brushed her cheeks and tickled her ears?

"I wouldn't do that to you," he said.

It was a perfect evening for dinner poolside. The sky was a vivid pink near the horizon, turning orange and then blue and then purple near a star-studded sky. Clouds were backlit by the setting sun, turning the edges bright silver, the insides of the clouds a purple so dark they looked like spilled ink.

"Do you eat out here a lot?" he asked, his words breaking Becca's nervous silence.

The question had her blinking and then mentally chastising herself for forgetting for a moment that she was having dinner, with a man, in the privacy of her backyard.

So? asked a voice. It wasn't like they were on a date.

"Actually, no," she said. "At least, not as often as I used to."

And there it was, the pin that always seemed to pop a balloon of conversation.

Randy.

The name was unspoken, but it might as well have been shouted from the rooftop.

"I'm sorry about what happened," he said, taking a sip of Michelle's famous pink lemonade.

"Thanks," she said.

"He seemed like a nice man."

"He was."

On some days.

But like any married couple, there'd been good days and bad. Still, she'd been deeply in love with him, and so she shouldn't be sitting across from another man wondering what would happen if she leaned forward and kissed him on the mouth.

She owed Randy more respect than that.

"I was surprised you stuck around the racing industry after everything that happened."

Becca flicked a cloth napkin open, kicking little

white pieces of fuzz into the air. The pool gutter slurped loudly, the pool sweep gurgled momentarily as it surfaced.

"I almost didn't," she said, leaning forward, picking up a nearby fork and stabbing a piece of chicken. "I almost chucked it all," she admitted, lifting up the lid to the tortilla warmer. "It would have been so easy to walk away."

"But you didn't," he said, grabbing a tortilla, too.

"Randy would have killed me," she said with a small smile. "He worked too hard to get his truck team off the ground for me to sell it off to a bigger team."

"Like Sanders' Racing?"

Becca nodded. "Blain and Cece would have bought it. They even offered. But I think after Randy died I needed to keep busy. We didn't have kids," she said, and even now, years later, she still felt the pang of regret.

But the time for "if only" had long since passed.

"Maybe if we'd had children I might have felt differently," she said, looking away. She didn't want Adam to see how much it still hurt that she'd never conceived. "But in the end I think the business became almost like a child to me."

"And you've done well."

Ha. But aloud she said, "Somewhat."

"Yes, you have," he said. "You've expanded the program, added a Busch and a Cup team. And you almost won a truck championship a couple of years back."

"Yeah, but then I lost my driver to a big name Cup team. We've been struggling ever since."

"You just need to give it time."

"I don't have time, *or* the luxury of unlimited funds. We're small potatoes compared to some of the other outfits."

"Your sponsors have stayed with you."

"Yeah, but for how much longer? They'll only put up with poor performances so long. Last year was a disaster and unless I get some decent drivers soon, they're going to bail. They may *still* bail."

"But that's why you were out at the track today. And why you'll be out there tomorrow. You'll find people to pilot your cars."

"Yeah. Maybe *you,*" she said, happy to remind herself of what the man across from her might ultimately mean to her. If he did well on Wednesday, she would have to offer him a job, which meant no more unprofessional thoughts. It'd be strictly business. But to be honest, she *wanted* to keep it that way—for Randy's sake.

"Maybe," he said. "Maybe not. I might choke the moment a TV camera is pointed my way."

"Doubtful," she said, taking a bite. But eating in front of him made her feel self-conscious. He watched the food enter her mouth, stared at her lips in such a way that she found herself blushing.

"You never know," he said.

They settled into silence, Becca telling herself to relax. It was just a harmless dinner. Nothing to get uptight about. Adam, as promised, was a perfect gentleman. She was grateful for that.

"Look, Becca. I want to thank you for bringing me out here. You've made Lindsey happier than I've seen her in years."

"Not at all," she said, her tongue starting to feel awkward in her mouth. Her heart pounded a bit too hard, too, because no matter how many times she told herself that it'd be a dumb move to get involved with a race car driver, she couldn't deny that she was attracted to him. And that was so completely disloyal to Randy, so totally out of character, she didn't know what to think—what to do.

"Your, um…your daughter did me a favor by showing up on my doorstep."

"Well, like I said, that remains to be seen."

"No. She did. You're lucky to have her."

And there it was again. The longing she felt

whenever she observed other people's children. She'd always wanted kids. She and Randy had even talked about it. But they'd always put it off.

And then he'd died.

"Becca?" he asked softly.

She looked up, surprised to see him staring at her in concern.

"You would have made a great mother."

She felt her throat tighten, felt her eyes heat up. "Thank you."

He reached across the table and to her shock, took her hand. There was nothing sexual about it. Nothing even remotely forward. It was the touch of a man who understood. Who only wanted to comfort her.

"Sometimes life isn't fair," he said.

"No. Sometimes it's not," she said, suddenly closer to tears than she had been in a long, long time.

"But you're such a good person, Becca. Your kindness shines through. Lindsey loves you. So does everybody out at the track. And so I have to wonder if God blessed you with such a kind heart so you could use it to help others."

"Do you think?" she asked through a throat gone thick with tears. "'Cause sometimes I wonder why I was left behind."

He shook his head, a lock of his hair falling across his forehead. "You were left behind because you're needed here," he said. "To help people like me and my daughter."

"I haven't helped you yet."

"Yes, you have," he said. "Lindsey's like a different kid. You should have heard her on the phone today. If nothing else, I know my little girl is proud of me. And that means the world to me."

"Yeah, but it helps that you've raised her so well. You're a good man," she said. "And you've got an amazing daughter."

"Thank you," he said. "But if she turns out half as amazing as you, I'll be a lucky man."

And for some reason that made the tears fall. It'd been so long since a man had given her a compliment. And he didn't do it to try to get on her good side or anything. She could see the sincerity in his eyes. She wiped away the wetness with a hand that shook. But as his grip tightened, other emotions began to surface, emotions that suddenly made her feel weak and vulnerable.

She pulled away.

"Our food is getting cold," she said. When she glanced up, it was just in time to see the disappointment on his face.

"Yeah, you're right," she heard him say. "It *is* getting cold."

But she had a feeling he wasn't talking about the food.

CHAPTER SEVEN

ADAM COULD hardly sleep that night. And while some of that might have something to do with the next day's testing session, he knew it had more to do with Becca Newman and their poolside dinner.

She was filled with such sorrow.

He nearly groaned every time he recalled the look on her face when they'd been talking about her having children. He wanted to rip his pillow apart. It wasn't fair that women like her went without children while women like his ex-wife up and walked away from them. What a waste.

But there were other emotions keeping him awake, too. Emotions that had to do with how he'd felt when he'd held her hand.

But then she'd pulled away. So that was that.

The next morning when he awoke, she was gone. Not surprising. He knew she'd do her best to avoid him today. Things had gotten a little too raw yesterday. And since she might end up being his boss, raw wasn't a good thing. He'd better stop imposing on her hospitality, anyway.

So he showed up at the shop, Becca nowhere in sight as he was put through his media training. That didn't surprise him too much since she didn't have any reason to be there. But he was a little surprised that she wasn't around when each of the drivers went through an interview with a faux print reporter. Then again, she might be watching on closed circuit television somewhere. His TV interview didn't go so well, or so he thought. He kept saying the wrong thing. Afterward, the PR specialist had grilled him on television dos and don'ts, most of which he'd already been told during the morning session.

The one bright spot to the day had been his commercial. Of course, it hadn't really been taped, but he seemed to be a natural actor and memorizing his lines had been a snap. Still, he couldn't help but feel a little out of place throughout the day. He was a thirtysomething has-been driver. Crap, he wasn't even a has-been. He was a never-was. Who cared that he'd *almost* won a Crown championship a few years back? Obviously he didn't have the goods.

And Becca Newman hadn't been around to reassure him.

He tried calling Lindsey on Brandy's cell, but

all he got was her voice mail over and over again. A glance at his watch told him she should be home from school. He dialed her the whole way back to Becca's house, his panic increasing with each unanswered call. Heck, he couldn't even get through to Brandy's mom.

He had his answer when he pulled up in front of Becca's home; Lindsey herself ran out and greeted him.

"Daddy," she squealed in delight, her face as bright as her loose red hair.

And as his arms wrapped around her, Adam knew he had Becca to thank for her presence.

"I'm so glad to see you!" she shouted.

"And I'm so glad you're here," he said, inhaling the scent of her. Instantly all the day's numerous debacles faded away. It didn't matter that he'd fumbled more things than he'd aced. It didn't matter that he hadn't seen Becca. All that mattered was that his daughter—the love of his life—was in his arms.

She drew back. "You should have seen it, Dad. I rode on a private jet with Lance Cooper. *Lance Cooper,*" she repeated, her eyes as wide as tire rims. "*And* his wife, Sarah. They were on their way home from visiting Sarah's mom in California and they made a special stop for me. Can you believe it?"

No, he couldn't believe it. Everyone's graciousness was unreal. He was beginning to think people in the racing industry were some of the most generous people on earth.

"How long have you been here?" he asked.

"About an hour. I was worried you might try to call Brandy's cell phone. And that you'd freak out when you couldn't reach me."

"You were right."

Her face fell. "But it's okay now, isn't it? I really wanted this to be a surprise. And Becca said we could both stay here with her. Ohmygosh, Dad, Lance and Sarah are so nice," she said, the words so close together Adam had a hard time making them out. "They would have stayed to meet you but Sarah wasn't feeling well. She's pregnant," Lindsey said, holding her hands out like she had a big belly. "It's their first child and she said she's been sicker than a dog and that she didn't want to go to California but that if she hadn't gone to see her mom, her mom would have come to North Carolina, which would have put her into early labor." She leaned toward him. "I don't think she gets along with her very well."

Which made him smile. She was so damn excited. He could see it in her blue eyes, which glowed nearly as bright as they did on Christmas day.

And in that moment he felt an overwhelming sense of gratitude toward Becca Newman.

"Where's Becca?" she asked, his daughter somehow reading his mind.

"I don't know."

"You mean you didn't see her today?"

"No. I didn't."

"Why not?"

"I don't know, Lindsey. You'll have to ask Becca."

She pushed her lips out, a habit she'd had since childhood. "Strange. She sounded like she'd be with you or something."

"Maybe she was," Adam said. "I have no idea if she was watching me do my television interviews."

That made her face clear. "How'd you do?"

"I think I blew it."

Her face fell. "What makes you say that?"

"I fumbled my newspaper and TV interview."

"But the other drivers might have done bad, too."

"Somehow I doubt it."

"But you don't know that for sure," she said, her hands moving to her hips like she was the adult and not a child. "You don't know anything until it's all said and done."

"I'm not going to kid myself, Lindsey. You shouldn't, either."

"And you shouldn't throw in the towel before the final lap."

They were words he'd used on her whenever she'd faced a difficult test or a challenge. Damn. What was the world coming to when your own daughter threw your words back in your face?

"Da-ad," she scolded.

"I know, I know," he said, once again feeling like the child in their relationship. "I haven't thrown in the towel." *Yet.* "C'mon. Let's go inside."

BUT HE DIDN'T FOOL Lindsey for a minute.

Holy crawdad, Lindsey thought as she stuffed her spare jeans into the top drawer of the elegant oak armoire that matched the bed behind her. Her dad had looked ready to puke.

"You want to go grab a bite to eat?"

Lindsey yelped, so engrossed in her thoughts that she hadn't heard him enter.

"Oh, um, sure," she said. And then she straightened suddenly. "Oh, wait. We can't."

"We can't?"

"We have to wait until Becca gets here."

"And why is that?"

"Because we're going to dinner with her," she said brightly, turning back to the armoire so her dad couldn't see her face, and the guilt that she was certain shone from her eyes like lightning bugs on a June evening. Okay, so she'd sort of orchestrated the whole thing. She'd called Becca's cell phone the minute her dad had left her alone, begging her to take them both to dinner. Becca Newman had sounded hesitant, but Lindsey had been persistent, and it was a good thing, too, because it was obvious her dad and Becca needed help in the romance department.

"I begged her to take us to Finish Line, you know, that race-themed restaurant we saw on TV. I'm dying to see what that place looks like for real and she said she'd be happy to take us there."

Okay. So maybe she hadn't used the word "happy."

"You asked her to take us to dinner?"

And now her *dad* didn't look happy, either. "Um, yeah. I called her to tell her I'd arrived safely. I have her cell-phone number, you know. She gave it to me when she arranged for me to come here. You should have seen it this morning, Dad," Lindsey said, trying to change the subject. "Brandy's mom dropped me off at a private terminal where all these fancy jets were parked.

And you should have seen the building where we waited for the planes to be fueled up. *Whew.* It looked like a fancy hotel with all this cool furniture—"

"We're not going."

Her mouth slammed closed.

"You should have asked me first before asking her to take us to dinner," he said sternly.

"But Da-ad."

"We're not going," he said again.

"Not going where?"

Lindsey looked up. "Becca," she squealed, darting by her dad and into Becca's arms.

"Hey there," she said, hugging her back. And any doubts that Becca Newman would make a terrific stepmom flew out the window when Becca said, "I missed you."

"I missed you, too."

"I hope it's okay that I arranged for her to come," Becca said. "Brandy's mom made sure the school knew what was going on. They gave her her homework to do. And she flies home tomorrow night so she'll only miss one day. I just thought you'd feel better if she were here for the final test session."

"He *does* feel better," Lindsey said. "Right, Dad?"

For a moment Lindsey thought her dad might do something stupid, like chastise Becca for going over his head. But he shook his head, saying, "I don't mind at all." Much to Lindsey's relief. "In fact, I'm grateful to you. I was missing her."

"Aw, Dad," Lindsey said, hugging him next. "I missed you, too."

"But that doesn't mean we should impose any more by asking that you take us to dinner," he added.

"Don't be silly," Becca said, "I don't mind taking you at all. It'd be good for me to get out."

Lindsey glanced back at Becca just in time to see…was that a blush on her face? Lindsey looked closer. It sure was, and Lindsey should know. Thanks to her red hair and fair complexion she was the queen of blushing.

Holy crawdad! Could her wildest fantasies have already come true? Could they be *majorly* crushing on each other and just not know it?

"C'mon," she said, "Let's get going. Dad, you have no choice, we're going out to dinner and that's that."

"Lindsey—" her dad warned.

"We're going," Lindsey said firmly. "I'm not letting you say no. I'm just going to go change my shirt. I spilled some orange juice on it on the plane." She shoved her dad out of her room, giving him the wide I'm-so-cute smile—which usually worked—before she shut the door.

Whew, she thought as she leaned against the cool wood. This might take some work. She'd have never guessed adults could be so clueless. Maybe they should study the book she'd gotten in Sex Ed, especially the chapter on physical attraction.

Jeesh.

BECCA HAD FORGOTTEN how precocious Lindsey Drake could be.

It was pretty obvious right from the get go that the girl was up to something. The moment they left the house she ran toward Becca's car saying, "I'll take the back," as if riding in the back would be the highlight of her week. Unfortunately, that put Adam in the seat next to her, a place that Becca didn't exactly want him to be. Not after last night.

She couldn't believe she'd bawled her eyes out right in front of him. She prided herself on her control. For heaven's sake, she'd somehow managed to hold it together all these years, hadn't she?

Until Adam Drake showed up.

But she smiled gamely and took her place behind the wheel. At first Becca had thought

Lindsey wanted the two of them side by side so they could get to know one another better, something that seemed almost amusing given their intimate conversation the night before. But as they made their way toward the restaurant it became more and more obvious that Lindsey Drake's goal was to convince Becca that Adam would make a great boyfriend or father or...something.

"And he cooks the *best* tuna casserole," Lindsey said. "My best friend's mom says my dad is the best cook in all of Kentucky."

"Really?" Becca said, biting back a smile when Adam said, "Lindsey," in a low voice.

"And he's not afraid to do housework, either. Of course, you have a housekeeper who doubles as a cook and so you're pretty lucky, too. But we can't afford that and so I'm pretty lucky to have the best dad in the world."

Out of the corner of her eye, Becca saw Adam rest his elbow on the window ledge, his finger rubbing his chin as he shook his head back and forth.

"Wow," Becca couldn't resist saying. "Does he do laundry, too?"

"Mmm-hmm," Lindsey said. "And the dishes and yard work...well, if we had a yard."

"Okay, that's enough," Adam said, shifting so he could peek back at his daughter, the smell of

him drifting to Becca on a stream of air-condition-
ing. It was early evening, and still warm even
though the usual summer thunderclouds were
nearby. "Lindsey, I'm sure Becca is thrilled that
I'm such a wonderful, loving, devoted dad, but can
we change the subject, maybe?"

Becca peeked a glance in the SUV's rearview
mirror, watching as Lindsey's face fell for a
second before suddenly clearing.

"Sure," she said. "Brandy's mom says hello,"
she said, her expression turning to one of satisfac-
tion. "You know she has a huge crush on you,
don't you, Dad?"

"Lindsey, please—"

"So Brandy's not a cousin or something?" Becca
asked, curious despite herself. "I thought since you
were staying with her that she might be family."

"I don't have any family, except my dad, of
course. I'm Brandy's best friend," Lindsey said.
"And I always stay with her when my dad has to
go out of town, which he does from time to time
when, you know, the mood strikes."

"What mood?" Adam asked. "And what the
heck are you talking about?"

"Come on, Dad. You don't seriously think
anyone believes you're actually *fishing* when you
drive down to New Orleans?"

Becca laughed. She couldn't help it. And when she caught a glimpse of Adam she laughed even harder. He looked so completely flummoxed, so thoroughly horrified that she *knew* his daughter was right.

"That does it," he said, swinging forward again. "I'm putting you up for adoption."

"Cool. Becca, you want to be my mom?" she asked.

Becca, still chuckling, shook her head. "After you just outed your dad? I don't think so. I have a few skeletons in my closet, too, you know."

"Somehow I doubt that," Adam said.

"You might be surprised," Becca said.

"You couldn't have any more skeletons than my dad. I once found a movie—"

"Lindsey!" Adam cried, cutting her off.

Becca just shook her head. *Dinner ought to be interesting.*

CHAPTER EIGHT

DINNER *WAS* INTERESTING, despite Lindsey's ultra-obvious matchmaking efforts. In fact, it was a great dinner. The food at Finish Line was always tasty. Becca did not even mind when a few fans approached and asked for her autograph.

Unfortunately, she had to cut the evening short because both Adam and Becca had a big day ahead of them tomorrow. And that should have been a reminder as to why she shouldn't get too close to the Drakes. But she couldn't help but start to like them, she thought as she drove home, the three of them settling into comfortable conversation about other race teams working out of the Moores-ville/Concord area. When they arrived back at her house Becca was almost sorry the evening was over.

It had felt good to get out.

"I guess I'll see you tomorrow," Adam said, Lindsey already at the front door. She tried to open it but it was locked, her sigh of exasperation clearly audible even though she stood a good twenty feet away, the porch light causing her red hair to glow almost gold.

"Do you want to ride over together tomorrow morning?" Becca found herself asking, her keys jingling as they walked to the front door. The nearby thunderstorms had turned the evening cool, one of the first cool nights they'd had, a light dusting of leaves on the ground signaling that fall was only a heartbeat away.

"I'm not sure," he said.

Neither was she, but at least he had the sense not to take her up on the offer.

What was she thinking? He might be her house-guest, but it was best if they drew the line there.

But was it wrong to wish—if only for a moment—that they could be more than boss and employee? That he could be her…friend?

"I understand," she said.

"Becca—"

She turned back to him, took a deep breath.

He'd paused at the edge of the lawn where the driveway met the front walkway. "Thanks for tonight. I know you recognize, too, that Lindsey is trying to get us together. She can be a bit…zeal-ous about things. I'll have a talk with her. But thanks for being such a good sport. She's young and so she doesn't understand that we could never be more than friends."

"No need to thank me," she said. "I enjoy my time with her."

Never be more than friends.

Why did the words cause her spirits to plummet?

"I'll see you tomorrow then, right?"

"Um. Yeah. Out at the track."

"Good," he said softly, and suddenly there was something there, something that hung in the air between them as thick as the night air, something that made her breathing quicken and her heart give a little flutter.

And when the silence stretched on, she realized he was waiting for her to say something.

No, she quickly amended, he was waiting for a signal from her, perhaps a word that she felt the tension, too, and that it was okay to maybe do what Lindsey so obviously wanted them to do— act on their attraction. But she couldn't go there. Not yet. Probably not ever.

"Good night," she said, turning away. Lindsey still stood by the door, a look of intense concentration on her face as she stared at Becca and her dad.

"Aren't you staying up?"

Ah. So it was back to that again. "No," Becca said. "I'll see you both in the morning."

Because it was better to end things now, not that there was technically anything to end. She and Adam might end up working together, and it was never a good idea to mix business with pleasure.

But it was more than that, she realized. Lindsey and her dad were wonderful, and in her experience "wonderful" never lasted. Something always happened to take it away. First her mom, then her dad, then Randy. She couldn't take that kind of pain again.

Not ever again.

SHE DREAMED ABOUT Randy that night, the kind of dream that seemed so real when you woke up that the pain of loss was fresh all over again. They'd been at a race, in Victory Lane, and he'd been telling her something. But she couldn't hear the words because the crowd was so loud. He kept mouthing things at her and she kept straining to hear and when she opened her eyes, Randy was gone.

She'd wiped away the tears and then forced herself up and out of bed, as she had every day since his death.

It was a big day today, she reminded herself. Actually, it was one of her favorite days because by the end of the test session not one, but two drivers' lives would change. Whether Adam was included or not, two men would get their shot at the big leagues.

She dressed quickly, her stomach complaining loudly as she left her room. But she didn't want to linger. If she lingered she might run into Adam. Or Lindsey. Lindsey might be harder to face because she had such high hopes for her dad. She didn't want to think about what it'd be like if Adam didn't do well.

They bused everybody up to Martinsville, Becca smiling when she caught site of Lindsey sitting in a seat next to her dad. Sure, it might have been faster for her to take a helicopter, or maybe even a jet, but unlike other team owners, Becca didn't own a private jet. She hated flying. Hated it so much she preferred to drive to race tracks. Yeah, it was probably irrational—planes crashed far less often than cars, but she couldn't contain her fears and so she preferred to ride with the drivers traveling on the special "Variety Show" bus.

When they arrived, Becca shot Lindsey and her father a small smile, then got off the bus as fast as she could. She didn't want to walk with everyone, but she especially didn't want to walk with Adam and Lindsey. All she needed was talk of favoritism.

So she hurried across the infield well ahead of the pack. Pop-up tents offered shade along pit road, toolboxes and tires stacked nearby. The drivers would go out one by one, changes to their truck allowed every twenty laps—just like in their first test session. Only today the crew chiefs would be making the call. Once they'd warmed up, they'd race against each other. During that time they'd be judged on how well they handled themselves in traffic. It usually made for an interesting day.

"Gonna be a hot one today," her NASCAR Craftsman Truck Series crew chief said, air ratchets whirring and tools clinking against each other as the crew members out on pit road examined the chrome-plated wrenches for flaws.

It *would* be hot, hotter than Concord had been the day before. She was glad she'd worn a team blouse, the white fabric hopefully keeping the sun at bay. "I think you're right, John, but at least it'll level the playing field." When they'd put the drivers through their paces beneath partly cloudy skies it'd made for some uneven lap times. Adam's had still been the best, but there'd been talk that they'd only been that good because of the cooler track conditions.

Today would tell the tale.

"I guess there'll be no second-guessing," she murmured.

"That's true," he said, his tan face wreathed in smiles. She'd employed John for two years now and she'd never regretted bringing him up from one of the touring divisions. She just wished she could find him a driver worthy of his talent as a crew chief. The last one had spent more time behind pit wall than on the track.

"Who've we got today?" he asked, his blue headphones resting around his neck.

"A few good ones," Becca said. John hadn't been to the test in Concord—too busy at the shop—so she took him down the list, weighing the pros and cons of each driver. When Adam's name came up she stated his strengths and weaknesses without bobbling once, but when she looked up and caught John's eye, he was smiling.

"He's the one, isn't he?" he asked.

"He's the one what?"

"The guy with the little girl."

Becca felt herself relax a bit. For a moment there she'd thought...but never mind. "Yes. That's the one."

"He seems pretty strong," John said, noting his lap times.

"Yeah, well, we'll see how he does under some

real pressure," Becca said. "The other day he didn't think he stood a chance. Today he knows he's competitive. That might mess with his head."

"Yeah," John agreed. "Today'll separate the men from the boys, that's for sure." He slipped his headphones on, clapping his hands and saying, "Let's get the show on the road," in a loud voice that Becca would bet reached all the way to the grandstands.

Cece arrived then, one of her ever-present Star Oil ball caps in place, her white polo-shirt the same as ever, too. She and Blain had flown out on their helicopter to the track, their smiles wide as they walked onto pit road. The three of them worked quickly to pair up the drivers for the test. Adam would go early that afternoon, and when Becca thought about what it'd be like to watch his test, her stomach heated and then turned. No matter how many times she told herself not to show favoritism, she really wanted Adam to do well. For Lindsey's sake.

The next couple of hours passed in a blur, Becca, Cece, Blain and the two crew chiefs watching from atop the Sanders' Racing hauler. It was still early in the morning, but the sun radiated up from the aluminum platform beneath their feet, and Becca felt sweat trickle around the plastic padding that rimmed her headphones. She pushed her sunglasses up her face, wishing she'd worn a ball cap like Cece's.

Out on the track a driver named Art Miller tried to bring his truck up to speed, but it became obvious after a few laps that the guy just didn't have it. John made changes to the truck on the driver's behalf, just as he would if this had been an actual race day, but it didn't help the driver out. If anything, his times dropped off, the rhythmic drone of his truck's engine echoing off the empty stands.

Four more drivers to go.

She felt sick.

But that was because those four drivers were in front of Adam.

You're too close to him.

Focusing her attention on other details didn't help, either. No matter how many notes she made in the margin of a driver's test sheet, her pages occasionally ruffled by a cool breeze that kept things bearable atop the hauler, she couldn't keep her mind off of Adam. Even when Sam Kennison went, the kid acing his solitary test, she didn't perk up.

Because right after Sam came Adam.

"Who've we got next?" John asked via his radio less than half an hour later.

Becca tensed even more, her stomach feeling like a tire that had come off a rim. Flip. Flip. Flip.

"Adam Drake," Cece said, and the way she said the name—A-dam Dra-ake—she sounded like a teenager teasing her best girlfriend.

"Oh, good," John said. "I'm looking forward to seeing him drive. His stats are impressive."

"His shoulders are impressive, too," Cece said with a wicked grin in Becca's direction.

"Oh, really?" her husband asked.

"Well, Becca thinks so," Cece said.

"I do not."

"Sure, you do," Cece teased.

Her friend had been giving her grief all morning, ribbing her about her fear of flying and asking impertinent questions such as if she'd sat next to Adam on the bus ride up. Or stared at him. Or had fantasies about him.

Becca wanted to push her over the aluminum balustrade that encircled the viewing pad.

A truck started up on pit road and suddenly there was silence. Well, not quite silence. Air compressors still rattled away. Air ratchets still whined. But Becca couldn't hear any of it. Her hand clenched around her pencil, her mind focused on one thing and one thing only: Adam's turn. This was it.

They all watched as he took off down pit road, his truck's paint glittering beneath the morning sun. Within a few minutes he had the truck warmed up.

She heard the first lap's time coming through her headphones, which she recorded.

"21.95," she reported to the group after Adam passed the start-finish line.

"Not bad for a first lap," John said.

His next lap was even faster, and when he came in for some adjustments, it wasn't long before he was running equal to or better than the lap time they'd set as the mark to beat.

"He's good," Blain said as Adam shut the truck down.

"Really good," John said. "His lines were awesome. And did you hear how smooth he was? He hardly revved the motor once, and when he got on the brake, he didn't cause the exhaust to pop."

"He's better than good," Cece said. "He's great. I only wish he was trying out for us."

And Becca said nothing. When she glanced at her lap it was to note that her nails had put dents in the yellow skin of her pencil.

Oh, jeez.

"Where you going?" Cece asked as she shot toward the opening in the platform's railing.

"Restroom," Becca said.

"Oh, great, I'll go with you."

Becca thought about telling her to stay put, but she knew Cece would see right through her and so she chose instead not to look her friend in the eye.

"Becca!" Lindsey cried practically the moment Becca's feet touched solid ground, the aluminum ladder rattling behind her as Cece came down. "Did you see him? Did you see him? He kicked butt out there."

"Is this Lindsey?" Cece asked after landing next to Becca.

"Holy crawdad," Lindsey said. "You're Cece Sanders."

"Guilty," Cece said with a laugh.

"I'm Lindsey Drake. Adam Drake's daughter."

"So I gathered. And it's a pleasure to meet you, Lindsey," she said, holding out her hand. "Lance and Sarah told me all about you the other night."

"They did?" Lindsey said, her red brows lifting. "Wow."

"They were very impressed."

"Well, I was impressed with their jet. Ohmygosh, it was *so* cool riding on that thing. I asked if they'd take me to Hawaii but they said no."

Cece huffed with laughter right as a masculine voice said, "Lindsey. You didn't really do that, did you?"

Becca's breath caught. Adam, his hair still mussed from his helmet, stood behind his daughter, his blue firesuit tied around his waist, a white fire retardant, long-sleeved shirt clinging to his wide shoulders. Jeesh. What'd he do? Jump out of the truck and run?

"Good job driving," Cece said, saying the words that Becca couldn't quite pass through her tight throat.

"Thanks," he said.

Becca felt his stare, knew she had to say something, too. "Are you ready for the next round?" she found herself asking, taking a deep breath before she met his gaze.

"Ready as I'll ever be," he said. He looked pale. And she was pretty certain his hand shook as he lifted it to scratch the back of his neck.

Oh, dear.

Please don't choke, she silently prayed, only to chastise herself immediately for even thinking that. It was none of her business if he choked or not.

Except somehow it was.

They heard more footsteps descending the ladder.

"Potty break," James, Sanders' Truck series crew chief, said.

"Adam, did you meet James on the bus?" she asked.

"No, actually, I didn't," he said, holding out

his hand. "But I heard your voice on the radio. Thanks for helping John with some of those calls."

"No problem," James said. "Nice driving."

"Thanks."

Becca looked between the two. There was an instant easing of both their shoulders as they shook hands, Adam's smile a bit forced, but genuine nonetheless. That was good. A crew chief was nothing without a good wheelman, and while James didn't work for her, it was nice to see that Adam seemed to appreciate everyone's help. There was nothing worse than a cocky driver who thought his talent was all that mattered.

"John told me I was the last one out," Adam said.

"You were. We'll start the group tests in just a minute."

"Who am I going out with?"

"Sam Kennison, Tate Evans and Jordan Fowler," Becca said with a reassuring smile.

"Sam, huh?" Adam said, a wry smile lifting his masculine lips.

"Yeah." Becca turned toward the garage. She hadn't really wanted to do that. With the bad blood between Adam and Sam's dad, this would make his seat time all the more stressful. But both Cece and Blain had thought it a good idea to pair the best with the best, pointing out that it was Carl

Kennison who had the problem with Adam and not Sam.

"Hey," Cece said. "It could be worse. You could be going out with the dad."

"Who's Sam Kennison?" Lindsey wanted to know. "And why would it bad if you drove with his dad?"

Becca looked between father and daughter. Lindsey remembered her mom leaving her dad but, obviously, she didn't remember the circumstances surrounding the breakup.

"He's nobody, honey," Adam said.

"Doesn't sound like nobody," Lindsey muttered.

Her dad ignored her. "I'm going to get something to drink. Lindsey, you need to find someplace out of the way where you can watch."

"How about on top of the hauler?" Cece asked, waving toward the race car transporter they'd just climbed down from.

"On top?" Lindsey said. *Cool.*

"C'mon, I'll show you how to get up there."

"I thought you needed to use the bathroom," Becca said.

"I will. In a minute," Cece said, waving Lindsey her way.

"Speaking of the restroom," James said, turning away.

That left Adam and Becca alone.

"I, um…I hope you're not nervous about this afternoon," Becca said into the silence that followed everyone's departure, well, silence but for the sudden clang of a dropped wrench.

"I'm not," Adam said.

Becca clasped her clipboard in front of her, that awkwardness she'd felt last night suddenly returning. "Good luck," she said softly.

"Thanks," he said.

"I mean that," she added, clutching the clipboard tighter. "Whatever happens, thank you for agreeing to come."

"Thanks for inviting me. And for paying me," he added. "Even if I don't make it, that money will come in handy."

Which reminded Becca that if he did make it, his sudden pay raise would dramatically change his life.

The question was: would he change hers?

CHAPTER NINE

HE COULD DO THIS.

Adam's hands tightened around the steering wheel, his body so tense it felt as if his helmet was digging into his temples.

He'd climbed into the truck again, had spoken a few words to Lindsey via his radio, then hooked his window net on the closing latches. Despite what he'd told Becca, he was more nervous than he'd ever been in his life.

Just a few laps around a track. Nothing to it.

But this was it.

This was *it*.

If he could just hold on to his truck in traffic, he might win the thing.

Holy crawdad, he might win.

His breathing echoed in his ears, the bars of his HANS device digging into his shoulder so that he could feel every beat of the pulse near his collarbone. His helmet suddenly felt too tight, pulse points pounding wherever the inner liner made contact with his head.

Becca had looked upset.

He'd wanted to tell her that everything would be okay. But he couldn't do that. They were just friends. That's all they'd ever be.

"Start it up," he heard John say.

Becca's image faded as Adam flipped the on/off switch with a hand that shook. *How'd it happen?* he asked himself. Two months ago he'd been working his fingers to the bone, trying to race and still make ends meet with a job at the local repair shop. Today he sat in the driver's seat of a race truck owned by none other than Randy Newman's widow.

"Everyone take two or three to warm up," John said. "Then we'll see what your lap times look like."

Two or three to warm up. No problem.

But behind him were three other drivers who wanted to impress the team owners, one of them Sam Kennison who followed directly behind him, his truck's red and white paint scheme a familiar one, though different from the red, white and blue trucks they'd driven on Monday. They were using real race trucks this time, not the trucks specially made for the first day's testing session. The Snappy Lube decal was affixed on the hood of

Sam's truck. Adam's boss hated the nationwide string of oil change stores, claimed they'd stolen business from him. And yet here Adam was in Martinsville, racing against the same race truck featured in their commercials. But what was even more surreal, what made it feel even more like a dream, was the logo on his own truck. TravelTime Hotels.

Un. Real.

Concentrate, Adam, he told himself after they told him to start the truck. He cruised down pit road, the engine so powerful he could feel its vibration down to his bones. On his left, the pit wall raced by like a white stream of paper, faster and faster. The grandstand began to blur, too, as he brought the truck through the gears. But unlike Monday, when he'd shown up at the track expecting to fail, today he knew he might have a shot. Everything seemed sharper somehow—the color of the infield grass, the empty blue seats, sunlight arching off the building's glass. His own truck's dark blue hood, the gold logo in the center refracting sunlight.

"Drop the hammer, boys," John said when they'd brought the trucks up to speed.

They'd been asked to start single file, Adam in front, followed by Sam, Tate and Jordan. But

Adam backed off a bit just before slamming down the pedal. Sam had to check up. So did Tate and Jordan. It was an old racer's trick, one Sam should have been expecting, but judging by how close he got to the rear of Adam's truck, Adam figured he'd been caught off guard. Good. The kid needed to remember he was up against a veteran.

Kid. Carl's kid. What the hell was he doing racing against Carl's—

No.

He wouldn't think like that. Instead he concentrated on steering his truck out of turn two, the back end breaking free. He had to work to keep the truck from spinning, but years of driving on dirt tracks stood him in good stead. At the last moment he found some traction, the back end hooking up and shooting him forward.

Close.

"How's it feel?" John asked.

"Loose."

"We'll fix it during the first scheduled break."

"Okay," Adam said, the pads of his fingers tingling thanks to his death grip on the wheel. His gaze shot toward his mirror. Sam was right on his rear spoiler and behind him he could see the front end of another car, one that had ducked down low. Tate was trying to pass Jordan. Well, good. Maybe that would keep them occupied while he worked to keep Sam off his ass.

They flew toward turn three and Adam's stomach knotted. He'd have to try to hold on to it. Backing off and letting Sam go by just wasn't an option.

Nothing ventured, nothing gained, he thought, shooting into the corner like a ball tied to the end of a string. His body slammed into the seat cushions. Gravity pushed against him, his head tipping to the left. The back end began to break free. Adam felt his breath catch as he inched closer and closer to the marbles. But instead of fighting the truck this time, he simply let it drift. And instead of the back end losing its grip, it sank down, seeming to squat as the traction bars kicked in, allowing the back tires to find some grip.

Sam fell back. Not a lot, but enough that Adam breathed a little easier.

"Nice line," John said, Adam catching a quick glimpse of everyone on pit road before entering turn one again.

"Thanks," Adam said.

"And nice lap time."

Adam almost asked what it'd been, but he didn't want to know. As long as he didn't wreck the truck and as long as he held off Sam, that's all that mattered.

But Sam gave him a run for his money. The kid was always there, pushing and pushing, looking for a mistake that he could capitalize on to pass Adam. The other two drivers, Tate and Jordan, were involved in their own battle, causing them to fall farther and farther back. Adam didn't have time to worry about them. He had his hands full. The kid ducked down low at one point so Adam had to force his truck to stay down on the apron, something that caused his back end to pitch sideways. That almost lost him the lead. Almost, but not quite.

"All right," John said after the first twenty laps. "Let's see how well you guys pit."

Adam's chest tightened, his heart squeezing so hard he could barely breathe.

Here was another test. And it was the one he most dreaded. Yeah, he had experience bringing a car down pit road, but never with as professional a crew as this. It'd be different.

Or maybe not, he thought as he spied the signboard bobbing up and down, the blue-and-gold 61 glowing in the sun. He hurled toward that colorful board as if he planned to bust through it.

"That's it," John said. "3,500 RPMs. Just bring her in nice and easy."

But it wasn't as easy as all that. His timing

needed to be perfect. Fast enough that he didn't lose valuable seconds by being overcautious. Slow enough that he didn't violate the mandatory speed limit. And while this wasn't an official race and he wouldn't be monitored by NASCAR, he would bet someone else was keeping a watchful eye.

"Five, four, three," John counted off. Adam kept an eye on the dancing sign, slamming down the brake pedal at the last minute and sliding to a stop with his nose against the plastic board.

Perfect.

Or at least he thought so. Hard to tell how close he was to the line without getting out of the truck. But it was already being hiked up on the right and Adam told himself to focus. He needed to be ready when John gave the signal to go. He kept an eye on the crew, especially John. The crew chief watched from near the front of the pit stall, upper body leaning forward, face as tense as if this were an actual race. Down went the right side and a split second later, up went the left. Fresh tires that were lower in air pressure replaced the worn tires that'd been on his truck before. He saw a tire changer duck down, the air hose snaking through the air as if alive.

"Go, go, go," John said.

Adam glanced in his mirror as he stabbed the

gas. Sam's pit stop was a little slower, but not by much, the two of them heading out almost together.

"Nice stop, everybody," John said to the crew. "That means you, too, Adam," he added.

"Thanks," Adam said, although he was pretty certain John said that to all the drivers. The crew chief was the laid-back type, his voice constantly in Adam's ear. That was a good thing because it calmed Adam down, helped him to focus.

He brought the truck up to speed, but something felt off. "Think those were the wrong adjustments," he told John.

"Roger that. We'll work on it some more during your next stop."

Suddenly it was all Adam could do to hold Sam off. Adam had to duck down low to block him, then drift up high. He battled Sam so hard he began to feel a vibration a few laps later.

"Think I've got a tire going down," he told John.

"You think?"

"Pretty sure," Adam said, wondering if this were part of the test. He backed off the gas and ducked toward the inside. Sam and the other two drivers roared past, Adam feeling as if he'd been passed by a multicolored rainbow.

"Damn," he heard himself mutter.

And then the truck pitched left.

"Shit," he cursed as he fought the front end, trying to keep the truck from careening into the wall. He wasn't going all that fast, thank God, but it was fast enough to send the car sideways. He felt the three good tires chatter in protest as they slid across the track. Smoke rose up around him, obscuring the view out of the front windshield. He flinched, waiting for a collision with the wall and when none came, glanced left and right so he could get his bearings.

He got his bearings, all right. He was facing the wrong direction. Turn two, the turn he'd just exited, sat in front of him. Adam felt a chuckle build then, then a bizarre urge to stay there so he could wave at the other guys when they rounded the corner.

"Unless we're racing in England, I think I need to turn this thing around," he said.

"You all right?"

"Didn't hit the wall, but the tire probably tore the fender all up."

Silence. Then, "Do you need a push?"

Adam flicked the starter switch. The engine roared to life with a puff of exhaust smoke. "Nope. But I'm going to nurse her in. Warn everybody there's probably debris on the track."

"Ten-four."

It was the slowest trip to pit road he'd ever had, compounded by the sound of the tire's outer liner beating against the fender wall. *Blam. Blam. Blam.* Over and over again. Not good.

"How's it look?" Adam asked when he came to a stop on pit road, trying to see for himself if the front fender had been damaged beyond repair. But he couldn't see anything other than the top.

"Like a dog's chew toy," John said. "But it's nothing a little duct tape won't fix."

He relaxed.

"We'll probably need to tighten it up. The damaged front end will make me loose."

"Ten-four," John said.

And then because he knew Lindsey was probably worried about him said, "Just be sure you leave some of that duct tape for me afterward. I could use it for my daughter's mouth when she gets out of line."

There. That should reassure her that he was feeling fine. He could practically hear Lindsey's "Hey!" from on top of the hauler.

But as he stared down pit road, he felt the first twinge of disappointment. Sam was good. Better than good.

Better than him.

The kid had almost had him, pushing him to the point that he'd worn the rubber off of his damn tires causing him to get a flat.

"Okay," John said less than a minute later. "Go on out. We've got track personnel out there cleaning up the debris so keep your eye on the flag man. We'll give you boys a green flag when you're good to go."

"Ten-four," Adam said, wanting to ask what the heck was the point. He wasn't as good as Sam, and now he'd be even worse. Frankly, he was surprised they didn't ask him to bring it behind the wall.

"HE'S SLOW," Becca said.

"He's in an inferior truck," Cece said from her position standing next to Becca atop the hauler, the headset she'd been wearing resting around her neck. The headpiece held down her long blond ponytail that stuck out of her ball cap.

"But his lap times are dropping off," Becca said after removing her own headset, hoping Cece didn't see how badly her hands shook as she flicked her hair over the top of it. She'd heard him spin out, Becca turning toward the back stretch and reaching for the call button a split second before John had done the same thing.

"Becca," Cece said, "given what he has to work with, I'm surprised he's keeping up at all."

Becca glanced down at Adam's lap times. Sunlight made the writing hard to see against a backdrop of bright paper. She blinked a few times, but she didn't really need to look.

"He's good," Cece said. "Better than good."

Considering what they'd given him to work with, he really was. She glanced up, her eyes unseeing as she stared out over the racetrack.

"Sam's good, too," Becca said. "He was gaining on Adam there for a little while."

Cece turned back to her. "Yeah, but he slowed down the moment he got out front."

"Maybe it's the truck. Maybe something's wrong with it," Becca said, glancing down at the guys out on pit road. They were following the drivers' progress around the track, a few of them stepping beneath one of the Easy Ups they'd erected to glance at the data that streamed across their engineer's computer screen.

"Doubtful," Cece said. "I think it's because he's not taking the same line Adam was, so it's slowing him down. And when he got into traffic with the other boys, he slowed down even more."

"Maybe Sam's truck doesn't like clean air."

"Becca, Sam and Adam's trucks are virtually

identical. Both of them were given the same, awful setup."

"Something could be wrong."

"Okay, then what about the other two guys? They're no spring chickens. The fact is they're not getting any better and Adam's still keeping up. He's the best of the bunch," Cece said, looking over to where Carl Kennison stood on pit road, his face as red as the gas can he stood by. He was chewing on something, his mouth doing double time in an obvious attempt to work out his frustration.

"He doesn't look happy," Becca said, looking away as the two trucks came out of turn four. Adam's front fender looked like a piñata that'd been burst and then resealed again, the light blue tape they'd used contrasting with the truck's darker blue body. But even with a bent fender and an inferior race truck, he still managed to tail the pack.

"If you don't hire him, we will," Cece said, and there was no need to ask who "he" was. "I mean it, Becca. Blain'll be all over him—"

"I know," Becca interrupted. "I know," she repeated more softly.

"Then why don't you look happier? Your search for a driver is over. This is the guy you've been looking for. He's got the goods and yet you look as glum as when you lost Bill Reynolds to RCS Racing."

"I do not."

"Yes, you do," Cece said, turning her body as Adam entered turn three, the other trucks' discordant motors seeming to vibrate the air. "What's the matter?" her friend asked. "Afraid you'll jump him the moment the two of you are alone?"

"Cece!" Becca said, glancing back at Lindsey who stood nearby, eyes never leaving her father. Adam and Sam roared by, the two vehicles seeming to rotate onto their sides because of the steep banking of the track. For a split second sunlight snaked atop their roofs in a neon glow.

"Admit it, you're afraid to hire him," Cece said, yelling to be heard over the sound of the trucks.

"I'm not afraid," Becca yelled back.

"You are," Cece said, her blond hair flicking across her shoulders as she shot Becca a glance. "You don't want him to get too close to you."

"Don't be ridiculous," Becca denied even as her stomach turned. "I'm delighted for Adam. And for his daughter." She peeked another glance at Lindsey, the girl's body once again rotating as she followed her dad's progress around the track.

"Becca," Cece said, her voice suddenly serious. "You need to move on."

Becca stiffened. The two trucks were forgotten as her friend touched her arm, squeezing it softly as if she worried she didn't have Becca's attention.

"It's been four years."

"I know."

"Then what's the problem?"

"I'm going to have to hire him, Cece. I can't think of him as anything other than an employee."

"Not if you keep your relationship under wraps."

Becca snorted. "Yeah, right. Like that's possible in this industry."

"It might be worth a shot."

"No. It's better to keep my distance."

Cece stared at her for a long moment and then to Becca's surprise, nodded in understanding. "After all you've been through, I guess you're probably right." She patted Becca's back. "But your luck's about to change, Becca. I feel it."

Becca just hoped her friend was right.

CHAPTER TEN

HE SUCKED.

Not only had he torn up one of their trucks, but he'd barely managed to keep up afterward. Granted, it was hard to keep up in a truck that wasn't as aerodynamic as the others, but he still should have been able to pass at least *one* other truck.

"Boss wants to see you," John said, taking his helmet and steering wheel from him.

Adam paused, having been in the midst of scanning pit road for her. "Where is she?"

"In the hauler," John said, his face giving nothing away.

Was it as bad as it felt?

Damn it, the words were on the tip of Adam's tongue, but he figured it must have been. Hell. Maybe they'd all been slow. Maybe the other guys going out after them were the good group.

Turning, he glanced over at Sam Kennison and his dad. Carl appeared to be giving his son a stern

lecture—about what, though, Adam couldn't hear.
The other drivers all looked at him strangely. He
felt like he'd just come in on the tail end of a joke.

"You going?" John asked, a weird smile on his
face.

"I'm going."

He looked for Lindsey on his way over. A
glance toward the hauler revealed that she, along
with everyone else, had left their perch. When he
looked for her on pit road, all he saw was Blain
and Cece Sanders glancing in his direction. He
gave them a nod and a wave, thinking yet again
that it seemed odd to be smiling at these people
as if they were friends. They'd been faces on TV
for so long that they sort of *seemed* like friends.

But where was Lindsey? Maybe in the hauler
with Becca, he thought, pausing at the back of the
big rig before going in. He was a sweaty mess. The
helmet had given him hat hair. Sweat beaded his
brow. He'd been so distracted he hadn't even
unzipped his firesuit in the sweltering heat. He
did so now, his hands shaking as he pulled down
the metal tongue. But the damn thing got caught.
Oh, well, he thought, opening the sliding glass
doors.

Cool air hit him in the face.

He'd seen haulers before. Hell, he'd had his own

fancy rig back when he'd raced the Silver Crown series. But things had changed a lot since then. Now there was a wafer-thin computer monitor attached to the rubber-coated countertop, not the clunky old-fashioned kind. Everything looked more high-tech, from the shock tester near the middle of the big rig to the flat screen TV that hung at the end of the long aisle. Then again, this was a whole other ballgame.

And he'd blown his chance.

He didn't know what upset him more: that he'd tried and failed—or how Lindsey would take the news. But she probably already knew. She was probably crying in the bathroom, Adam thought as he knocked on the office door near the front of the hauler where someone had told him he could find Becca.

"Come in," Becca said.

Adam took a deep breath, his hand clutching the chrome door handle for a second while he pulled himself together. He didn't want Becca to think he was upset. Or Lindsey, if she was inside.

But Lindsey wasn't inside. When he glanced around the twelve-by-twelve room, it was to see Becca swiveling to face him in an office chair pushed up next to a desk. A matching desk sat in the opposite corner.

"Have you seen Lindsey?" he asked, worried.

"She needed to use the restroom."

Just as he thought. Off crying. "Look," he said, wanting to get this over with, "I appreciate you giving me a shot, and I'm sorry I wrecked your truck."

She smiled a bit, her red hair curling around her shoulders attractively. She'd applied some lip gloss before he'd come in. Either that or she'd just licked her lips…and *that* wasn't a good direction for his thoughts to take.

"Adam, sit down," she said softly, the blue team polo shirt she wore turning her eyes turquoise. He eyed the empty chair opposite her, then reluctantly sat at the desk. The chair squeaked as he spun it around.

"Are you going to ask me to give the money back?"

"What money?" she asked.

"The money you paid me to come down and test."

Her brow cleared. "Not hardly," she said, something slipping into her green eyes. It was a look that could almost be called amusement. Or was it derision? "In hindsight we probably shouldn't have made you go through this at all."

The words stung even though he'd told himself he wouldn't get upset. "Yeah, you're probably right. Lindsey shouldn't have blackmailed you like she did."

"Are you kidding? Lindsey did me a favor."

Suddenly he felt like he'd missed part of the conversation. "Lindsey wasting your time couldn't be considered a favor," he said.

She tipped her head sideways again and Adam was reminded of the first time they'd met. From nowhere came the image of that damn belly button ring. Did she have it on now?

"She didn't waste my time, Adam."

Adam had to replay the words in his head, his mind stuck on the memory of her belly button ring.

"She didn't?"

Becca smiled then, her wide lips spreading into a grin that could only be called beaming. And yet…and yet, there was something missing from that smile, something that didn't quite reach her eyes.

"And the reason why you shouldn't have had to test this way is because you're good. So good, in fact, that if we'd had a look at you during a normal test session we'd have hired you on lap times alone."

"What?"

"The test is over," she said. "We're not even going to look at the second group. Actually, we'd never really planned on doing that. They were just there as a backup in case one of the first round picks tanked."

"But…I don't understand."

"No. You probably don't. Let me start by telling you that John was told to give you changes that would make you go backward, not forward."

"But…that's not possible. At one point I even told them what adjustments to make."

"And he didn't do it. We wanted to see how you'd drive given a not so great setup."

"You're kidding."

She smiled. "No, I'm not. We try our best to test drivers under every circumstance. Every one of you had a not so great truck. And yet you were still kicking everyone's butt at the beginning of the session and so John made you go backward even more. That's why you blew a tire trying to hold Sam off. Your truck was crap, and yet you still held him off. Hell, you held the whole field off."

"Are you trying to tell me I did *good?*"

"Better than good, Adam. Given what you had to work with, you were extraordinary."

He leaned back, his whole body feeling as if it might float off the ground. "Son of a bitch."

"And so I'd like to offer you a job."

No. This wasn't really happening. She wasn't really going to—

"I'd like you to come work for me."

Tears threatened to fill his eyes.

"Ohmygosh! *You* want *him* to come *work* for you?"

They both looked up. Lindsey stood at the door, jaw hanging wide open.

His eyes burned even more.

"Yes, Lindsey, I want him to come work for me. Actually, I want to try him in a race or two," Becca said. And finally, her smile reached her eyes.

His daughter stared at Becca for a second before crying out, "Daddy!"

Adam almost let out a sob. He held back his tears with the fiercest of efforts.

"Oh my gosh," she said as she flung herself at him. "You did it."

"I did it." He held his little girl in his arms, wondering how he could have thought pursuing a full-time driving career might be the wrong thing to do. If he'd known how badly Lindsey had wanted this for him he'd have done it long ago.

"Shh," he soothed, taking a deep breath to stall off tears. Wouldn't do for Becca to see him cry. "We've a long way to go before anything's for certain, Lin."

"I know," his daughter said, pulling back and wiping at her eyes with the heel of her hand. "It's just that I'm so *proud* of you."

His ears buzzed for a second as he felt a lump in his throat.

He'd done it.

"I *knew* you could do it," she said.

"We still have to calculate your score," Becca said, and when Adam looked back at her, he was floored when he noticed her own red-rimmed eyes. "But it's pretty obvious that you did great."

"Are you sure?" Adam asked. "This morning you had three other drivers who were faster than me."

"Yeah, but they scored poorly in other areas. One of them didn't take direction well. Another one's lap times weren't consistent. It's one thing to drive fast once or twice. What you need to do is do it all the time. You have that ability."

Lindsey hugged him again, her little limbs managing to give him a death squeeze despite her petite frame. "You did it," she crowed again.

Yes, he thought. *I did.*

Son of a bitch.

CHAPTER ELEVEN

SHE HAD TO LEAVE.

Becca had felt like an interloper from the moment Lindsey had entered the room.

"I'll let you two celebrate," she said, getting up from her chair.

"No, you don't have to—"

But she'd already left the office. She had to leave the office because if she didn't, she'd do something completely unprofessional.

Like start bawling in front of them both.

"Becca," she heard him call.

She pretended not to hear him.

Footsteps rang out behind her. She sped up. She didn't know where she was going, just wanted to find someplace where she could catch her breath, maybe get rid of the stupid tears that kept welling up in her eyes every time she pictured the look on Lindsey's face.

"Becca," she heard him say again.

She reached the end of the hauler, slipped out the door and stepped into bright sunlight. Their spare parts hauler was parked right next door and so she slid between the two big rigs, hoping he'd think he'd lost her amongst her crew members that were moving about and trying to clean up.

She should have known better.

"Hey, Becca. What's up?" He appeared between the two haulers, too.

The sides of the truck were white, so if she turned back to him the light would refract up the makeshift alleyway, revealing her watery eyes—

His hand caught her shoulder. "What's wrong?" he asked, stepping in front of her.

"Nothing," she said brightly, too brightly, wiping quickly at her eyes.

"You were crying."

"No, I wasn't."

"Why?"

Because she was terrified. Because she envied what he had with his daughter. She'd never felt so alone. But she couldn't say that. "I thought you and your daughter might want some time alone."

He held her gaze. "You could have stayed."

"No. You and Lindsey needed privacy."

"You're part of this, too."

Her heart lurched. "No, I'm not—"

"I wouldn't *be* here if not for you."

"I'm not the one that drove the wheels off that race truck."

"Just the same, thank you," he said, squeezing her shoulders.

"You're welcome," she choked out. His hands felt warm. She suddenly felt cold.

"For everything," he added. "I'll never be able to express how much this all means to me. And to Lindsey."

But he would try. She could see it in his eyes and that scared her to death because if he knew how much she wanted him to succeed, he might think she cared.

You do care.

"I have to go," she said, her throat so tight with unshed tears that it was hard to get the words out.

"Becca."

He stepped closer to her. She stopped. His hand tried to pull her close. She resisted.

He closed the distance between them.

She gasped. And the moment he touched her she lost the will to do anything other than move into his arms.

She was tired of always being strong.

"Adam," she mumbled weakly.

He rested his cheek against the top of her head

and held her. That's all he did, hold her, but her legs grew weak just the same. She leaned back, tried to pull away, but his head began to lower. Their breaths mingled and for a moment she thought—

"Well, well, well."

They broke apart.

Carl Kennison stood at the entrance to the alleyway, arms crossed, the white truck reflecting light onto a face that was a scorching, angry red.

CHAPTER TWELVE

"So this is how it works," he drawled. "It's not about driving skills, it's about your ability to seduce the boss."

"Mr. Kennison—"

"Shut the hell up," Adam interrupted, taking a step toward Carl. "You have no idea what's going on here, so I wouldn't be so quick to leap to conclusions."

"What conclusion is there to leap to other than you were about to kiss Becca Newman?"

Adam lunged. Becca caught his hand just in time, tugging him back. "Don't," she warned him when he glanced down at her, only to try to tug away from her. "Don't," she repeated. "It's not worth it."

"Oh, it'd be worth it, all right."

"No, Adam, it wouldn't. You know what he'd tell the media."

"Oh, I'll be talking to the media, all right," he said, his blue eyes flaring like an arc welder.

"Go ahead," Adam challenged. "We've got nothing to hide."

"No? I'm sure the media will have a field day with this, anyway."

With a nasty smirk, Carl turned away, Becca letting go of Adam's hand only when he disappeared from the opening of the makeshift alleyway.

"That son of a b—"

"Adam, forget it. We didn't do anything wrong."

But they'd almost done something wrong.

"I know we didn't, but that won't stop that you-know-what from spreading nasty rumors."

"Then we shouldn't do anything that might be interpreted wrongly."

"What I do is my own business."

"Not when it involves me. Not now that you work for me."

"Becca—"

"No, Adam. I know what you were about to do, but you can't—" she took a deep breath of resolve "—you can't kiss me," she finished in a low voice.

"Becca, there's something here," he said, touching his heart. "I know you feel it, too."

"All I feel is a healthy respect for your driving ability and a fondness for your daughter," she lied.

"That's *all*. And so in the future you'll refrain from touching me."

"Becca—"

"I mean it, Adam," she said, crossing her arms when he took a step nearer. "Or I'll rescind my offer and I think we both know that would break Lindsey's heart. She wants this for you, probably more than you want it for yourself."

His jaw had begun to flex stubbornly. "You're fooling yourself, Becca."

"Am I? Or are you fooling yourself? You wouldn't be the first driver to have a crush on me."

His eyes narrowed, but that was good. She'd angered him. Maybe now he'd get the point. There was nothing between them, and there never could be.

Not as long as he was her driver.

"This isn't over," he said as she slipped past him, their shoulders brushing, Becca's breath catching.

"Yes, Adam, it is."

"It isn't, Becca."

She turned back to him, crossing her arms in front of her. "Then I guess that means I can't hire you."

"DAMMIT!"

"Dad?" Lindsey asked, suddenly blocking the entrance to the alleyway. "What's going on?

Becca just walked past me and she looked really, really mad."

Her dad ran his hand through his hair, the look on his face one she recognized from the many times she'd gotten into trouble.

Uh-oh.

"Nothing," he said, running his hand through his hair yet again, another sure sign that he was P.O.'d. If her face was going to freeze into a permanent cow grimace, her daddy was going to go bald by the time he turned forty with the way he always tugged at his hair.

"Look, Dad," she said, glancing behind her before stepping between both trucks. "I may only be ten, but I know when something's wrong. You should have seen the look on Carl Kennison's face. I thought he might punch something."

"It's nothing, Lin."

Lindsey watched her dad try to calm down. She could always tell he was doing that by the way he flexed his hands over and over again. It was like yoga for him.

"Did Carl catch you two kissing?"

"What?"

"Come on, Dad. It doesn't take a rocket scientist to know there's something between you and Becca."

Her dad stared at her for a long second, only to run his hands through his hair again. "Why do I have a feeling you know a lot more about the birds and the bees than I want you to know?"

"Da-ad. Nobody calls it the birds and the bees anymore."

He shook his head. "I don't want to talk about this. Let's go."

"What did Carl say?" Lindsey asked, refusing to budge. "Did he say something to Becca to make her cry?"

"Was she crying?"

And he said the words so quickly Lindsey knew he'd begun to care for her already. *Awe. Some.*

"No. But she looked like she might."

"Son of a—" He shook his head again. "We're leaving."

She shrugged out of his grasp. "Dad, don't. We need to talk about this. What's going on between you and Becca is only about the most important thing in your life. You can't let that Carl Kennison guy do something to ruin it."

She didn't think her dad would answer, but to her surprise she saw his shoulders relax, saw the look in his eyes change from one of irritation to one of acceptance. "He caught me just as I was about kiss Becca."

"So?"

"She doesn't want to hire me now."

"She doesn't? But that's ridiculous."

"Lindsey, it's not up to me."

"Maybe you shouldn't give her a choice."

"I can't force her to hire me."

"You can if you threaten to go to work for another team."

"She'd let me go."

"No, she won't. Not if she's as smart as I think she is."

He appeared to consider that, the look on his face thoughtful and then serious. "You make it sound easy."

"It *is* easy," she said. Jeez. Sometimes adults could be so stupid. "Just go to her and tell her you're sorry and ask if you can drive for her."

"I think Becca's afraid if she hires me some-one will believe Carl Kennison when he says we're an item."

"That's just dumb. All anyone'd have to do was look at your lap times."

"He'll claim they were doctored up or some-thing."

"No way."

"He might," he said.

"Does that mean you're not even going to try?"

She watched him closely to make sure he really thought about her words because she couldn't, just couldn't let him quit. Not when practically her whole entire life depended on it. For years she'd been a total outcast. Well, okay, she had Brandy for a friend. But that was it. All those popular girls looked down their noses at her. But if her dad became a famous race car driver they wouldn't be able to do that. Sure, she'd be going to another school by then, but just the thought of them seeing her and her dad on TV filled her with glee.

"Dad?" Lindsey prompted, still holding her breath.

"I'll talk to her."

"Yesss!" Lindsey said, punching the air. "Yes, yes, yes. That Frances Pritchert will be *so* sorry she ever called me white trash."

"She *what?*"

"She's one of the popular girls, Dad, and she's a total you-know-what. She's always making snide comments about my clothes, my shoes, my hair—"

"What's her name again?"

"Dad, it's no big deal. I've gotten used to it. But I can't wait until you have your first autograph session. I'm going to make sure she knows about it."

"Lindsey, I may not be able to convince Becca to hire me."

"You'll do it."

"And why didn't you tell me about that girl before?"

"I don't know," Lindsey said. "Stuff like that happens all the time, so I hardly notice it anymore. But getting back to you and Becca, all you have to do is talk to her. She'll realize she's made a mistake when Blain and Cece offer to hire you."

"They haven't done that."

"Bet you they will."

"I don't know. But I guess we'll see."

Lindsey stared up at her dad, noting the worry in his eyes. "Talk to her," she said.

"Not today. Let me wait a day or two."

Why did she have a feeling it'd be longer than that? "You promise?"

"I promise."

Good, because if he didn't talk to Becca, *she* would. And if that didn't work she'd do something else.

She just didn't know what.

SHE RODE HOME with the truck driver.

Becca knew it was the coward's way out, but when it came time to leave she just couldn't face Adam.

Or Lindsey.

Neil, one of her big rig drivers, wasn't the talkative type, which was good. She had a lot to think about on her way home.

She had to hire him.

She knew that. Cripes, she hadn't gotten as far as she had in this business without making sound business decisions. And the truth of the matter was she needed to find *someone* to drive her race truck. Her financial situation had gotten dire, so much so that she was thinking about putting feelers out for an investor. She didn't really want a partner, but she'd do whatever was necessary to keep her team.

When they got back to the shop she headed immediately for her car in its private parking spot near the back of the shop.

Adam was sitting by the curb waiting for her.

"We need to talk," he said, the light fixtures overhead making him look pale. Her, too, probably.

"Where's Lindsey?"

"Inside," he said, motioning with his chin toward the shop. "The guys who stuck around to unload the haulers are keeping an eye on her."

She nodded, fishing her keys out of her purse at the same time she asked, "What's up?"

"You know what's up."

She met his gaze, her keys jingling as she pressed the unlock button. "I told you what the deal is, Adam."

"Did you? I didn't hear any deal. All I heard was that you didn't want to hire me."

That was how it'd come out sounding. And to be honest, at the time she'd meant the words. "I was wrong," she admitted, shaking her head. Her face felt burnt from her long day in the sun, and she was exhausted, both physically and emotionally.

"Does that mean you've changed your mind?"

She looked him in the eye. "I'll let you drive for me, Adam—on one condition."

"Name it."

"We can't cross the line."

"What line?"

"You know very well what line I'm talking about."

"Maybe I don't. Maybe you should explain it to me just so we're absolutely clear."

Maybe she should. "We can't be friends. We can't…"

Kiss.

"Socialize," she ended up saying. "We can't be seen together. We have to keep things on a professional level."

"I see."

"Do you?" she asked. "Do you really, Adam? Because this is nonnegotiable."

"I understand," he repeated, crossing his arms in front of him. He wore the same polo shirt he'd had on earlier, his big shoulders looking twice as wide all of a sudden.

Maybe that was because she wanted to lean on them.

"Then you agree to my terms?"

"I agree."

"Good. When you get your things in order, give me a call. I'll get Sylvia started on finding you an apartment."

"Fine."

She opened her car door.

He was there at her car door before she could stop him.

"What is it?"

"I just wanted to say thank you again," he said, resting his hands across the top of the door frame.

"You're welcome."

"Lindsey will be thrilled."

"I'm sure she will be."

"You won't regret your decision," he added.

"I hope not," she said with a flick of her head.

Adam watched her drive away, and if Becca

had looked back at that moment she might have rethought her decision.

"We'll see about your 'rules,' Becca Newman," he muttered as she drove off. "We'll just have to wait and see."

PART TWO

The tragedy is not that love doesn't last.
The tragedy is the love that lasts.
                              —Shirley Hazzard

One Guy And A Precocious Baby
By: Rick Stevenson, Sports Editor

Sometimes there's truth to the rumors you hear, and sometimes there're ten-year-old girls who aren't afraid to tell it like it is.

Most of you have no doubt heard the stories swirling around Newman Motorsports's newly hired driver, Adam Drake. I don't think there's a Web page anywhere on the Net that didn't post at least a sentence or two about Carl Kennison's recent allegations. Most of us dismissed the tale as sour grapes—his son didn't win *The Variety Show,* but there was quite a buzz about the matter, especially when Kennison refused to let the matter drop and Becca Newman refused to comment. For the most part, I ignored the story—until Drake's ten-year-old daughter called my radio show last week.

I don't usually publish stories told by children, but this one's too good to keep under wraps. Plus I was able to verify most of what the daughter told me, and after the response from my listeners, I don't think I have any choice *but* to write about it.

So here goes. Let me start with some backstory. Seems Lindsey Drake's responsible for her dad getting his shot at the big league. She personally rode down to North Carolina—on a Greyhound bus, and without her dad's knowledge—and begged Rebecca Newman to give her dad a look. Becca Newman did, and Adam Drake blew the doors off the competition.

As far as the allegations of a romantic entanglement between driver and owner, Lindsey Drake denies them. She said her dad has never, not once, kissed Becca Newman. That's not to say Adam Drake's daughter wouldn't like Becca Newman and her father to start dating. Ms. Drake thinks Ms. Newman is "totally awesome." She also told me that she's pretty certain her dad thinks she's "totally hot." Given the fact that lots of men around the country also think Ms. Newman is "totally hot" (present company included), I can't really fault the guy for that.

But now that the rumors have been laid to rest, a question comes to mind:

Does Rebecca Newman think Adam Drake is "totally hot," and if so, what is she going to do about it?

CHAPTER THIRTEEN

"LINDSEY SAMANTHA DRAKE! Get out here *now*." Adam yelled, his arms crossed as his daughter emerged form her room.

"Yeah, Dad," she said sleepily, wiping at her eyes.

He stood in the doorway of their tiny kitchen, a multitude of boxes filled with appliances, utensils and cookware sitting at his feet. He was half tempted to find the box with the spatula, bend her over his knee and give her a good spanking— except he'd never spanked her in his life and so she'd see right through his threat.

"I just got off the phone with KYZX channel 21," he said.

"Really?" she said, still blinking up at him.

"Guess what they wanted to talk to me about?"

"What?"

"You know."

And there it was, just a glimmer of discomfort. "I know what?"

"It appears one of the reporters at the station heard your call in to *NASCAR Live!*"

And now she winced, her hand falling back to her side. But he had to give her credit. She recovered quickly, her freckled face stretching into a grin so wide she would give a slice of watermelon a run for its money.

"They heard me? Really?"

At least she didn't deny it. "They heard you," he said, and the look he gave her should have had that smile fading—only it didn't. That was the thing about his daughter. Even when she'd done something outrageous—like call into a national radio show and tell the world about how he came to be employed by Becca Newman—she always brazened things out, making it seem as if she'd done nothing wrong. He admired that about her even when it made him want to throttle her.

"Wow, Dad. That's wild. I didn't expect anyone local to hear."

"Really?" he asked, arms still crossed. "And what did you think? That nobody in Kentucky had radios?"

"No," she said, shrugging. "I just didn't think about it, I guess. It's kind of weird, actually. I mean, what are the odds that someone from our own hometown would be listening to *NASCAR Live!* at the same time I was on—"

"Lindsey!" Adam snapped. "Rick Stevenson wrote a piece about it. The column's in this morning's paper."

"So?"

"So," he repeated, flabbergasted. "The media's going to be all over this and I'm not so certain Becca Newman wanted the story out."

The phone rang again.

"That's probably another damn reporter wanting to know if I really *do* think Becca Newman is 'totally hot.'"

At last she looked a bit cowed. Well, at least as cowed as his daughter *could* look, which was to say her smile faded, but only a bit.

"Aren't you going to get that?"

"No."

"Why not?"

"Because I'm half-afraid it's *her*. What do you think she'll say when she hears what you've been up to?"

"She should be happy. I was setting the record straight. That Carl Kennison was all over the place talking about how you slept with Becca to get your job. That's wrong. You didn't sleep with her." Her eyebrows squished together. "Did you?"

"No!" he shot back, exasperated.

"See. So he's a bald-faced liar. I couldn't let him get away with that. So I called the show."

"And told the world that Carl Kennison is a 'butthead.'"

"He *is* a butthead."

The answering machine kicked on, Drake listening to his daughter's innocent voice asking people to leave a message.

Innocent. Right.

"Hello, Mr. Drake," said a sexy feminine voice. "This is Christy Lawson from *We* magazine. We're doing a story on employees attracted to their bosses and wondered if you'd be interested in giving us a quote."

"I don't believe it," Adam said, turning to the answering machine and dialing the volume down as low as it would go, but they could still hear her—like a tiny little person was captured inside the phone. He shook his head and faced his daughter again. "Not only does Rick Stevenson have a radio show, but he's also a stringer. His columns appear in newspapers nationwide. There's no telling what you've unleashed."

"Da-ad. All I was doing was setting the record straight."

"That's not the point and you know it."

"It's not?"

"You shouldn't have done it, Lin. I might get fired. Again."

"Becca wouldn't do that," Lindsey said. "She likes you too much."

Okay, that did it. He couldn't let her go on living in a fantasy world. "Lindsey, there's nothing between Becca Newman and I."

"There is. You almost kissed her."

"Once."

"And she was about to let you."

"We don't know that for sure."

"The point is she didn't pull away."

He sighed in exasperation before saying, "Look," and swiping a hand through his hair. "My attempt at kissing Becca was a mistake, one I won't repeat, and so there is nothing between us. You can stop your matchmaking machinations right now."

"Matchmaking? I'm not doing that. And what's a machination?"

He gave her a long look. "It means you're trying to manipulate someone."

"Oh," she said, starting to look uncomfortable.

The phone rang again. They both dropped into silence, Adam even leaning forward to hear who it might be. Yes, even after he'd turned the damn volume down, some perverse part of him wanted to hear who it was. A few seconds later he had their answer.

"Mr. Drake, this is Sylvia Munroe from Newman Motorsports. Becca Newman would like to speak with you at your earliest convenience. Please call us back…."

"Damn it," Adam said.

"Dad, she might be calling about something else."

He gave her a hard look.

"She might," she said again, weakly.

"Yeah, right," was all he said.

"HE'S NOT RETURNING my calls," Sylvia said later that same afternoon. Her assistant stood at the entrance to her office, her hand on the door. Down in the shop someone was banging away with a rubber mallet, its rhythmic *thud-thud-thud* giving Becca a headache.

"Okay," Becca said. "Keep trying."

"Will do," Sylvia said.

When the door closed with a soft click Becca put her head in her hands, one of her stack of phone messages sliding out from beneath her elbow and onto the checkered flag carpet below. She left it there.

Three calls from her truck team's sponsor, numerous calls from the media and one slightly strange call from the president of *Singles.com,* who would like to sponsor her race truck as long as she'd allow them to frame a reality show around her and Adam's courtship.

"Courtship," she mumbled, rubbing her temple. "Unbelievable."

Someone knocked. She grumbled a reluctant, "Come in."

"Hello, Becca."

She shot up from her desk, tugging at her white silk blouse that persisted in clinging to her body thanks to the static in the air, static that seemed to charge every particle of her body the moment she spotted him.

"Adam, er, Mr. Drake," she said, resisting the urge to tug down her knee-length black skirt, as well. Why did it suddenly feel like it was riding up her legs? "What are you doing here?"

"Guess," he said, walking into her office like a man who wasn't afraid of anything.

"Rick Stevenson," she said.

He nodded. "When Sylvia called this morning I decided I better drive over and talk to you about it face-to-face."

"You didn't need to do that."

"I thought it might make it easier if you were about to fire me. Again."

"Fire you? No, I'm not going to fire you. I'm not happy about it, but in all honesty it's been great publicity. We can probably get extra mileage out of it if I ask our PR gal to spin it. Is Lindsey with you?"

"No. She's at school."

"I see."

"Becca, about what happened in Martinsville—"

"No, Adam. There's no need to talk about that again. I have the utmost confidence that you'll respect my wishes to keep things on a professional level."

"You do?"

"I do," she said firmly.

She saw something in his eyes then—pique, maybe, or disappointment. "Great. Then I guess I really didn't need to drive down here."

"You didn't."

He took a step toward her. "Do you want me to talk to the press when they call? Or should I field all interview requests through you?"

Becca almost took a step back, but she stopped herself just in time, crossing her arms as she looked up at him. "We can handle them."

He nodded.

"How's the packing coming along?"

"We're almost there."

"I hear Sylvia found you and Lindsey a nice apartment."

"I don't know. I've only ever seen pictures. But maybe I'll take a drive by there today."

"Maybe you should," she said, straightening some papers on her desk.

"Well, I've got some people coming in, so I better get back to work."

But he didn't move, didn't nod, didn't do anything but stand there.

"What is it?" she asked.

"Martinsville."

"No," she interrupted. "I told you. We don't need to go there again."

"Actually, I think we do."

"No, we don't."

"Yes, we do, Becca. We do because I know you felt the same thing I did."

"I didn't feel anything," she lied.

"Yes, you did. You felt the same jolt I did. I saw it in your eyes."

She looked away, her chest rising and falling as quickly as a piston.

"And so I have to ask myself, maybe the reason you fired me the first time wasn't because I tried to kiss you, but because you *wanted* me to kiss you?"

"Adam," she said softly.

"And if you *want* me to kiss you, then why didn't you let me?"

"Because I'm your boss."

"No," he instantly contradicted. "That's not it. That's got nothing to do with it."

"It's got everything to do with it."

"You don't want me kissing you because you're still hung up on Randy."

She didn't answer. What could she say? It was true. She would always be "hung up" on Randy. The sooner he realized that, the better.

"But, Becca, I never got anywhere by quitting. And I've learned that in life, some things are worth fighting for."

The implication was that he wanted to fight for *her,* and God help her, those words made it all happen again—made her body warm and then tingle like it had when they'd been standing together between those two trucks.

He made her *feel* again.

She looked away again. Her gaze landed on the trophy case.

No.

No, she repeated with a inward shake of her head. She wouldn't give in. She owed Randy that much.

She sucked in a breath, forced herself to look him in the eyes. "I appreciate your honesty," she said. "But I'm not ready for a relationship." Even as she said the words, she wondered if she lied.

"Fine," he said. "I'm willing to accept that excuse." He leaned toward her. "For now."

He turned on his heel and walked out of her office without another word. When he was gone, Becca sank down into her chair, the thing squeaking as it rolled back a bit.

Adam Drake had just propositioned her. No, not propositioned her, *warned* her. He wanted to pursue her. And instead of backing away from her when she'd sent up the usual roadblocks, he'd accepted the challenge. Given what he did for a living she supposed she shouldn't be surprised. What did surprise her was how that made her feel. She wasn't mad. She wasn't furious. She didn't want to fire him.

She was...excited.

She put her head in her hands again, her whole body beginning to shake. She felt excited and afraid and so terribly guilty that she could feel that way about any other man than Randy.

It's time to move on.

Cece's words echoed in her ears. But as Becca sat there, she had only one question.

Was it?

SHE AVOIDED HIM over the next week, as Adam had assumed she would. To be honest it wasn't hard to do. In between moving from his place in Kentucky to a new apartment in Mooresville, he wasn't at the shop a whole lot. And even once he *was* settled, he still didn't see her. As an owner, she had far too many duties, most of which involved the day-to-day operation of her race teams, to concern herself with him. He wasn't supposed to have a whole lot to do. Most drivers let the specialist build their cars. But Adam had spent too many years racing on a shoestring not to know a thing or two and so he felt comfortable offering John, now his official crew chief, advice. Granted, he wasn't familiar with the tracks he'd be racing at, nor all that familiar with truck chassis, but John was, and between the two of them Adam thought they might have a shot at building some pretty awesome trucks.

Plus, it kept him close to Becca.

With her office overlooking the shop he often found himself looking up to the plate-glass windows. He'd never caught her staring, but he knew *she* knew he was there. Through the week he'd watched her escort visitors around the shop, hold meetings in her office and generally stay busy for ten-, twelve-, sometimes fifteen-hour days. And on the one occasion they'd crossed paths and he'd been tempted to get close to her, he'd kept his distance. She needed time. And space.

But he wasn't going to wait too long.

Adam didn't know when he'd decided to make a play for her. Probably when he'd burst into her office and seen Becca looking worn and tired and just plain lonely. Something happened to him then as he stared at her, something to do with recognition. He knew what it was like to be alone. Knew how it felt to have the weight of the world on one's shoulders. But it didn't need to be that way.

Someone had to make her see that.

"You ready for the race this weekend?" someone asked, bringing his focus back to the race shop.

"I don't know," Adam said honestly, glancing at the rear end specialist who'd built the thing. "It's one thing to sign up for this gig and another thing to actually have to do it for a living."

"That's for sure," Chris said.

He was a kid, or at least it looked that way to Adam. With his mop of blond hair, he resembled a surfer, not someone who worked for a race team. In reality he was probably in his early twenties, the product of North Carolina's Institute of Racing Technology.

An Important Message from the Editors

Dear Reader,

Because you've chosen to read one of our fine novels, we'd like to say "thank you!" And, as a **special** way to thank you, we're offering you a choice of <u>two more</u> of the books you love so well **plus** an exciting Mystery Gift to send you— absolutely <u>FREE</u>!

Please enjoy them with our compliments...

Pam Powers

Lift here

Peel off seal and place inside...

The Reader Service — Here's How It Works:

Accepting your 2 free books and gift places you under no obligation to buy anything. You may keep the books and gift and return the shipping statement marked "cancel." If you do not cancel, about a month later we'll send you 3 additional books and bill you just $5.24 each in the U.S., or $5.74 each in Canada, plus 25¢ shipping & handling per book and applicable taxes if any.* That's the complete price and — compared to cover prices starting from $5.99 each in the U.S. and $6.99 each in Canada — it's quite a bargain! You may cancel at any time, but if you choose to continue, every month we'll send you 3 more books, which you may either purchase at the discount price or return to us and cancel your subscription.

*Terms and prices subject to change without notice. Sales tax applicable in N.Y. Canadian residents will be charged applicable provincial taxes and GST.

If offer card is missing write to: The Reader Service, 3010 Walden Ave., P.O. Box 1867, Buffalo, NY 14240-1867

BUSINESS REPLY MAIL

FIRST-CLASS MAIL   PERMIT NO. 717-003   BUFFALO, NY

POSTAGE WILL BE PAID BY ADDRESSEE

THE READER SERVICE
3010 WALDEN AVE
PO BOX 1341
BUFFALO NY 14240-8571

NO POSTAGE
NECESSARY
IF MAILED
IN THE
UNITED STATES

"And now you have a bunch of people watching you," he said.

He did, thanks to Rick Stevenson's article. The reporter had sat down and interviewed Lindsey again last week—this time under Adam's watchful eye. Once more the phones had started to ring, or so Connie had told him, but Adam had to admit, the piece Rick had written was pretty good even if it did make him sound like racing's version of Cinderella. But the end result was that a lot of people were no doubt watching to see if he'd be any good.

They'd know the answer in three days, sooner if you counted qualifying. He hadn't been able to race that past weekend thanks to a licensing snafu—Adam's application for a permit hadn't gotten to NASCAR in time, so he'd been forced to sit it out. Although to be honest, that hadn't been a bad thing. It'd given Lindsey and him time to settle into their new home—and Lindsey her new school, which she appeared to love.

"So you're the new boy."

Adam and Chris looked up to see Jason Ingle standing above them, the NASCAR NEXTEL Cup Series driver's arms crossed and a sneer on his face.

"Hey, Jason," Chris said, and Adam could tell

by his tone of voice that he didn't think much of the driver.

"You the one they hired to replace me?" Jason asked, not acknowledging the two crew members.

"Well, I don't know about that," Adam said, thinking the guy looked older in person than he did on TV. Twenty-eight, maybe twenty-nine years old. Black hair. Errol Flynn mustache.

Jason glanced at the race truck currently on jack stands, the blue and gold paint scheme reflecting back bars of light from the fluorescents overhead. The smell of parts cleaner hovered in the air. They'd drained the rear axle and both Adam and Chris had rear end grease all over their light blue coveralls.

"I read Rick Stevenson's article," he said, face impassive, arms still crossed, one side of his wannabe mustache lifting.

"Oh, yeah?" Adam said, wiping his hands with a blue work towel. The grease wouldn't leave his fingers.

"Yeah. And I have to wonder. What kind of driver has to be persuaded by his ten-year-old daughter to test for a race team?"

"You wouldn't ask me that if you knew my daughter," Adam said as he tossed the towel onto a bright red work cart, making light of the situation since it was obvious Jason was trying to get his goat. There was intense dislike in the man's blue eyes. Not surprising. Everyone in the shop knew he was on his way out, including Jason. The only reason Becca kept him around was because she didn't have anybody better to take over his ride. And while he wasn't a bad driver, he'd never be the best. Becca knew that. His NASCAR NEXTEL Cup Series team knew that. Heck, Jason probably knew that.

"Sounds like your daughter has bigger balls than you."

"Jason," Chris said, standing up.

Adam straightened. "Look, I don't know what your deal is and, frankly, I don't care, but I've got a long ways to go before moving to a Cup team, *if* I get to that level, and so there's no need to throw darts my way."

"Yeah," the guy said. "You're probably right. Besides, I guess we'll discover how big your balls are this weekend."

"I guess we will."

"But just so you're prepared, I'm entered in the truck race, too."

Swallowing his pride, Adam smiled. "Well, good, maybe you can give me a few pointers."

Jason smirked. "You'll probably need all the pointers you can get."

Adam nodded. "I probably will."

Jason held his gaze a moment longer, probably trying to think of another way to insult him. In the end he apparently gave up, although not without a scathing look of condescension.

"See ya Friday," he said. "Don't forget to bring your helmet, rookie."

"Whatever," Adam muttered under his breath, turning back to Chris.

"Man, that guy is one hundred percent. Ass. Hole," Chris said when he'd walked away. "I'll be glad when Becca fires his sorry ass."

"You think she's really going to?"

"No doubt about it," Chris said. "That cat is toast. She'd have fired him before now except all the good drivers want to drive for the multicar teams, not Newman Motorsports. "

"Yeah, well, we'll just have to prove to them that Newman Motorsports is the place to be," Adam said with a glance toward the entrance to the shop. Jason was just pulling open the door.

"I don't think it helped that he made a play for Becca."

"He what?" Adam asked, swinging back to face Chris.

"Tried to come on to her after a race one day last year. Probably a last-ditch effort to hold on to his job. She shut him down faster than a coon dog catches fleas. She's been giving him the cold shoulder ever since."

Adam knew he shouldn't be gossiping about Becca, especially given the fact that he'd been the recipient of some of that gossip in recent weeks, but still.

You wouldn't be the first driver to have a crush on me.

The words came back to him, and now Adam realized that she'd been talking about Jason.

"I'm surprised she didn't release him," Adam said. Then again, she hadn't fired *him.*

"They exchanged words. I think he threatened to make it look like she propositioned him. Or at least that's the shop rumor. Someone claims to have overheard the conversation. But whatever really happened, she's treading carefully around the putz now."

"That's no good."

"No, it's not." His gaze held Adam's. "Watch yourself Saturday night. That guy's trouble and you, my friend, have a big ol' target painted on your ass."

"Jason Ingle to Ms. Newman's office," a feminine voice announced over the PA. "Jason Ingle to Ms. Newman's office."

Adam and Chris looked up at the glass windows of Becca's office.

"Uh-oh. Looks like someone's in trouble."

"You think?"

"I'll wager my favorite engine that he is."

"WHAT DID YOU say to him?" Rebecca snapped the minute Jason Ingle entered her office.

"Nothing," he said in that smooth voice he used when trying to act the innocent—or get down someone's skirt.

"I saw the look on your face," she said. "And it wasn't *nothing*."

"What's the matter, baby?" he asked, sauntering up to her. "Worried I'll get your new boyfriend upset?"

She stood, slowly. Though on the outside she undoubtedly looked cool and professional, on the inside she was shaking with rage.

"He's not my boyfriend," she said.

He lifted a dark brow, his smile more of a snicker. "That's not what I'm hearing."

"Any more than *you* were ever my boyfriend."

"Your loss," he said.

"No, your loss," she shot back. "And here's

something else you're going to lose," she said, leaning toward him, her fingers splayed across the cherrywood surface. "Your ride in my Cup car."

"You wouldn't fire me. If you did that you'd lose your sponsor for sure."

"Don't tempt me, Jason. You're on shaky ground with me. I might chuck it all just for the joy of tossing you out on your butt."

"Yeah?" he asked with a flick of his head. "We'll just see about that, won't we?"

"Yeah," she said, matching the tone of his voice. "We will."

She held his gaze. His own eyes swept her up and down, taking in the crisp black slacks and rust-colored shirt. "Is that all?" he asked, his words and the look in his eyes seeming to suggest she might want him for something else, like an afternoon tryst.

God, she wanted to fire him.

"That will be all," she said, settling back behind her desk and picking up some paperwork.

"Call me if you change your mind," he said.

"Only if hell freezes over," she muttered under her breath, half hoping he heard her.

When the door closed behind him she set the papers down again, her gaze shifting to the wall of windows. Adam stared up at her.

She looked away, wondering if he'd seen what happened, and if he could tell from all the way down there how much she loathed Jason Ingle.

But the truth of the matter was she couldn't fire him. Sponsors liked their cars to have an outside chance of finishing well, and as sad as it seemed, Jason was the best thing out there right now. Once Silly Season started, that might all change. Thank God with The Chase now in effect, drivers started moving around much earlier in the year. With any luck she'd find someone then.

Or maybe Adam could take his spot.

She glanced at the windows again, but he was gone. She wondered where he was, but then the phone rang and she had to focus on yet another problem. That was what she did all day. Solve problem after problem after problem. And her troubles were mounting every day, so much so that she'd made an appointment with a potential investor. She hadn't wanted to do it, but it seemed she had no choice.

BY THE TIME she turned down her street, Becca was so tired and so depressed she truly wondered if she might cry.

And then she saw Adam's truck in her driveway.

She slowed. Actually, she almost stopped and put the car in Reverse. But to be honest, she was too damn tired to skulk away.

"What are you doing here?" she asked. She hadn't meant to sound terse, but the words came out that way, anyway.

"I came to see you," he said over the sound of nearby frogs. They always croaked at dusk.

"Well you've wasted your time, Adam. I don't have the energy to fend off your advances."

"I know."

"Good, then go home," she said, grabbing her briefcase from the back of her Cobra. The sound of the trunk slamming shut stopped the frogs from croaking for a moment.

"I saw you with Jason Ingle today," he said, causing her to turn back to him. "I don't know what you two talked about, and I don't need to know. I just think you should watch yourself. That man is trouble."

"You think I don't know that?" she asked. "Jason Ingle's cost me more money in fines than any other driver who's worked for me. I know exactly what type of man he is."

"Then why haven't you fired him?"

She sighed. "I can't. I need him to keep the sponsors happy. At least for now."

He didn't say anything, just stood there, the setting sun highlighting his hair on one side.

"Look, Adam. I appreciate your concern, but there's nothing to worry about."

"Have you gotten any sleep recently?"

She looked up sharply. "What?"

"You look exhausted."

"Thanks," she said, turning away again.

"Now you look like you're about to cry."

"You're imagining things," she said.

Keep on walking, Becca. If he knows you well enough to sense that, you better keep on walking.

"I just thought you could use a friend."

"I don't have time for friends."

"Is that what you've been telling yourself since Randy died?"

Once again she found herself facing him. "Don't bring Randy into this."

"I know what it's like to be alone," he said softly, ignoring her. "To have nobody but yourself to count on. I know what it feels like to be so damn tired that it's all you can do to stand up, because if you sit down you know you're going to fall asleep from exhaustion."

"So?" she said, telling herself that just because her throat tightened it didn't mean she would cry.

"So?" he said, moving toward her. "I'm telling

you I understand. That I know what it's like to be so overwhelmed with responsibility it's all you can do to hold on to your sanity. I'm a single dad, Becca, with a daughter I love. But you don't have anybody to love you. There's nobody there for you to prop your spirits up when you're feeling down."

"I have Blain and Cece," she contradicted, the words sounding thick even to her own ears.

"It's not the same," he said. "It's not the same as talking to someone who *knows*. Who's been there."

"Someone like you."

"Someone like me," he said, holding her gaze so that her breath caught and her heart beat in a way that had nothing to do with sorrow and fear and everything to do with wanting to just…escape. Escape into his arms for a moment.

Or a night.

"I know what it's like," he said, walking toward her, reaching out a hand and trying to clasp her own.

"Adam, no."

But he grabbed her hand, anyway. And that's all he did. But somehow it felt like the most intimate of caresses.

"Becca," he said, and his voice was so gentle and full of compassion. "You don't have to do this alone."

Her lips began to tremble.

He ducked down. She tensed. He gave her time to pull away.

But she didn't.

His kiss was as soft as the brush of dandelion seeds, his hand tightening around her own and pulling her closer. She leaned back to resist him, but then she felt his tongue brush her own lips and she suddenly didn't care that they were in front of her home, or that someone might drive by and see them. She just didn't care.

His big hand ran up her arm, and then down again, and then lowered even farther, slipping around to find the small of her back. That was all he did. Touch her right behind her hip, but he might as well have done so much more.

"Adam."

His other hand slipped between them, unbuttoning her shirt. She felt the silk part a little, static making it stick to her body like wet cloth. She heard the crackle of electricity as he pulled the shirt down, then felt a different kind of charge when his lips left hers and landed at the crook of her neck. Her head tipped to the side.

Headlights were coming down the street.

That snapped her out of it. She stepped back and hastily buttoned her shirt. Adam backed away, too, no doubt hearing the car's engine. Or maybe not. Maybe he'd been waiting for her to call a stop to things.

"Becca—"

"I've got to go."

"You don't have to run away."

Yes, she did.

"I'm willing to wait."

Wait? Wait for what?

"I'll be here. Waiting for you."

Then it would be a long wait.

She unlocked her door and slipped inside, leaning against the door after closing it behind her.

A picture of Randy sat on the hall table. That was good. His picture centered her. It reminded her of all that she'd shared with him. That kind of thing couldn't be found twice. It was precious and rare. What Adam offered was common and crass. A temporary release that would disappear as quickly as it'd come.

Then why don't you indulge yourself?

She shook her head at the question because the answer was simple. She wasn't into one-night stands, and that's all she could allow herself with Adam.

Randy owned the rest of her nights.

CHAPTER FOURTEEN

IT WAS EASY to avoid him for the rest of that week, although Becca suspected Adam was deliberately giving her space. Before she knew it, his first race had arrived. Unfortunately, she couldn't be there for practice and qualifying, although ultimately that might be a good thing.

But she couldn't avoid him forever, and so she forced herself to attend. As it turned out it was a good thing she went. Adam's outstanding qualifying performance at such a hard to handle track—Bristol—seemed to be the topic du jour. The prerace interviews helped to distract her, but not for long enough. She was a nervous wreck, not so much because she was worried about Adam's safety, but because a good performance would mean so much.

She *needed* him to do well.

She didn't expect him to win, she admitted, holding on to the clipboard so tightly she lost feeling in the ends of her fingers. What she wanted was a good finish, something tangible she could show to the investor she'd met with this week. Something she could use as proof to show that things weren't as grim as they appeared on paper. Something that she could point to as a way of convincing the man that he didn't deserve controlling interest in Newman Motorsports in exchange for his influx of cash.

Then again, she'd sign just about any deal at this point. Things had gotten that bad.

"Hey there, Becca," someone said as she passed by.

It was night, the race being held under the lights, but those lights were bright enough to illuminate the darkest corner. And the thousands of fans who sat in the stands.

"Hey, Perry," she said to one of the other team owners. "You seen my driver around?"

"Last I saw he was in the driver's meeting."

She nodded, turning back toward her hauler. The crowd roared; Becca looking up in time to see a large American flag pass by, the red, white and blue fabric suspended high above a flatbed truck. The wind dragged at the ends, causing it to snap and crackle, the sound still audible over the spectators' yells. She closed her eyes, trying to let the familiar sound soothe her. Didn't help.

Tonight she would find out if her program had a snowball's chance in hell of succeeding, or if she should just throw in the towel.

Things had gotten that dire.

"You looking for me?" a slightly amused voice said, and when Becca opened her eyes, Adam stood there, his dark blue firesuit hugging wide shoulders, hair slightly mussed, a tiny smile lifting the edges of his mouth.

"I am," she admitted. Crew members ebbed and flowed around them, last-minute preparations under way. A hand truck of tires rolled by, filling the air with the bitter smell of rubber, the scent mixed with oil and race fuel, burning her nose.

"What'd you need?" he asked.

She remembered their last conversation, remembered his kindness even though she told herself not to. Business. She needed to keep her mind on business.

"I wanted to congratulate you on qualifying fifth."

"Thanks."

"And to tell you how much I hope—" She swallowed, trying not to sound too anxious. "How much it would mean to Newman Motorsports if you did well tonight."

"Just Newman Motorsports?"

She nodded.

He didn't say anything, just crossed his arms in front of him. Becca thought she saw a hint of disappointment in his eyes. Or maybe anger. Or maybe that was just his game face. Becca didn't know. All she knew was that having him standing there, clothed and ready for battle, tripled her anxiety.

"You missed Lindsey," he said.

"She called me on my cell phone."

"Did she?"

Becca nodded. "She told me if I didn't show up tonight she'd disown me as a friend."

"Oh, yeah? Sounds like Lindsey."

"Look, I'm ah… I'm going to watch the race from on top of the hauler."

"Not the pits?"

John came up behind him. "Adam, they're calling the drivers to their cars."

"I don't like watching races from pit road."

John shot her a look of incredulity, not surprising since she was usually seen atop a pit box on race day.

"But good luck," she said, reaching out a hand and patting him on the arm.

He looked amused by the impersonal gesture.

She turned to John. "Tell the team to have a good race."

"Why don't you tell them yourself?" John said, still baffled.

"I'll tell them when I get on top of the hauler," she said. "Have a great race," she told John.

But even though she told herself not to look back, she couldn't stop herself. She couldn't seem to keep from taking one last look. Adam stood there, watching her, John saying something, although by then she was far enough away that she couldn't hear.

She lifted a hand. He nodded.

And that was that.

"THAT WAS ODD," John said as she walked away.

"Yeah?" Adam asked.

"She's usually in the pits with us," John said, his crew uniform nearly matching Adam's firesuit. TravelTime Hotels was scrawled across both their chests, the gold lettering looking brown beneath the klieg lights.

"I guess not tonight," Adam said, watching as she walked away.

"You nervous?" John asked.

Adam shook his head. Maybe he was still too green to be nervous. Maybe it was because this all still felt like a dream, but whatever the reason, he felt as calm as could be. Whenever he glanced up into the stands, he couldn't help but think that those people were there to watch *him* race. Well, him and about forty other drivers. But just one quarter section of a grandstand would probably fill the seats of his old track. Heck, it'd probably make it standing room only.

Unbelievable.

He glanced toward Becca again. She'd disappeared between the haulers that were set up in the garage, their backs open so that crew members could pull out equipment. "Nope," he said. "Not nervous at all."

"Good, because it's time to get into your car," John said after lifting one side of his headphones to listen to whatever someone had said. "And I gotta warn you again, Jason's going to be all over you. That cat's probably pissed as hell you qualified better."

"Well, that cat's gonna realize soon enough that I specialize in short tracks," he said.

John smiled, the two of them walking toward his car. It was a night race, which should have made things seem more familiar to him, but of course it didn't. And maybe that was why he didn't feel nervous. He felt way out of his league. Chances were he would blow it tonight, but John had told him that was okay. Nobody expected him to win, not like they did some of the other drivers who walked by, faces Adam had only ever seen on

TV. Since the NASCAR NEXTEL Cup Series cars were racing the day after tomorrow, more than one driver was doing double duty this weekend. As such, some of NASCAR's biggest names would be out on the track with him. Forget Jason Ingle. Adam would have his hands full with names like Waltrip, Schrader and Biffle.

"Wait," he heard a voice yell just as he lifted a leg to crawl inside his race truck.

Adam turned.

Lindsey flew toward him, loose red hair flicking from side to side behind her, blue eyes wide. Becca's assistant, Connie, raced behind her. "Daddy, wait!"

"Lindsey," he said in surprise. Kids were allowed on pit road just before the race, but Lindsey was supposed to be up in a suite watching the prerace show.

His little girl threw herself into his arms. "Good luck, Daddy."

Her tiny arms wrapped around him and suddenly Adam knew why it was all right. It didn't matter how he finished today. Didn't matter if he never raced again. As long as his little girl could wrap her arms around him, that was all that mattered.

"Thanks, kiddo," he said, bending down so he could inhale the scent of her hair. It was something he'd done at least a thousand times before, but he never got tired of her baby powder and apple smell.

She drew back, looking into his eyes. "Go kick some butt."

"I will," he said.

"Time for her to leave," a NASCAR official warned.

"I know," Adam said to the man. Then to Lindsey, "Go."

She smiled once, a big smile full of confidence and pride. "See you in Victory Lane." Connie reached for Lindsey's hand, and the two turned back to the suites.

He smiled back, shook his head and turned away. John helped him get in, handing him his helmet and his HANS device. He slipped his earpieces in, then positioned the metal safety device over his shoulders. His newly painted helmet came next, the one that matched the colors of his truck. Lastly, he plugged in his mic.

"Check, check," John said, squeezing the on/off switch on the side of his headset.

"I'm here," Adam said.

"Good," he heard the crew chief say, his voice popping into his ears. He tapped the top of his cab. "Good luck."

Adam lifted a hand in acknowledgment, and suddenly the calm he'd felt earlier while holding Lindsey in his arms disappeared. His heart began to beat against his chest so hard he would bet it vibrated his firesuit.

Calm down.

For the first time in his life he understood what it felt like to be on the verge of an anxiety attack. Blood rushed through his ears and sweat beaded his brow, the foam insides of his helmet absorbing the moisture.

"One minute," John said.

Adrenaline crashed though his body. His fingers began to tingle, not from the rush of blood, but from his grip on the steering wheel. Out of the corner of his eye he could see pit crews moving around the stalls, fidgeting with equipment, sweeping out pit box, standing on the wall. But he couldn't move. He was strapped into his race car like a fighter pilot about to take off down a runway.

"Start 'em up."

He had to blink the sweat out of his eyes in order to focus. He took a deep breath to calm himself before reaching for the toggle.

Vaa-room.

There was no sound like it in the world. The reverberation caused by 358 cubic inches slammed into the air, rebounding against his chest.

Adam glanced at the NASCAR official standing near the hood of his truck. Her white firesuit seemed to glow beneath the overhead lights, the woman's arm up, her eyes firmly fixed on the other officials. But then that arm dropped and the field of cars rolled off.

This was it.

No going back. This would be the test. The test of whether or not he had the goods.

"Check your gauges," John said.

"All good," Adam replied after a quick scan of his oil, water, fuel pressure and voltage meters.

"Okay, they're saying five laps. Copy that? You should be green to go in five laps."

John sounded so perky that Adam almost smiled. "Roger that," Adam said, his voice surprising even to him given the panic that had threatened to choke him.

First gear. Second gear. He cycled up, shifting the steering wheel left and right as he went along.

Thirty-six degrees of slope made the truck seem like it might tip over, the track's grandstands rising up so high Adam felt like he was inside a giant bowl. In less than half a minute they made a lap, and then another, the roar of the field echoing off the high banks to his right. His tires had warmed and the truck was sticking to the asphalt, the stench of rubber leaching beneath his helmet and filling his nostrils with its burnt-oil smell.

"One to go," his spotter, Brian said. "They're telling us one more. Pace truck should be ducking off now."

Adam didn't answer. His breaths came faster and faster, the air inside his helmet thickening. The visor started to steam up. He squinted his eyes, trying to calm himself by focusing elsewhere. He fixed his gaze on the truck in front of him, eyeing the Buzz brand paper-towel logo on the tailgate. The white cylinder was supposed to look like paper towels but it resembled a toilet paper roll instead, Adam thought. And who'd come up with that particular shade of green? It looked like nose snot.

"Green, green, green," Brian said calmly.

He released a breath he hadn't even known he'd been holding, the instant rush of oxygen that flowed to his brain sharpening his mental process. Everything suddenly clicked as the part of his brain used to the routine of going fast switched on. Adam mashed the pedal to the floor.

He'd passed the truck in front of him by the end

of the first lap, John coming on the radio and saying, "Take it easy there, hot rod." But amusement hovered in his words.

"She feels good," Adam said, his head tipping sideways as he entered a turn, his HANS device straining against his shoulders. "Maybe a bit tight, but not bad. I think I might be able to knock off a few more in a lap or two."

"Forty," John said the next lap around. "Leader's a ninety-one."

And those tenths of a second were adding up. In a matter of minutes he had the leader firmly in sight. Adam was shocked to realize he might actually lead this thing.

"Seven truck's coming fast," Brian said.

"Who's that?" Adam asked because the truth of the matter was, he didn't have all his fellow competitors memorized.

"Todd Peters."

NASCAR NEXTEL Cup Series driver. Series champion two years ago. "What's he running?"

"One-seventeen flat."

That was good. Better than him, Adam thought as he worked on catching the leader. They'd caught up to the tail end of the pack, the slower cars making it more difficult to pass.

"Where's my buddy Jason?"

Adam heard the tail end of a chuckle. "He's dropping through the field like a sack of bowling balls."

"How far back?"

There was a pause and then, "You're about ready to lap him. He's coming to the line right…" Another pause. "Now."

Shit, Adam thought as he came to the start/finish line a few seconds later. That wasn't that far ahead. With his luck he'd catch the bastard and then have a real battle on his hands. Or maybe not. Maybe Jason had left his attitude at home.

Yeah, right. But to be honest he wasn't all that worried about it. The longer he ran, the better he got.

"They're talking about you on TV," John said.

"Are they calling me a handsome devil?"

Another laugh caught midchuckle. "No, they're calling you seriously deluded."

"That might be true," Adam said, blinking against the glare of the overhead lights that arched off the front windshield. It got more and more difficult to see as the race wore on, sludge from the track spotting the windshield.

"They're actually talking about how you look like you might lead the race."

"Might? There ain't no *might* about it."

Because just like he had a hundred times at his

local short track, Adam shot his truck down to the inside, the nose edging up to the back end of the vehicle in front of him. Closer and closer he drew, up to the guy's quarter panel, then the doorjamb.

"Outside high," Brian said, indicating the guy was still there.

"Damn it," Adam muttered.

"What's the matter?" John asked.

"Can't get 'em."

"Well there're plenty of laps left to do that. Just hang tight, driver."

Adam did as asked, hoping that an early race caution might help him gain positions. It didn't. He went back out right where he was before, and after the restart, he realized the other truck had gotten better.

Crap.

He wanted to win so bad—for Lindsey's sake, and Becca's—and so with every lap that passed he analyzed the driver in front of him, looking for holes, maybe a weakness. Was he loose off the corner? Tight going in? And if he was, could he capitalize upon the flaw?

"Yellow flag," his spotter said. "Go low. Low, low, low."

Smoke billowed up in front of him. Adam resisted the urge to close his eyes as he dove into the bulbous white cloud. To his right he caught a glimpse of something moving fast.

"Shit," he muttered, ducking the wheel left.

They almost collided. The truck behind him wasn't so lucky, Adam glancing in his rearview mirror in time to see the impact.

"Watch for debris," his spotter said.

Boom.

Adam gasped as his truck lurched forward. "What the—"

He checked his rearview mirror. Jason Ingle lifted a hand, perhaps in apology for the hit, although Adam somehow doubted it.

Damn it. "Where'd he come from?"

"He got better after that last caution. Worked his way through the field," John said.

Great.

Just ignore him.

Boom!

"Son of a—" Okay, that did it. Once could be excused But not now. He cued his mic. "Somebody better tell that jerk to back off," Adam said.

"Stay calm, driver," John said. "We saw that. He's just trying to rattle your cage. Jason's known for that."

"He's gonna get his own cage rattled if he doesn't watch it."

Another glimpse out of the rearview mirror showed Jason backing off only to surge forward again.

There was no place for Adam to go, what with the leader still in front of him, so he swerved the truck right. The next "tap" almost pitched him sideways.

"That does it," Adam muttered, hands clenching around the steering wheel as he prepared to turn it—right into Jason's side.

"Adam," Becca said in warning. "Don't you dare."

His foot froze above the brake.

CHAPTER FIFTEEN

"JUST STAY CALM," Becca said. "I'm about to give him a warning, and in another minute, I bet NASCAR will, as well."

"Somebody better warn him to back off," she heard Adam say, and he sounded pissed as hell.

Becca watched him from high atop her race truck's hauler, her heart pounding as she watched Jason Ingle—her own frickin' driver— go after Adam.

"Just stay calm," she said, wincing as Jason raced forward again. He hit Adam with enough force that the truck lurched forward.

"That little—"

Becca echoed her driver's words, just before she switched frequencies on her radio. "NASCAR, this is Becca Newman. Number twenty-six doesn't seem to want to stop rear-ending my truck."

"Roger that," an official said. "We're on it."

"I'm gonna pound the bastard's face in," Adam said.

"NASCAR's on it," Becca said.

"I mean it, Becca. Someone better tell him to stop or I won't be responsible for my actions."

"Pits're open," his spotter said.

Thank God. Adam sounded like he was on the verge of losing it. Not that she blamed him. What Jason did was wrong—not that it was unheard of, but NASCAR wouldn't tolerate it and neither should Adam. But what pissed her off the most was that Jason drove for *her*. Sure, he might be in someone else's truck tonight, and he might know he was on his way out—after trying to lip-lock her not too long ago he *should* be out—but that didn't give him the right to beat up her equipment.

Adam tried to lip-lock you, too.

That was different, she told herself.

Oh, yeah?

"Watch your RPMs," John said.

Jason backed off, NASCAR's warning apparently having worked. Or maybe it was just that they were about to pit. Whatever the reason, Becca suddenly began to feel sick. This could get bad. With Jason starting right behind Adam, all it would take was one more tap and Adam would be in the wall.

Stop it.

This was Bristol. And while the wrecks here could be spectacular, they wouldn't be at the same speeds as, say, Talladega.

You can't afford to lose such a good truck.

She knew that. Just as she knew it was out of her hands. Still, she closed her eyes. Gripped the edge of the aluminum balcony.

"That's it," she heard John say, his voice seeming to come from a distance. "3,500 RPMs. We're right after the 'Carpet Direct' pit stall. That's the number ten truck. Here you come. Three…two…turn, turn, turn."

Thump. Thump. Thump. Thump went her heart.

She couldn't stand it. She was going to have a heart attack. She needed to get off the roof of the truck and down to pit road where she'd feel better.

"What the—?"

Becca froze.

"I'm going to kill that rat-faced bastard."

She whipped her gaze around, finding her pit box, but it was empty. She looked toward pit road.

There he was. Sideways, the nose of her truck pushed up against the pit road's wall. Jason Ingle's truck sped away.

"What happened?" she asked, her hand shaking as she clutched one side of her headphones.

"That son of a bitch ran into me, that's what happened!"

"Are you okay?" John asked.

"No. I'm not okay. I'm pissed as hell."

"Are you injured?" John clarified.

"My truck's injured, but I'm okay."

Becca felt her body relax, but only for a second. Her heart began to pound again.

Not the truck. Not her *best damn truck*.

She'd kill Jason Ingle herself.

He'd ruined her equipment. Not to mention, the lowlife could have *hurt* Adam.

"Do you need to come into the garage?" John asked.

"I don't think so." She heard the sound of the engine firing for a split second. A puff of smoke came out of the back.

"Front end's messed up," he said, backing up.

"How're your gauges?"

"All fine," Adam said.

"Water pressure?"

"Radiator's fine. Front end feels toed out," Adam said, Becca hearing him shift through the gears as he exited pit road. Beams of light from the overhead fixtures reflected on and then off his rooftop, making the sheet metal glisten.

"You think it'll drive?"

"Oh, it'll drive, but I'm gonna drop back faster than an elephant in a horse race."

"Ten-four," John said. "Just do your best."

Becca darted off the balcony, taking the steps three at a time. She arrived inside her hauler just in time to see the replay.

"I can't believe it," David, a shock specialist, said, one ear covered by his radio, the other exposed so he could listen to the TV announcer. "He ran right into him," he said, bunching his fist at the TV screen as if he could reach inside and hit Jason in the face.

"It was Jason's fault?" Becca asked, pulling the left earphone away to listen to David's words. The network went back to a live shot of the race. John had the crew working on Adam's truck, trying to get it back out there.

"Yeah, it was Jason's fault," he said. "Adam was clear of him by a mile. Jason sped up and ran right into him."

"Crap," Becca said, dropping the earpiece back in place.

It seemed like it took forever to get the truck ready to race again, Becca watching the repairs from pit road. Her crew ran around, trying their best to pull out the twisted sheet metal, angry faces echoing how she felt.

"Go, go, go," John said a good five minutes later.

She queued her mic. "Adam, you better behave out there. I know Jason deserves to be punted, but let NASCAR take care of that."

"I won't give him anything he doesn't deserve," Adam said ominously.

"Adam—" she warned, her anxiety suddenly returning tenfold.

She moved to the toolbox that sat in front of the pit wall. On the TV monitor that was set into the box, Adam brought the truck up to speed, his smashed front end looking like a tin can that'd been kicked one too many times. Fortunately this was Bristol, one of the few places where aerodynamics didn't really matter. But Jason's truck had hardly a scratch on it, and that just wasn't right.

Jerk.

Becca wiped a stray lock of hair away from her face, her hands still shaking so badly she hoped David didn't notice.

"You should fire his sorry ass," David said, dipping toward her so he could be heard. "He's been a pain in the ass for months now. Really, Ms. Newman, nobody would blame you. We're all tired of him bad-mouthing us. He seems to think his inability to drive a Cup car is everyone's fault but his own."

And she was tired of being the employer of one of racing's worst bad boys.

Out on the track, Adam's truck picked up speed. So did Becca's heart. Becca wondered if maybe she should start on over to the NASCAR trailer. Might as well give herself a head start, since she was almost certain she'd be summoned there soon.

"You're ten laps down," John reported.

Damn it. Ten laps. Impossible to win a race from that many down, especially when it became patently obvious Adam wouldn't be as fast as the other trucks. She watched as he dropped to the inside, swerving low as the front runners came up on him—including Jason.

She tensed. Adam dropped even lower. Jason came up on him. Adam let him pass.

Or so she thought.

A split second before Jason cleared Adam's truck, Adam swerved, cleanly and skillfully nosing Jason in the rear quarter panel.

"Yee-hah," David screamed as Jason's truck collided with the safety wall, the back end collapsing like an accordion. Other cars whipped by, but everyone managed to avoid Jason and Adam.

"Way to go," David added.

Adam's truck had spun out, too, Becca gasping

as, on TV, her race truck stalled in the middle of turn three. Another truck hurtled right by it.

Becca couldn't look away. She was breathing so heavily now she'd begun to feel light-headed.

"Oooh," David said. "That was close."

"My apologies to the twenty-six truck," she heard Adam say as the other cars drove by. "Something must be broken in my front end for it to lurch to the right like that."

David snorted, then said, "You know, I think I like this new driver."

"I think I'm going to be sick," Becca muttered.

David turned toward her. "You okay, Ms. Newman?"

No, she was very definitely *not* okay.

"Tell Adam to come see me after the race." She turned away.

"Ms. Newman?" David called after her.

But Becca was gone and sprinting toward the bathroom, because she really *was* going to be sick.

CHAPTER SIXTEEN

"IT WAS AN ACCIDENT."

Becca looked up at him like he'd just told her going to the moon had been an accident, too.

They stood at the end of the long aisle that ran up the middle of the big rig, fluorescent fixtures casting white light over them. Outside the stands slowly emptied of fans, although a few diehards stuck around—some to watch the infield empty, many waiting for pit road to open so they could go down and get autographs.

"Somehow," Becca said, her voice sounding tired, "I doubt NASCAR will see it that way."

He'd had to park his truck after taking Jason out, not because he'd been ordered to do so—NASCAR had asked the two of them to appear at their trailer after the race—but because it was wrecked too badly to continue.

"You shouldn't have done that, Adam."

"He deserved it, Becca."

"You could have been hurt."

"I'm fine," he said, squeezing her shoulder.

To his surprise, she let him touch her—but only for a split second. When the sliding glass door opened, she pulled back, quickly glancing toward the front of the hauler where a crew member entered with an armful of brake duct vents.

"You were lucky this time," she said softly, crossing her arms in front of her. "Next time you pull a stunt like that you might not walk away."

"There won't be a next time, Becca," he said softly. "I promise."

"There better not be. I realize the truck was wrecked beyond repair, but at least some parts might have been salvagable. Now I have nothing."

"I'm sorry."

"You should be," she said. "As it stands, NASCAR might take your license away. You're driving on a *provisional* basis. They could pull your permit just like that." She snapped her fingers. "And if they do that you won't race again until next year."

"So? I don't care if I have to wait a few months."

"But *I* do," she said, and suddenly her exhaustion looked more pronounced. "I'm running a business here, one that needs a victory in order to help bolster confidence in its investors."

"You have investors?"

"I was speaking figuratively," she said, swiping her hand through her hair, the look in her green eyes tinged with fatigue—and something else, something he couldn't put his finger on. "What I meant were my sponsors. They need a win in order to help generate some publicity. Publicity means TV time and that's why they put their name on the hood of my truck. Positive TV time, not you smashing the front of your truck—one with *their* logo on it—into the side of someone else's truck."

He gave her a smile. "But you gotta admit, the fans loved it."

"You can wipe that smile off your face, Adam, because it's not going to make me feel any better about what happened. If NASCAR suspends you, I'll have to terminate your contract."

"Would you really do that?"

"I might," she said softly. "I *would*," she corrected, "because I wouldn't have a choice. I need this team to succeed, and I can't afford to let my personal feelings enter into it."

"It just about killed you to watch me out there, didn't it?"

He watched her swallow, watched her mouth

open and close before she said, "I've watched a hundred men drive around a track before."

"But not since Randy have you cared about one."

She looked away, shook her head. "Don't," she said softly. "Don't do this, Adam."

"Don't do what?" he asked, moving close to her again because he knew what he'd said was true. "Don't tell you how much I care for you?"

She met his gaze again, only suddenly something changed in her eyes. "Don't put yourself in the same category as Randy."

That hurt, but she'd meant it to. "I'm *not* Randy," he said. "I'm Adam Drake. Randy is dead."

She nodded, saying, "I know exactly who you are. And that's the problem."

"What do you mean?"

"Just that you should focus on driving a race truck. Nothing more."

"Hi, Becca."

They both turned. "Hey, Lindsey," she said.

Lindsey glanced between the two. "Umm, hi. I, uh, hope I'm not interrupting."

"We're finished," Becca said. "I'm going to meet with NASCAR now," she called out over her shoulder, stopping by the entrance, her hand on the glass door. "You'd better hurry. They don't appreciate being made to wait."

A cool breeze that smelled like oil and solvent slipped inside the trailer as Becca stepped outside.

"Boy, she's mad."

"That she is," Adam said, frustration causing him to run his hands through his hair.

"Did you two break up?"

"Lindsey, it'd be hard to break up when we're not even a couple."

"But you should be together, Dad. She's a great person."

As if he didn't know that. He held up a hand. "Lindsey, please, let's not talk about this now."

"Okay," she said, "even though it might help if we talked about it—"

"Lindsey—"

"Okay, okay," she said holding up a hand. And then her face brightened. "That was a great race, Dad. The way you took out Jason Ingle. Awe. Some. Everyone in the suite was cheering you on."

"Thanks," he said, opening his arms when she moved toward him.

"Don't be worried about NASCAR," she said as she hugged him. "Nobody blames you for taking Jason out."

"I know," Adam said.

"And don't be worried about Becca. She'll come around."

"Lindsey, I'm not worried about Becca. I was just thinking about my meeting with NASCAR and how I better get over there."

John came up behind him then, the crew chief motioning him toward the entrance of the hauler. "Don't you have a meeting to go to?"

"I do," Adam said, stepping back and ruffling Lindsey's hair. "Keep an eye on her, will you?"

"Will do," John said.

"Don't go far from the hauler," Adam ordered.

"I won't," Lindsey said after a roll of her eyes.

"I'll be back in a few minutes."

"*Okay,*" Lindsey said impatiently, waving him away. "Jeesh," she muttered.

"What were they talking about?" John said, lowering his voice as he glanced toward the entrance. "Brent said Adam and Becca were arguing."

"They were," Lindsey said.

"That's not good," another crew member said, having entered the big rig right after her dad had left, a pair of headers in his hands.

"No," Lindsey said. "It's not. And it makes me think a 911 is in order."

The two guys stared down at her with amused looks on their faces, but Lindsey was used to grown-ups looking at her like that.

"You know," her dad's crew chief said. "I really pity your father."

"And Ms. Newman," the other guy added.

"Why would you feel sorry for them?" Lindsey asked. "Once I get the two of them together they'll realize how perfect they are for each other. Until then, I'm going to keep doing what I can to help them along."

"*That's* why I feel sorry for them," John said. "Because I have a feeling they have no idea what they're up against."

CHAPTER SEVENTEEN

LINDSEY ACTED that night, not that her dad knew what was going on. Oh, no. All he heard when he walked into the hauler after getting a polite but tersely worded warning from NASCAR was, "Lindsey's gone."

Adam paused, the glass door gliding to a smooth shut behind him. "Gone?" he asked John. "What do you mean gone?"

"She disappeared right after you left for your meeting. Said she'd be right back and I haven't seen her since."

"Did she say where she was going?"

John shook his head, not looking him in the eye, Adam assumed out of guilt. "I thought she was running to the bathroom, but we've been so busy packing up, I didn't bother to ask if that's where she was going for sure."

"Maybe she's still there," Adam muttered.

"Maybe," John said.

But something was up. The look on John's face was one he recognized from years of putting up with Lindsey's antics. Not to mention, there was something hovering around the edges of the other crew member's mouth, something that looked suspiciously like laughter.

"What's going on?" Adam asked John, giving his crew chief a look that would have put the fear of God into Lindsey—had she been around.

"Nothing," his crew chief said with a small shrug.

"Bull," Adam said. "My daughter's up to something and you're in on it. Spill."

John looked above Adam's head, to the left of Adam's ear, anywhere but at Adam. But then he said, "All right. Fine." Guilt hovered in his eyes. "I was supposed to stall, to give her time to get away, but I can't do that to you. Here," he said, pulling out a piece of paper. "She wanted me to give this to you."

Adam looked between John and the piece of paper for a second before snatching the thing away. "Dad" was written on the front, the A in the shape of a heart.

Nice try, kid.

Okay, so I know you really like Becca Newman. Maybe not love, but that could happen if you stop dilly-dallying around. So I say go for it. She's perfect for you. Plus I think she needs you. I was watching her during the race through a pair of binoculars. Dad, she looked really freaked. You should get her alone and try and figure out what's wrong. But I know you won't while I'm around and so I'm spending the night in Blain and Cece Sanders' motorcoach. (They have an XBox!) I know, I know. I should have asked your permission, and Cece won't let me stay unless I do that. And so I'm going to write her cell phone number down at the bottom. Call her and tell her it's okay, all right, Dad? You *need* to do this. If you wait too long, I have a feeling it might be too late. Go, Dad. Go, go, go. I'll be cheering you from the stands (or Cece's motorcoach) just like I always do.

Love,

Lin

Adam scanned the number down below, Cece having jotted a line down next to it:

She'll be fine. Go to Becca. Like Lindsey says (and you have a very bright daughter!), Becca needs you. I think something's wrong,

but I don't know what. She won't talk to me.
Maybe you'll have better luck. And in case
you're wondering, she doesn't have a motorcoach. She's staying at the Giraldi Hotel.
Cece.

And so there it was. A conspiracy. One he
appeared to be hip deep in.

"Mrs. Sanders told me it'd be all right to let
Lindsey go with her. I hope you're not pissed."

Adam scanned his emotions. He wasn't exactly
mad. Maybe a little peeved, because if his daughter
had told him what she'd planned he would have
told her exactly what was wrong with Becca
Newman.

She was still in love with her dead husband.

"No, I'm not mad," he said.

Becca came in behind them, not even looking
him in the eye as she passed. John's brows hiked
up like a drawbridge. Adam shook his head. Their
meeting with NASCAR hadn't gone all that well.
And while Adam hadn't been suspended, he'd
been put on probation. Becca had been fined, and
as she'd confessed on their way back—in clipped
vowels—it was money she could ill afford.

Shit.

The only good news was that Becca had promised to fire Jason. That made things barely more tolerable.

He swiped a hand over his face. John kept staring at him. Behind and around them the crew continued to pack things up as they prepared to leave. The aisle continued to grow more and more crowded with toolboxes, tire carriers and other items that didn't fit into the dark gray cabinets. Any minute now Becca would come out of the lounge with her stuff, nod goodbye to him and take off for her rental car.

And that's exactly what happened. She stepped around a tool cart, around a spare tranny and over some brake duct tubing, never making eye contact as she shuffled by him and a few other crew members. "Good job, guys," she said, smiling in the direction of a tire changer. "See you next week."

And that was that. She flicked her hair over her shoulder, slid open the door and slipped outside.

"Well?" John asked, his blue crew uniform looking rumpled.

Adam glanced toward the glass doors, the light from inside the hauler casting a silver sheen on top of the glass and making it impossible to see outside.

"Damn it," he said.

"Go," John said.

When Adam looked back, it wasn't just John

staring at him with raised eyebrows, the other guys staring, too. "What, does everybody know what's going on?"

"Yup," John said. "Might not be obvious to you, but it's obvious to us. Becca Newman needs someone like you, Adam, someone who's not afraid to confront Randy's memory."

"And it wouldn't bug any of you guys if we got together?"

"Are you kidding?" John asked. "We'll all be jealous as hell, but glad for Ms. Newman. She's an amazing lady."

Funny how those words struck him. He'd thought to himself that he'd like to be with Becca Newman, but until that moment he hadn't realized how much. He shook his head, wondering how it was that he could care so much about a woman he'd only just met.

Because it was like John said—she was pretty incredible.

"Guess I'll be on my way," Adam said.

"Have fun," John said.

"Don't do anything I wouldn't do," someone else added.

Adam nodded, cool air hitting his face as he all but jumped onto the car lift that someone had lowered, his battered race truck poised at the edge of the ramp. Later on it would be loaded onto the hauler, but for right now it stood there, waiting, its smashed front end looking worse beneath the overhead lights, radiator fluid leaking out and leaving lurid green drops on the oil-smeared ground.

"Mr. Drake, can I get your autograph, please?" someone asked. Adam was suddenly aware of the race fans milling around as he stepped into the darkened evening.

"Adam? Can you sign this for me?"

He looked left. Becca had reached the end of an outbuilding, her red hair easily recognizable beneath the overhead lights. It looked like she, too, had been asked to stop and sign autographs.

"Sure," he said, taking a Sharpie from the out-stretched hand of a teenager.

"Good race," the kid said as Adam signed the program. "I loved the way you took Jason Ingle out."

"Yeah, that was great," an older man said. "The guy's a total putz. Someone should pull his NASCAR license."

"Or they should kick him out of the Series," someone else added.

And then it became surreal. Suddenly he was surrounded by race fans. Oh, not as many as if he'd been doing the Cup Series. Or maybe so, he thought, taking another look at Becca. She'd disappeared into the shadows.

"Thanks for your support," Adam said absently, trying to sign faster. His name became nothing more than a straight line with a few bumps near the end by the time he'd worked his way through, saying, "Catch you at the next race."

Served him right for getting caught. He hadn't bothered to change out of his firesuit, something he normally did first thing after a race. But he'd been too distracted with Becca to remember to do that, and then in too much of a hurry to meet with NASCAR to have time to change afterward. And so now he raced after her, his run attracting the attention of other fans whom he waved off apologetically. Unbelievable. And this after only one race.

She'd already crossed the steep-banked racetrack and slipped beneath the massive grandstands. Parking wasn't allowed inside the infield—crews had to walk to an exterior parking lot—so Becca had been swallowed up by a dark hole. Adam hurried his steps. He was going to miss her.

But when he came out from under the grandstands, his gaze lit upon her red hair again. "Becca," he called.

But she either didn't hear him, or ignored him. He moved so fast he nearly lost his footing, the asbestos soles of his racing shoes having little traction against the black asphalt.

"Becca," he called again.

She had to be ignoring him. There was no way she couldn't hear him now, the concrete barrier passenger cars were allowed to park against only a few feet away. He vaulted over the white barricade, then charged down the main road that separated the rows of parked cars. He lost sight of her for a second amid the vans and SUVs common to team parking lots. Luck helped him spot her, a car starting up near where she'd parked, drawing his eye. She'd just pulled open the door of her Explorer.

"Becca," he called again. "Wait up."

She slid inside the car and Adam thought she might just take off on him. He rushed forward, arriving just as she rolled down her window a crack.

"What's up?" she asked, wiping at her eyes. There were lights in the parking area, fluorescent lamps on tall poles directly overhead, so he could see her face perfectly.

She was crying.

CHAPTER EIGHTEEN

"WHAT'S WRONG?" Adam asked.

Becca shook her head, tempted to roll the window up and drive away. "Nothing."

Except I needed a good performance tonight to bolster the race team's profile.

At this rate no one would want to lend her money. "What do you need?" she asked, her palms starting to feel clammy, her heart beating so hard and so fast she started to panic all the more.

Calm down.

She hadn't lost the team yet.

"I need to talk to you," he said.

She swallowed even harder, knowing she needed to get on the road and drive—do something, anything to turn her thoughts.

"I can't right now," she said. Her hands shook as she started the ignition. "I need to go."

He opened the car door.

Becca gasped and drew away. His big hands

reached inside. He grabbed her by the upper arms and pulled her toward him.

"Adam, what the hell do you think you're doing?"

"We're going to talk."

"I don't think—"

He turned and sat on the edge of her seat, Becca shifting away.

"What's wrong?"

She almost gave in to the urge to tell him then, almost broke down and told him everything.

"Nothing's wrong."

"That's a lie. There's something wrong. I can see it in your eyes, and at the shop when you think I'm not looking. Or didn't you realize I can see you sitting at your desk with your head in your hands? I see the stress on your face while you're studying paperwork. Something's wrong and you're keeping it from me. Keeping it from the team."

She looked straight ahead, started to shake her head.

"Becca," he said. And out of the corner of his eye she could see him move, feel a hand touch a cheek and turn it toward him. They were so close now their hips touched. "Talk about it."

"I can't," she said, the feel of his hand against her cheek making her want to close her eyes.

"You don't always have to be so strong."

"Yes," she said softly, and—oh, God—was that her voice sounding so weak? So miserable? So close to tears? "Yes, I do."

"No," he said, shaking his head. "You don't."

"Adam—"

"Come here," he said.

What was he about to do? And then she realized he wanted to hug her. "No."

"Shh," he soothed. "It's all right."

His arms wrapped around her. She froze. He pulled her to him.

And she didn't resist.

She told herself to. Told herself to pull back, to tell him this was way out of line.

But then he rested his head atop her head, just like Randy used to do. But rather than drive a wedge between them, it made her want to bow her head and cry.

She missed Randy.

She'd missed having someone to talk to.

"Shh," he soothed again, his body so warm against her own if she'd been wax she would have melted right onto him. "I understand what it's like. I know how hard it is to hold on. But I'm here for you, Becca. *I'm here for you.* Whatever the problem, I'm here for you."

He did understand, she realized. She'd sensed that about him from the moment they'd met. Maybe that was why there was such a strong attraction between them. She couldn't deny that as he held her she started to feel other things, things that had nothing to do with the shop or her financial situation.

"Please," she said softly. "Let me go."

"No."

She tried to draw away, but she couldn't with her back against the seat. She glanced up, saw the look in his eyes.

And almost gasped.

There was a heat there, one so scorching it made her flushed cheeks feel merely lukewarm.

"Adam—"

He didn't move. She didn't, either. One of his hands began to move in circles, gently at first, but then bigger and bigger, lower and lower. It dropped to the small of her back, and then moved lower still, to that spot just above her hips. The jeans she wore hung loosely there, allowing him access to her bare skin. Two fingers dipped beneath the fabric.

She gasped.

"Becca," he said softly, his lips nuzzling her hair.

No. She shouldn't. *Randy.*

But she was tired of thinking about Randy. God, was she tired.

His hot fingers found a sensitive spot right above her hips, his touch sending sharp tingles of excitement down the backs of her legs.

His hand sank lower. "Becca," he said again, her name pronounced in wonder. She felt his mouth nuzzle her ear, felt his lips work their way around her lobe. Warm breath misted her flesh, and then a searing heat as his tongue licked at the shell of her ear.

She fell apart.

"Adam," she sighed, tipping her head sideways.

He caught her top lip between his teeth, nipping her and then releasing her, his tongue taking the place of his teeth.

"Adam," she whispered again. Or maybe she didn't whisper. Maybe it was all in her head. Maybe this was all in her head. If it was, it was such a good dream, she didn't want it to end.

A car door slammed shut.

They pulled apart.

Adam stared down at her, eyes dark and intense, his breathing just as harsh as her own, she suddenly realized.

"Let's go," he said.

"Let's—" she swallowed "—go?"

"I'm taking you to your hotel, Becca. We're going to finish what we've started. No more backing away. No more shutting me out. We're going to finish this, the way you know we both want to."

Her body flushed. Yes. She could see that that was exactly what would happen.

"Adam, I—"

He kissed her, pushing her up against the side of her car, his tongue pushing into her mouth when she gasped. But then she was kissing him back, and moaning and gasping and wanting…just wanting to forget.

"Don't say no," she heard him murmur. His hand reached up to cup the side of her face, and this time he said the words more gently. "Don't say no," he said softly. "Please."

And so help her, she didn't.

CHAPTER NINETEEN

SHE WOKE UP in his arms the next morning.

Or, at least, she thought she did.

But when Becca turned to look at Adam, she quickly realized it wasn't Adam at all and that she was staring at....

Randy.

She gasped, sitting up.

"Hello, Becca," he said, his dark hair rumpled and curling around his head like it always had.

And all at once she started to cry. Tears fell from her eyes as she covered her mouth with a shaking hand. "Randy."

His light blue eyes twinkled as they gazed down at her, his lips quirking into the smile he'd always given her whenever she'd done something silly.

"How you doin'?"

It was the question he always used to ask. Not *how are you doing,* but *how you doin'* in that Jersey accent of his.

"Not good," she said, her voice thick with tears.

"Come here," he said.

She sank into his arms, a part of her knowing this was a dream—he only came to her in dreams—but caring little. His body was warm against her own, his breath misting her shoulder, wiry chest hairs pressing against the cool flesh of her cheeks.

"Don't leave," she begged, just as she always begged. "Please don't leave me again."

And then he was gone and Becca was at the funeral, standing at the edge of an open patch of earth.

Oh, God.

"I'm so sorry," Blain Sanders said softly, the grass he stood upon so bright it was as if a can of green paint had been upended beneath them. "Damn it, Becca, I'm so very sorry."

She looked up at her husband's longtime friend, seeing his own tears stream down his face, tears matched by those in her eyes.

"I'm so sorry," he said again.

"Please. I think I'm dreaming—"

And she was. She knew that. The flowers around the edge of her husband's grave were just a little too bright—yellow, white and dark purple blooms nearly blinded her. The people who stood around them looked too waxy, the grief on their faces frozen in time.

"Let me know if there's anything I can do for you," Blain said.

She'd heard the words, began to shake her head because this was a dream—just a dream.

"Mrs. Newman," the pastor was saying.

"No," she said, knowing what was coming next.

"It's time."

No, her heart screamed. No.

But in her dream her hand clenched around a piece of metal she'd been holding.

Randy's lucky penny.

The hole where the chain had been was twisted and scarred. She'd stared at the thing in dismay, the metal warm in her hand. But then it turned cold—ice-cold.

Oh, God.

She felt the tears build again—not just one or two, but a flood of them, a whole river of them, a whole ocean. And though she tried to hold them back, she couldn't. Her lips grew numb about the same time a horrible pain began to build in her heart.

Gone.

He was gone.

"Becca," she heard someone say.

Her knees gave out, the penny she clutched in her hand digging into the middle of her palm.

She heard voices. Saw legs around her. She curled into a ball. Someone said something again, she didn't know what—she just knew that there, over there, past the murky edges of her dream world was the body of someone she loved. Only it wasn't Randy's body.

It was Adam's.

She was alone.

Again.

"BECCA," Adam said again. "Wake up."

"No," she murmured over and over again.

"Becca?" he said again gently.

The name hung in the air like a wrecking ball.

"You were dreaming," he said.

"Adam," she said after blinking her eyes more than once.

"You okay?" he forced himself to ask.

"Yes. Dream," she said. "Just a dream."

About Randy.

He looked away. He'd just spent hours making love to her. He'd held her and kissed her places so intimate she should be blushing right now. She'd even cried after the first time, and then had held him tight. And he'd held her, too, something moving through him at the same time she'd cried out his name.

But she hadn't been dreaming about *him*. She'd been dreaming about Randy.

Randy. Always Randy.

"What was it about?"

"Nothing," she said with a small shake of her head.

"It was more than nothing," he said. In that moment he knew that he could choose to ignore the ghost of her dead husband, or he could confront it right now. "You were dreaming about Randy."

She flinched, then looked away, her eyes darting around her hotel room as if contemplating a lie. It was early morning, gauzy curtains casting a filmy gray light onto the dark brown carpet below, but he could see the panic in her eyes.

"Becca, tell me."

He thought she might ignore him. Thought she might leave the ghost of her dead husband hanging between them.

To his shock, she didn't.

"It's the same dream I always have."

"And *was* it about Randy?"

She didn't answer.

He waited, knowing she'd only talk to him if

she wanted to. There'd be no forcing this issue, not without upsetting her.

"Becca. I'm here for you. You can talk to me about anything."

Her gaze became unfocused, her face growing slack. "Can I?"

He reached out, gently touched the cheeks he'd kissed so lovingly last night. She felt cool to his touch. Last night she'd felt so warm and alive.

His.

"You know you can."

But she shook her head, resisting him still. Her gaze darted away, catching on the clothes that they'd discarded last night. "It'll be too hard."

"It's not going to get any easier."

He watched her fingers flex and unflex. He waited.

"Sometimes I dream about his funeral," she admitted, scooting back in bed so that she could prop herself up against the headboard, white sheet drawn up beneath her arms.

"What happens?" he asked.

She took her time forming an answer, green eyes staring at the foot of the bed. "Usually, he talks to me," she said, shoving hair away from her face. "And it's like he's still alive. For a second I almost think he's still here. And it's so good to see him. And then I'm suddenly at his funeral."

And Adam could see pain spill into her eyes. "It all turns horrible then," she said softly. "I relive each moment—each moment of the funeral—the conversations I had, what the pastor said, the lowering of the casket." She shook her head, her face completely devoid of emotion.

He rubbed his thumb against her cheek, trying to soothe her, to bring her back to the present. To *him*. "Have you talked to someone about this?"

"Right after he died. I went through therapy, but it didn't help and so I stopped. There was nothing anyone could tell me, nothing anyone could say that would make me feel better."

"But it's still affecting you," he said gently.

"Only sometimes," she said, meeting his gaze. "When I'm under stress."

"Are you stressed because of us? Or are you still upset about whatever's been bothering you?"

She shook her head, her eyes misting a bit as she looked up at him. "Last night was wonderful."

He wanted, oh, how he wanted, to bend down and kiss her then. But he knew the timing was off. She was still upset, and though she smiled up at him, it wasn't a real smile—something was missing from her eyes.

Something that scared him.

"Then what is it? The team?"

She clutched the sheet, the soft fabric crushed by the palm of her hands. "Adam, I'm not in the best of financial situations."

"I know that. Everybody knows that. That's why you needed to find a new driver. Someone to bolster your program." He smiled softly. *"Me."*

"Yeah, but no one knows just how bad it really is."

"So tell me."

She sucked her bottom lip. "I don't know if I should," she said softly.

He'd just spent the night making love to her. They'd been as intimate as two people could be.

And she didn't think she should?

"How bad is it?" he asked.

He saw her take a deep breath, the sheet rising and then falling just a bit, a hint of cleavage showing. "Bad enough that I've put out feelers for an investor."

That explained the hotel room. He'd heard most owners stayed in suites. But Adam would swear Becca's room was smaller than his. "Have you had a response?"

"One."

"From who?"

"William Black."

Adam sat up straighter, not sure how he felt about that bit of news. William Black was rumored to be a cutthroat, someone who would do whatever it took to win. On one hand, that might be good for Becca. On the other, a person would have to look closely before getting into business with someone like Black.

"How far has it gone?"

"What do you mean?"

"Have you signed any papers?"

"He wants me to. And to be honest, I'm desperate enough to do it."

Adam opened his mouth, about to tell her to think long and hard. But what business was it of his? He didn't own the team. All he did was work for her. And if he started interfering, she might take it the wrong way, and the last thing he wanted was for that to happen. Their relationship was too new. Too fragile.

"Have you talked to anyone else?"

"There've been other nibbles, but none as serious as Will's."

"What about Blain and Cece? Couldn't they help you out?"

"They offered," she said, the expression on her face as pensive as he felt. "But I refused."

"Why?"

"Because they're friends," she said, tipping her head sideways in that endearing way of hers. "I don't want business to get in the way of that friendship."

"Then what about us?" he found himself asking before thinking better of it.

"We're not friends. We're lovers," she said, something in her eyes causing a pit to open up in his stomach.

"Funny. I thought we were friends, too," Adam said, unwilling to let her trivialize what had happened last night.

"Adam," she said softly. He watched as her mouth opened and then closed. She battled with herself, he saw. The look he'd seen earlier returned, only this time he could put a name to it: detachment. She'd shut off Becca the woman and turned on Rebecca the boss. "Adam," she said again. "You know we can't let this go any further."

"Do I?" he asked softly. He wanted to yell the words.

"It'll lead to trouble. Tension among the team."

"Are you kidding? The whole team helped set this up, including your friend Cece."

"And I'll have a talk with her about that. She's not my pimp."

He sat up, the sheet falling away from him and

landing in his lap. "Is that what I am to you? A john?"

"No," she said, looking horrified. "Of course not. I just think we should keep what happened to ourselves, and that we're better off remaining—"

"If you say 'friends,' so help me God, Becca, I'll quit."

Her jaw locked into place. He'd never seen her do that before and he didn't like it now. "Would you?" she asked, clutching the sheet around her, the look in her eyes growing more and more aloof.

"I would."

She tipped her chin up. "Well, maybe that'd be for the best, anyway."

"What? Are you serious?"

"You were the one to suggest it."

"Only because I refuse to stay away from you, Becca. Whether you believe it or not, there's something between us. You're just too wrapped up in self-pity to notice it."

She slid sideways, wrapping the sheet around her as she stood. She looked furious when she turned back. "Maybe you should leave," she said softly, ominously.

Crap, he thought, grabbing the remaining bed-covers and tugging them around his waist. Ridiculous to be suddenly self-conscious in front of her, but that's how he felt. "Becca, look. I didn't mean that the way it sounded—"

"You're fired."

"What?"

"You heard me, Adam. You're fired."

"Don't be ridiculous."

"I'm not being ridiculous," she huffed, and for the first time he caught a glimpse of the temper that went along with that red hair. *"You're* the one being ridiculous. You can't separate your personal life from your professional one."

"That's the pot calling the kettle black."

"Get out."

"No."

"Fine. Then I'll leave," she said, bending down and scooping up the clothes he'd so tenderly removed last night.

"Becca," he said, getting up, too, the bedspread heaving in his hands. "Don't," he said, shifting the corners of the spread to one hand. He used the other hand to touch her.

She jerked away. "I'll make a formal announcement that you're leaving Newman Motorsports today."

"Don't you dare."

"Don't I dare?" she shouted. "Don't you dare *threaten* me."

Damn it. How had it gotten to this? How had they gone from lovers to enemies in the space of a few short minutes?

"I just don't want you to do something stupid."

"And choosing to fire someone who threatened to quit on me is stupid?"

"I didn't mean to threaten you."

"You could have fooled me."

He knew then that he was fighting a losing battle. The light was gone from her eyes. All that remained were explosive sparks as brilliant as exhaust flames.

"Leave, Adam."

"I don't think that's a good idea—"

"Fine, then I will," she said, looking as cool as a beauty queen contestant as she pulled her sheet tighter around her and headed toward the bathroom. He knew she'd emerge a few minutes later, dressed, and that she'd leave him in her hotel room without a backward glance.

Son of a bitch.

Because he refused to allow her to do that. He banged on the bathroom door. She ignored him.

"Becca," he called out.

When she finally pulled the door wide, she breezed past him looking completely unruffled. "Goodbye, Adam."

"Becca, don't." He followed her out into the hall, tried grabbing her arm, but she wrenched away. So he followed her to the elevator. He probably would have followed her inside the damn thing except when it opened up, an older couple stared at him in shock.

"Becca, please," he implored as she stepped into the five-by-five box.

"Goodbye, Adam," she said again.

And as the door closed between them she never, not once, looked him in the eye.

CHAPTER TWENTY

"SHE *FIRED* YOU?" Lindsey asked, staring up at her dad incredulously.

Her dad stared right back at her, his face as grim as that time she'd tried to lighten her hair with lemon juice and turned it orange.

"She fired me," he said again, although not because Lindsey hadn't heard him. She suspected he repeated it because he had a hard time believing it himself.

Ba-ro-ther.

They stood outside the Sanders' motorcoach, which was parked near Bristol's infield. Her dad had come to collect her at the crack of dawn—or so it felt like to Lindsey. She'd expected him to spend the morning with Becca after a night of wild debauchery (a term she'd overhead Cece say to her husband). Instead he stood before her now, expecting her to just take off.

"Dad. Can't you talk to her after the Cup race

today? It seems kind of silly to just pack up and leave."

He gave her The Look, the one he gave her when he preferred she keep her opinions to herself.

"We're going home," he said flatly. "Now."

"Okay, okay," she said, holding up her hands. "Just let me go inside and get my stuff."

"What stuff?" he asked. "Or did you pack a bag I don't know about before inviting yourself to stay with the Sanderses?"

"Actually, Cece went to their souvenir rig last night and got me a shirt to sleep in. It says 'Lance Cooper' on it and it's really cool," Lindsey said, trying to remain upbeat when inside her mind was going a hundred miles an hour.

"Ask her how much it cost and I'll reimburse her."

"Okay, sure," she said, knowing better than to argue with him. "I'll be right back."

She ducked back inside the swanky motor-coach that Blain and Cece stayed in while at a track. The couple was already up, their three-year-old son having woken them earlier than Lindsey would have believed possible. The kid obviously didn't need sleep.

"What'd he say?" Cece asked where she sat on

the floor, a rainbow-colored array of Mega Bloks spread out around her. Cece's son had a whole row of the things plugged together, the little boy taking great delight in snapping them in place and then beating the things apart. *Boys*.

"He said we're going home."

"Going home?" Cece repeated, scooting up from the floor.

"They had a fight."

"Is that what he told you?" Cece asked, her long blond hair pulled back in a ponytail. She didn't look like the glamorous co-owner of Sanders Racing Lindsey was used to seeing on TV. That was the weird thing about all the people she'd met. They were all so down to earth and so…nice.

"Are you kidding? If my dad won the national lottery, he wouldn't tell me until the day he went to collect the check. That's the way he is. But I can tell something happened. He's as surly as a herd of monkeys with missing bananas."

"Darn it," Cece said, turning and then pacing the family room floor—if one wanted to call the area near the front of the bus where the two slide outs expanded a "family room." "I can't believe it."

"*You* can't believe it? What does this say about my dad's skills as a boyfriend?"

Cece spun toward her, mouth open. She looked like a woman who'd just been licked on the tongue by a dog. But then she put her hands on her hips. "Lindsey Samantha Drake. I can't believe you just said that."

Why did everybody call her by her three names? *Why?*

"Me? You're the one that said they were in for a night of drunken debauchery."

"I did not say 'drunken.' I said 'wild.' And I can't believe you heard that."

"I heard it."

"Brother," Cece mumbled, her gaze moving away. But her face lit up a second later when she spied something on the kitchen counter. A cell phone, Lindsey noticed. One with NEXTEL written in yellow letters across the front.

"911," she cried into the phone's receiver after pressing the direct connect button. "911. 911. 911."

What? Cece Sanders was calling 911 over this? Was she psycho?

"Cece, what is it?" Blain asked after a loud chirp, his voice sounding panicked. "Is it Randy?"

Oh. That explained that.

"No. Randy's fine," she said with a glance at the toddler who still snapped blocks together only to swing them like a bat and break them apart. "It's that darn Becca Sanders that has something wrong with her."

And Lindsey could hear the way Blain's voice had relaxed when next he spoke. "What'd she do now?"

"She fired Adam."

"She *what?*"

"What?" Randy echoed, looking up at his mother. He reached out his tiny hands, saying, "Talk. Daddy?"

Cece shook her head, "In a minute, BamBam. Let Mommy talk first."

"Bam. Bam," their son said, picking up blocks and tossing them at the floor.

Cece just rolled her eyes. "I need you to come here for a second," she told her husband after her son had stopped yelling.

"Why?" Blain asked.

"Because we're going to offer Adam Drake a job."

"Yes!" Lindsey cried, bouncing up and down on her toes and causing Randy to glance up at her curiously, his big blue eyes wide. "Yes, yes, yes," she said to him with a big smile.

"Yes," Randy echoed back.

"ABSOLUTELY NOT," Adam said when Cece invited him in a few minutes later.

"But, Da-ad. What are we going to do? Go back to Kentucky?"

"Did she put you up to this?" Adam asked Cece. He'd been surprised when the team owner had invited him in only minutes after Lindsey had gone in to fetch her stuff. He'd thought she was being polite, but now he could see they had ulterior motives.

Women.

"Actually, it was my idea," Cece said. "I'm the official owner of our truck team and so it's my decision as to who I hire."

"Yeah, but what about your current driver?"

"We have a lot of drivers in our development program, including Sam Kennison."

Adam winced at the mention of that name.

"One more driver isn't going to hurt us. In fact, we would love to have you since you came in first at the time trials."

"What do you think Carl Kennison's going to say if you bring me in to drive for you?"

"What Sam's father thinks is immaterial."

It'll be material when we're out on the track, Adam thought. "Look, I appreciate the offer, but I don't think it'd be a good—"

"It would piss off Becca," Blain interrupted from the doorway.

All three of them turned toward the door, Randy abandoning his blocks and screaming, "Daddy!"

Blain scooped his son up while he was still standing on the bottom level of the motorcoach's steps, his little boy delighted to be at almost eye-level with his dad.

"I play blocks," he told his dad.

"I see that," Blain said with a grimace at the mayhem on the floor.

"Mr. Sanders, look—"

"Blain," he quickly corrected.

"Blain," Adam said, a part of him still finding it hard to believe he was on a first-name basis with Blain Sanders. *The* Blain Sanders. "I really appreciate the offer your wife made, but I think it's a bad idea."

Lindsey let out a huff of exasperation. "So you're really going to move us back to Kentucky?"

"I don't know what we're going to do, but I'll find something. Maybe wrench for one of the teams. I just think it's best if I stay away from the track."

And Becca.

"So that's it?" Cece asked. "You're just going to give up. Like that?" she snapped her fingers.

Adam almost smiled. "In case you haven't noticed, I've been chasing her all over Mooresville. I think maybe she needs more space."

"Space is what we've been giving her for years. She doesn't need any more space," Cece said. "She needs a man."

"Dad, you can't say no to driving. You just can't. You're *good* at this. And I don't care how much space you think you should give Becca, or how much I like her, I think it's silly of you to let her interfere with your driving career."

"I have to admit," Blain said, "I agree with your daughter."

"Me, too," Cece said. "You're good, Adam. The way you raced last night only proved it. You were aggressive, and every owner in the garage applauded the way you took Jason out, not that they'd ever admit that to your face, and if you tell people I said that I'll call you a liar. But the fact is we're not the only one that's going to offer you a job. And since I've taken such a shine to your daughter," she said, pulling Lindsey close—his daughter making a funny face when Cece hugged her a little too tight, "I don't think you have a choice in the matter. You're driving for us and that's that."

Adam shook his head, but Blain said in a low

voice. "You better give in right now. They won't leave you alone until they get their way. They're a mutant species. That's why men used to keep them locked away in harems."

But Adam didn't laugh. He was already shaking his head. "I just don't think it's a good idea."

"Give in, man," Blain said. "It's a conspiracy."

"This is ridiculous," Lindsey shouted, startling Randy, who hugged his dad tighter. "Sorry," she said to the little boy. "Dad," she said after turning to him, "this is our future we're talking about here. Are you really going to let Becca Newman ruin that?"

You know, he really hated it when his daughter sounded like an adult. And she'd been doing that since she was five.

"I'll think about it," was all he said.

But she must have taken that as a yes because she bounced up on her toes, her face lighting up as she said, "Right on."

Let's All Be Silly
By Rick Stevenson, Sports Editor

Everyone knows how crazy it can get around a certain time of year. "Silly Season," as they call it, usually means owners are swapping crew members like chess pieces on a game board, and drivers are suddenly backing out of contracts two years before said contract is up.

But I ain't ever heard about no driver being fired the day after his first race.

Forgive my lapse in grammar there, folks. You can credit it to my absolute shock that Adam Drake, Newman Motorsports's newest talent (and I do mean talent), has been released from his contract less than a month after being hired by Becca Newman, and this after a promising debut in the NASCAR Craftsman Truck Series race this past Saturday.

The garage was abuzz on Sunday after

Ms. Newman made the announcement—understandably so when you consider the rumors of a romantic entanglement between Ms. Newman and her newest driver—rumors I've heard are true. Yes, folks, more than one crew member has reported that the beautiful Ms. Newman is, shall we say, smitten with Adam Drake.

And so I ask myself, was Adam Drake fired because Becca Newman has been scorned? That would certainly add fuel to the fire that women make lousy race team owners—something I don't personally believe. Or is it that Ms. Newman feels that employees should not become, er, *good friends,* which is what she proclaimed Mr. Drake to be…right before she informed the racing community that he'd been released from his contract.

I'll have to admit, my money's on the "woman scorned" theory, but I suppose only time will tell. In the meantime I'll butter some popcorn, because this promises to be very interesting.

PART THREE

Woman inspires us to great things,
and prevents man from achieving them.
                                    —Alexandre Dumas

CHAPTER TWENTY-ONE

"DAMN IT," Adam said, slamming down the phone for the tenth time.

"Daddy, you shouldn't swear," Lindsey said from her position on their new couch.

Adam glanced in her direction, squinting against the glare that sparked along the surface of Lake Norman. Their condo overlooked one of the popular coves, sailboats and motorboats anchored only a few hundred feet from his back window.

Boy, how things had changed.

"Don't tell me not to swear," he grumbled. "I'll swear if I want to."

Okay, so he'd sounded younger than Lindsey just then, but he didn't care. Becca Newman was driving him nuts. Not only did she refuse to return his calls, but every time he dropped by the shop, she avoided him there, too. Heck, he'd even gone to her house, hoping to run her to ground like he had not so many weeks ago. No such luck. She must have seen his car in her driveway and driven right on past. Or hidden her car in the garage and not answered the door.

"There's no need to act like a jerk," Lindsey said, her homework spread out around her on the dark brown couch. "You'll see Becca next weekend."

"Not if she can help it," Adam grumbled.

Lindsey shot him a quick glance, all but rolling her eyes. The faux-suede couch she sat on was new, thanks to the signing bonus he'd gotten from Cece Sanders when he'd agreed to drive for her.

"I would have never figured you for a quitter," his daughter said.

"I'm not quitting."

"You sure sound like it."

He swiped his hand through his hair thinking you couldn't *live* with women and you couldn't keep them medicated so that they did things that made sense. What a messed up world.

He crossed over to the tinted glass that was supposed to keep sunlight from baking the insides of their living room. Didn't help. Even though it was still fall, he had to keep the AC buzzing in the background to ward off the heat.

"You *are* going to try and see her at New Hampshire, aren't you?" Lindsey asked.

"You shouldn't be worrying about my personal

life, Lindsey. You should be worrying about your homework," he said.

"Dad, I've been worrying about your personal life for years. Nothing's going to stop me from doing it now."

He turned to face her, crossing his arms in front of him. "Your new teachers aren't going to be happy with you if you fail your classes."

"You totally don't need to worry about me and my grades. And I've got hours and hours to finish my homework. But if you try calling Becca Newman one more time, I'm worried she'll have you arrested for stalking. You should wait until this weekend."

"Stalking? I'm not stalking."

"Just about," his daughter muttered. "So confront her at the track. All three NASCAR series will be there. She will be, too. You can hook up with her there. Lock her in a storage closet and lay a big ol' wet one on her. That'll get her to forgive you."

"Lay a big ol'—" The sentence log-jammed in the back of his throat. "Just finish your homework, will you?"

"Whatever," she said in a way that boded ill for his sanity through her teenage years.

Lay a big ol' wet one on her. He felt like telling

Lindsey he'd tried that back at the hotel. Becca had shut him out, just like she was doing now.

But his daughter was right about one thing. He would see Becca in New Hampshire and when he did, he wouldn't let her slip away. Oh, no. Not this time.

SHE HID in the spotters' stand, high atop the grand-stands, in plain sight beneath a partly cloudy sky. It was the only place she could think of where she knew Adam wouldn't look for her.

Other spotters stood around her, including her own. Brian kept peeking glances at her in between keeping an eye on her race truck. He wasn't the only one. It wasn't unheard of for an owner to traipse all the way up to the catbird seat, but it was unusual enough that everyone seemed uncomfort-able with her around. It made her rethink her choice to hide there. But it only took one glance at the track to solidify her resolve. Adam was out there. And instead of watching her own race truck with its new driver behind the wheel—the third place winner at *The Variety Show*—she couldn't keep her eyes off the green-and-white Sanders' Racing truck.

This had to stop.

She was driving herself slowly crazy by thinking about him. Well, she was already halfway crazy, she admitted. She didn't have far to go to make it all the way over the edge. But Adam might just put her there.

She turned away, the sound of the truck seeming to grumble as it made its way around the track behind her. A stiff breeze kept sweeping her hair across her face, the loose red strands starting to annoy her. Turning toward the exit, she waved goodbye to her spotter. He looked surprised that she was leaving, but that was to be expected. She had a new driver behind the wheel of her race truck and she really ought to keep an eye on him.

She told herself she could still hear Brian and John's voices dropping into her ear from the headphones resting on her shoulders.

Tate Evans wasn't as good a driver as Adam, she thought as she climbed down the narrow steps that led to a utility door, then through a narrow corridor and to the top-most level of the grandstands. The announcer's booth was to her right, as was the media center, network production office and scoring stand, but she kept on walking, climbing the stairs to the upper level of the deserted grandstands. There she found a seat, leftover peanut shells crunching beneath her feet as she slid onto an aluminum bench. It was colder beneath the overhang of the suites above her, but Becca didn't care. She wore a long black jacket that kept her warm and so she ducked down into it like a turtle beneath a shell as she blindly watched the trucks make circles around the track.

Adam looked good.

Stop it, she told herself. She shouldn't care if he looked good or bad or otherwise. He didn't drive for her anymore. And it was over between them.

Her new driver nearly wrecked, Becca noticed, wincing at the sound of his tires screeching across the asphalt. But he kept it out of the wall, thank God. Still, she could feel adrenaline begin its familiar trek throughout her body, causing her heart to beat faster and faster.

Just hold on, she told herself.

Things would get better soon. She almost had her deal worked out with Will Black. Once the financial burden she was under disappeared, things would get better.

They *had* to get better.

"Anyone seen Becca?"

Becca jerked, and when she came back to reality she realized final practice had ended and they were trying to find her via the radios.

Jeez.

"I'm here, John," she said, dumbfounded that she'd been so deep in thought she hadn't even noticed that the trucks had left the track, a rainbow array of vehicles lining up for final inspection. "What do you need?"

"Adam's looking for you."

And there it went. Her pulse.

Thumpthumpthumpthump.

She'd never had anxiety attacks before, but this new deal with Will Black and her falling out with Adam had nearly pushed her over the edge.

"Tell him I'll catch up with him later."

Silence. Then, "You can't avoid him forever."

"Is he standing right there?" Becca asked, peering down at the garage. It was impossible to see through the outbuildings and so she had to take John at his word when he answered, "No."

"I told you I don't want to see him."

"I know. And I told him the same thing. But he's not giving up, Becca. I think you better resign yourself to having it out with him."

Not if I can help it.

"Thanks. I'll keep that in mind."

Silence again and then, "Where are you?"

"Up with the spotters."

"Liar," came Brian's voice, and she could hear laughter behind the word.

Okay, that did it. "Guys, I really don't appreciate you interfering in my personal life. Now, if everyone wants to keep their jobs, I suggest they mind their own business."

"Yes, ma'am," Brian said, all traces of humor gone.

She'd been too terse. But, damn it, she didn't have a choice. Things had gotten out of hand. It had to end. Now.

"One of the spotters said he saw her heading toward the grandstands," she heard over the radio.

"Damn it," Becca said, shooting up. She opened her mic. "Brian. You're fired."

"Hello, Becca."

She gasped.

Adam stood over her, looking out of breath and out of sorts, the green-and-white firesuit that clung to his body meaning he must have parked his truck and run all the way up here.

"How'd you find me?"

"Spotters," he said. "Your spotter told my spotter who told me you were on your way down here."

Damn them. Damn them all to hell.

"Adam, look, I really don't want—"

"I'm falling in love with you, Becca."

It felt like a defibrillator had shocked her. Her

chest actually stung from the force of the adrenaline that his words sent through her.

"You don't mean that," she said softly.

The smile he gave her was a humorless one, the twist of his lips seeming to be almost self-deprecating. "Unfortunately, I do."

She shook her head. "Impossible."

"No. It's not. I've watched you, Becca. I've seen you when you think I'm not watching. You have a light about you, one that seems to glow even with the dark cloud hanging over your head. You're goodness and light and you have so much love to share that I used to ache every time I saw you with Lindsey."

"Adam, don't. Please," she said, feeling her throat tighten up. "Don't. I can't. I don't think—"

"Don't think," he said quickly, shocking her by going to his knees while still holding her hand. "Don't. Think," he said firmly.

But she couldn't stop herself from doing exactly that. Nor could she pull her hand out of his grasp, not after their one night together—

But she couldn't think of that because thinking brought it all back. The joy. The tenderness. The pain of seeing Randy in her dreams.

"I'm not ready," she said softly.

I don't think I'll ever be ready.

"You have to let go."

She started to shake her head again. The breeze kicked up, ruffling his black hair. She resisted the urge to straighten it. "It's not that," she said softly.

"Then what is it?" he asked, suddenly shooting to his feet. He turned away from her, shoving a hand through his hair, the undersides still damp from being beneath his helmet. "What is it?" he asked, turning back to her.

She recoiled from the anger she saw in his eyes, the anger and the desperation. She was hurting him. She could see that.

"It's not that stupid argument we had, is it? Because I see now that it's better that we don't work together. You're right. It would've caused problems. Jason Ingle illustrated that point perfectly. But we're over that now, Becca. I don't work for you anymore and so the way I see it, there's no reason why we can't get involved."

"How about the fact that you work for the competition?"

"Cece and Blain aren't the competition. They're your friends. You know as well as I do that they wouldn't care if we dated."

"But *I* do."

"You do what?"

"Care," she said, standing. "I already care," she

admitted in desperation. "It was me who told all those owners to call you. Me," she said when she saw his eyes widen in disbelief. "I did that for you, Adam, because I understand how important racing is to you. And because I didn't want anyone to think you were fired because you'd done something wrong."

"I thought it was the Rick Stevenson article that got people's attention."

"No. It was me," she said, pointing a finger at herself. "Nobody would have called you if they'd thought I'd fired you for any reason other than personal differences."

"Is that what you told them?"

"I didn't have to tell them anything. Everybody in the garage knows about our affair."

"Is that what bothers you? That people will talk?"

"No," she said, shaking her head sadly, wondering how much she should admit, deciding he deserved the truth. "My problem is that you're a driver."

He blinked across at her, his green eyes looking almost hazel in the grandstand's half light. "Are you afraid it'll happen to me? That I'll end up like Randy—"

"No," she interrupted, wiping a strand of hair

out of her eyes. "It's everything that comes along with your being a driver. I lived that life once before. I've watched what happens. It's not easy being the woman behind the man."

"But you wouldn't be behind me. You'd be right alongside."

She shook her head. "That's how it might start out, but it wouldn't end up that way. As your star rises—and it will rise, Adam, you're too good for it not to—I'll be left behind."

"You could never be left behind. You're Becca Newman. You're more famous than me."

"I'm famous because of Randy. For no other reason."

"But your dad—"

"Was a racing legend. But no one would know my name if not for Randy. And just like with Randy, I'd be there, watching your career soar. I'd become Becca Newman, Adam Drake's girlfriend. All my hard-fought independence, it would disappear. I'd lose myself again, just as I did before."

"That would never happen with me."

"Yes, it would. You forget I've lived through it once before. I'd want things for you, Adam. I'd want you to be at the top of your game. To be successful and in the limelight and happy. That's the type of person I am—"

"And what's wrong with that?"

"Nothing except that all too soon I'd disappear."

Again. Just like she had with Randy.

"I won't let that happen ," he said softly. "We'd be a team, you and I—"

"Oh, yeah? she asked softly. "For how long? What if you got tired of me? What then?"

"Don't say that."

"I'd be a laughingstock. It'd be worse than it was with Randy. At least when he died I had some dignity."

She looked away from him, knowing she shouldn't admit it, but unable to stop herself. "If things ended between you and me, I'd have nothing left."

"Yes, you would, Becca," he said.

She stepped back when he tried to enfold her in her arms. "I care for you, Adam," she said as his arms fell back to his sides. "I think I'm in love with you. But I don't want to be. I swore that I'd never fall in love again. That I'd never lose myself like I did with Randy."

He didn't say anything for a long moment, even looked away for a second before facing her squarely again. "So what are you going to do? Never date again?"

"No. One day I'll settle down, but with a nice ordinary man. Someone who's far removed from this lifestyle."

"Like an auto mechanic from Tennessee?"

She didn't say anything.

"Is that what you want? Would that make it better? Do you want me to give up driving?"

"No, I'm not asking that because that would be ridiculous. It's stupid. It makes no sense." She lifted her chin. "But maybe that *is* what I want."

Down in the garage she heard cars start, the crack of exhaust incredibly loud even all the way up in the stands. Time for the next series to practice. Adam didn't even flinch. All he did was say, "You know I can't."

"I know," she said, her voice suddenly thick with tears.

"It's all I've got."

"I know." And ultimately, it was more important than her. It always was with drivers.

Another car started. Then another and another. But the two of them were in their own little world, one where the only sound they heard was the beating of their own hearts.

"It would break Lindsey's heart," he said at last.

Just as it would break hers. "I know," she said again, her eyes stinging.

And she'd known that's what his answer would be. She'd known it would come to this. That's why she'd been avoiding him. She'd known it and she hadn't wanted to face the fact that, having come to care for him, she would have to give him up.

"And so I'm saying goodbye," she said softly.

"We don't have to do that."

"Yes, we do," she said quickly. "I'm going to end this now, Adam, before one of us ends up getting hurt."

"I'm already hurt," he said. "And so is Lindsey."

Lindsey. Just the mention of the little girl's name brought her closer to tears than ever before. "Tell her I'm sorry," she said. "I know she was hoping... that she thought..." She shook her head. "Just tell her I'm sorry."

She turned away, heading down the long row of empty seats, her steps echoing against the roof above and away from Adam.

"Becca," he called.

But she kept on walking.

"Don't do this!"

She had to. For his sake and hers.

But mostly, she admitted, for *hers.*

CHAPTER TWENTY-TWO

SHE WAS WALKING AWAY.

Adam fought the urge to go after her. And the harder he fought, the angrier he became.

What was she thinking?

What was she doing?

Didn't she realize what it was that she gave up? How could anybody do that out of fear of losing themselves? For a man who faced death for a living, it was nearly an impossible concept to grasp.

But she did give it up.

He watched her long hair sway from side to side as she reached the end of the aisle, turned right and then climbed the steps to the top. Out on the track, a car began to go through the gears. A part of him counted the changes in tempo. First gear, second, third and then fourth. By the time the driver reached fourth, she was gone.

He stood there. But only for a moment. Without

thought, he sank into the seat next to where she'd been sitting.

She'd broken up with him.

Because she didn't like what he did for a living.

The irony of the excuse wasn't lost on Adam. But what he didn't understand, what pissed him off more than anything, was that he wasn't at all like Randy Newman. Sure, Randy had been a brilliant driver, but he'd also been a jerk. There wasn't a weekend on the circuit that he hadn't spun someone out. Adam never drove like that, and while he hated to speak ill of the dead, the man had always put his needs above Becca's. Everyone said so. Adam would never do that.

He turned on his heel, walking in the opposite direction. He wouldn't go chasing after Becca. Not this time. Not ever again. And with each step he took, his anger grew.

His watch refracted light onto his face as he checked the time. Four hours until qualifying. He had four hours to prepare himself mentally. Four hours to get his head on straight.

He'd prove to Becca he was the better man.

HE STARTED the race fifth. It would have been higher but he had misjudged one of the corners and almost lost control.

It wouldn't happen again.

Remembering the look on Lindsey's face when he'd told her what had happened between him and Becca had only fueled his determination. His little girl had idolized Becca. That she'd asked him to give up racing had just about broken her heart, too.

"Fire 'em up."

It was Friday night. Time to race. Time to concentrate.

With a hand that was absolutely level, he flipped the switch to start the engine.

Nothing happened.

He switched boxes and tried again. Still nothing.

"I've got no ignition," he said, his voice dead calm. He wasn't worried. He was going to win this race whether he had to start from the back of the field or not.

A NASCAR official came up to his truck and tapped his window, motioning him to get a move on, the safety shirt she wore glowing beneath the neon lights. He splayed his hands indicating that he couldn't. With a quick wave the official waved for help in pushing him out of the way, but his crew had only been a few pit boxes away and they were already there, Adam shifting it into Neutral. Someone already had the hood pins off by the time he'd been pushed into their pit box, someone else leaning under the hood.

And still Adam didn't panic.

He could see a tiny sliver of what was going on between the front cowl and the hood. Someone jiggled some wires. His crew chief told him to try it again at the same time trucks started rolling by, the *woosh-woosh-woosh* of engines echoing in the truck's cab.

Vaa-roof.

It wasn't a roar so much as an explosion of sound, six-hundred-and fifty horses all kicking and galloping at the same time.

He pulled out the minute they had the hood secured.

"NASCAR's telling you to take your position."

"Roger that," Adam said, ducking to the inside and passing cars one by one. The flagman waved at him to catch up when he crossed under the stand.

"Three laps. They're telling us they'll start in three laps."

Adam registered the comment, but that was all. He was focused on warming up his tires, on checking his gauges and testing out the handling. Two laps later and he readied himself. This was his race to lose.

And he was not. Going. To. Lose

Jason Ingle might have something to say about that, a little voice said. The man was toward the back of the field, but Adam didn't care. It was obvious to everybody that Ingle was a better NASCAR Craftsman Truck Series driver than he was a NASCAR NEXTEL Cup driver. But for some reason he suspected Jason blamed him for his demise. He'd tried patching things up after a driver's meeting not too long ago, but Jason hadn't wanted a thing to do with him.

Fine.

He wasn't in the sport to make friends.

They picked up speed, the lampposts surrounding the track sliding past his car faster and faster. The distance between them seemed to shorten the faster he went, an optical illusion that told him they were almost up to racing pace.

"Green, green, green."

He didn't need to be told. He saw the flag man jerk the green flag back and forth. He didn't slam the pedal down, he pushed it gently, feeling his whole body relax the moment he crossed over the start/finish line. He didn't see the stands anymore. Didn't catch a glimpse of the leader board. Didn't see the infield grass flash by. Didn't see anything but the back end of the truck in front of him, the sponsor's logo like a giant target on the truck's back end.

He pointed his nose right for it, ducking down at the last minute to pass the guy before a single lap had passed.

"Clear high."

He jerked the wheel up, steering the truck into the groove, his eyes on the track in front of him. Lights flickered off the hood of his truck, the green-and-white sheet metal vibrating beneath the force of the draft. One down.

"You're looking to be about a half second faster than the leader," his crew chief said.

Adam didn't bother to answer. The next truck was in sight. He kept his gaze focused on the guy's rear tires, registering his position on the track without conscious thought, looking for weaknesses as they went into turn three and four, noting the way he lost bottom end exiting the turns. Easy pickings.

He waited half a lap before making his move, following the guy around and then ducking up high, near the marbles, his back end breaking free for a second. But his competition didn't have the horsepower to keep up with him, even with Adam running the high line.

One more down.

It was like that with the next truck, too, Adam

suddenly in a position to lead. And so he would. It wasn't a matter of if, it was a matter of when. The guy in front of him was going down. Now.

Lights flickered on and off like neon signs when he steered the truck into the bottom groove. The guy was fast. Almost as fast as he was. But the leader didn't have anger urging him on. Adam didn't care how he had to win, he just wanted to win. And so he took a risk he probably shouldn't have. His truck pushed. He slid right into the side of the leader. Tires squealed. His truck lurched. Adam held on.

"Still outside," his spotter said.

As if Adam didn't know that. They were trading paint like a couple of targets on a paintball field.

"Still there."

But he was pulling him. Inch by inch he gained ground until…

"Clear high."

"Good job, driver," his crew chief said, excitement causing his voice to rise. "Just ride around the front now."

And stay out of trouble.

But it wasn't as simple as that. Halfway through the race the fifty-one truck challenged him. He lost the lead for a few laps, but a good pit stop and a fresh set of tires put him back in front again. No, his biggest challenge came from none other than Jason Ingle. Big surprise. But he didn't come from behind. Adam had to pass him and put him a lap down. Unfortunately, he had to do so with twenty laps to go. And Jason wasn't going to let it be easy. Oh, no, he had a bone to pick. But Adam didn't even flinch when Jason checked up, hoping Adam would run into the back of him. Adam pulled the wheel to the left and ducked beneath him.

"Nice try," he said.

"You've got company," his spotter said.

Adam glanced in his rearview mirror. But it wasn't Jason behind him now. It was Sam Kennison, his new teammate.

"Somebody better tell him to play nice," Adam said. "I'm not going down without a fight."

"Ten-four," his crew chief said. "I'll tell him you said that but somehow I don't think it'll help."

And probably it wouldn't. Sam had been posting decent lap times all night. Adam knew that, having been kept in the loop of who was fast and who was not.

Suddenly, he had a race on his hands.

And, suddenly, Adam was smiling. There were twenty laps to go. He was racing for a win and his main competition was his own teammate. Sure, it was the son of an old rival, but Adam trusted Sam. The kid would make it interesting.

Sure enough, less than two laps later, Sam darted into the bottom groove right when Adam dropped down to keep the line closed. But Sam forced Adam to hold the high line, his spotter calling, "Low, low, low," in his ear.

He could hear the air pressure change as wind from Sam's truck buffeted the sides, rattling the catch net to his left. For the first time that night, Adam felt his knuckles tighten, felt the adrenaline surge. One foot, two—Sam began to pass him. But Adam hung on, holding on to the high line through the turn's exit.

Sam fell back.

Adam had better top end, but that was the only thing that saved his ass. Sam would push on him again through the next turn. And the next. And the next.

And so it went until Adam heard the words he'd been dreading. "Ducking down," the spotter said. "Looking for a pass."

Sure enough, Sam shot to the bottom, nudging up along his back quarter panel. Metal touched metal.

"Low."

Obviously, Adam was tempted to answer, but

the adrenaline was pumping now. Sam would have to work harder to pass him.

Or wreck him.

"Coming again."

Adam tried to hold his line, but his truck pushed high. Sam moved up. Adam held on to it, the straightaway once again providing the room needed to accelerate. Sam fell back once more.

Two to go.

He couldn't take much more of this. But the problem didn't end. The next lap Sam tried to take the high line.

"Almost there, driver," his crew chief said. "Hold on to it."

"White flag," said his spotter.

But he didn't think he could hold on to it. His truck didn't run as well down at the bottom, but that was exactly where Sam forced him go. Around turn two they went, bumping into each other in the middle. Adam's back end broke loose. He could feel the truck begin to turn, feel his back quarter panel touch Sam's. They were like two magnets, drawing together and then repelling one another, Adam pulling away only on the straightaway.

"Checkered flag."

Two more turns. Would he make it?

"Come on," he muttered to himself, knowing Sam was there, waiting for Adam to make a mistake. One more turn to go.

Sam began to catch him, the nose of his truck almost even with his own.

No.

The word was a shout in his head. He wouldn't let it happen. He was better than Sam. Older. More experienced. He'd been pushing cars to the limit while Sam was in high school.

And there it was. The checkered flag. Right in front of him. He already had the pedal to the floor, but he mashed it harder, his toes growing numb, hands clutching the steering wheel as they both charged toward the dotted line.

CHAPTER TWENTY-THREE

HE WON.

Becca watched as Adam's truck crossed the start/finish line first, just inches ahead of Sam.

"Well, I'll be damned," he heard his crew chief say, though not to the team. No. John had to watch their own truck limp its way home to a twenty-ninth place finish.

"He won it," he said, meeting her gaze.

She knew what he was thinking. They could have had that victory if she'd kept him on board. Now they were forced to watch fans scream and yell in honor of another team's driver. Blain and Cece's driver.

She jerked her headset off. "I'll be at the hauler," she said as their own truck crossed the start/finish line. Around her, crew members jumped down from their pit boxes, shook hands and congratulated themselves on finishing the night.

Becca hardly noticed.

Out on the track she could hear Adam's tires squeal in protest as he did a burn out, then another one, the sound of the engine mixing with the roar of the crowd.

He'd won.

Well, good for him, she thought. She'd known he had the goods. It's why she'd hired him. Why he'd been snapped up by another race team in a matter of days. Adam was good. Good enough to go all the way to the top. She wished him well.

So why was she crying? Why was she suddenly finding it hard to breathe? Why did she feel such an odd combination of joy and sorrow that it made it hard to think, hard to focus on where she was going?

Somehow she found her way back to her rig, nearly bumping into a few of her employees as they buzzed around gathering items that needed to be stowed away.

The crowd roared once more. Adam must be out of his truck. She slipped inside her hauler, keeping her eyes averted from the flat screen TV at the end of the long aisle. But she caught a glimpse of him, anyway; a mirror someone had hung off one of the cabinets reflecting the image back to her. She stopped in her tracks.

He stared right at her, a smile on his face, Lindsey clutched in his arms as he gave a postrace interview. The sound was turned down, so Becca watched in silence as he gave a commentary. Behind him someone shook a bottle of something—Gatorade, it looked like—over his fellow team members, some of it hitting Lindsey, who squealed. Adam glanced back just in time to spy Cece coming up behind him. He stopped whatever it was he was saying and gave his team owner a hug.

Becca had to look away. She pushed open the door to the lounge, locking herself inside for good measure.

She couldn't take it, she thought, all but collapsing into the chair that someone had pushed beneath her desk.

But, of course, that was stupid. And it was wrong. She was a team owner. She would have no choice but to watch him race. That was part of the job. She'd sit there and watch him race against her own drivers weekend after weekend and she'd learn to get used to it.

But for now, she just wanted to hide. And so she did, placing her head in her hands, resting her elbows on her desk. Her laptop hummed, the LCD screen closed, an LED blinking—but she hardly noticed. Tears pooled on her lashes. She wiped them away. But more came. Second after second, minute after minute, more came.

Someone knocked on the door a long while later. "Be there in a minute," she said, wiping at her eyes. She needed to get herself together. They had a truck to load. Things to pack. A postrace meeting to coordinate.

"Becca."

Becca's head snapped up. That sounded like—

"Open the door, Becca," he said again.

"Adam." She shot up, wrung her hands, then turned away from the door, only to turn back toward it again.

You can't run away forever.

No, she couldn't. She was a professional. Time she acted like one.

Reluctantly, she opened the door, taking in Adam from his green-and-white firesuit—slightly damp and spotted with red Gatorade—to his mussed hair, still pressed down flat around the edges where the helmet had rested.

"I won," he said.

Behind him her crew members still worked, packing up things but not so busy that they didn't glance her way.

"You won," she said, her left hand still resting

on the door handle—as if she might swing it closed in his face if things got out of control. But they wouldn't get out of control. She would listen to what he had to say, but that was it.

"I won the race for you."

Her breath caught. He took a step toward her. She retreated, but only up against the door. And then, to her complete shock, he bent down, cupped her face—and kissed her.

Once.

Becca gasped.

That was all he did, just hold her face in his hands and kiss her once.

Then he drew back.

She didn't move.

His head lowered again.

She knew in that moment that she was kidding herself. She wasn't *falling* in love with Adam, she was *in* love. In love with the way his hands shook every time he held her. In love with the way he looked at her just before he kissed her—as if he couldn't quite believe he was about to do exactly that. In love with the way he always seemed to know just exactly what type of kiss she wanted.

This one was no different.

He didn't pressure her. Didn't force himself on

her. He kissed her. Softly. Gently. Tenderly moved his mouth against her own. They were little baby kisses, ones she could barely feel, his soft lips capturing her lower lips between his own. Nibbling…nibbling…nibbling and causing her legs to grow weaker and weaker and weaker.

And then he stopped.

She opened her eyes. He didn't move. Neither did she. After a moment or two she realized he was waiting for her to say something.

She knew instantly what it was.

I love you.

Don't go.

The words lodged in her throat. She opened her mouth, tried to say them. But in the end she just couldn't.

"I love you," he said gently, and the words weren't a taunt, or said as way of prompting her to say it back. The words were a statement of fact with maybe even just a hint of surprise thrown in. "I love you," he said again, straightening.

I know.

But she didn't say the words aloud because he was stepping back, moving away.

"Goodbye, Rebecca."

I love you, too.

"Adam," she said softly.

But he ignored her. And this time she knew it was over for good. This time she knew he wasn't coming back.

"WHAT DID SHE SAY?" Lindsey asked the moment her dad came out of the hauler.

Her dad checked up. "Lindsey," he said, stopping in the middle of the road that separated the permanent garages from the haulers that parked across from the structures. "What are you doing here?"

"I followed you," she admitted, having to move out of the way of a man pushing a cart of tires. Everyone hustled about, fans working their way through the crowd in search of autographs. She saw a few heading their way. "Everyone thinks you ran off to go to the bathroom, but I knew better. You have a bladder like a camel."

Her dad shook his head and started walking again. "We need to get back to Victory Lane."

"What did she say?" she asked, falling in step beside him.

He smiled at a fan who thrust a piece of paper out in front of him, signing his name without thought. A few people called out their congratulations. Lindsey marveled that even with it being so dark out—the only light came from the inside of the still-open garage—everyone seemed to recognize her dad and know his name. But that was the way it should be, because her dad rocked and one day *everybody* would know that.

"Well?" she asked. He didn't say anything, and she paused to swipe away a gnat that buzzed around her face. Now that it was dark the bugs were out in full force.

"We'll talk about it later," he said, turning just past the garage and heading toward Victory Lane.

"Dad, wait," she said, grabbing his hand and turning him toward her. "*What* did she *say?*"

"Nothing," he said, looking away from her and swiping a hand through his still-damp hair. "She said nothing."

Lindsey felt her eyes widen. "Did you tell her you love her?"

"She doesn't care."

"But did you tell her?"

"Of course I told her," he said, standing there, his big body tall and stiff and yet somehow slumped. "I told her that." He looked away. "Yesterday I told her that, too. But she doesn't care. She's too focused on what it was like being with Randy to realize I'm a different man. A better man."

"And you thought by winning tonight's race you'd win her heart, too."

His gaze snapped back to hers. In the halogen glare of the garage lights, she could see him look at her in a strange way, his eyes darting all around her face only to connect with hers again. "You really aren't a little girl anymore, are you?"

"I am," she said softly because she could see the hurt in his eyes. "I'll always be your little girl, Daddy."

She thought he would continue to stand there, hoped that he wouldn't, so when he stepped toward her and pulled her up and into his arms, she felt tears come to her eyes. His big arms wrapped around her just as they had a hundred times, her feet dangling off the ground. Two weeks ago she might have told him she was too big for that kind of hug, but tonight she didn't care. She loved her dad with everything she had, and she wanted to kill that Becca Newman for turning him away.

"I love you, kiddo," he said softly, his face buried in the crook of her neck.

"I love you, too," she said back.

He pulled back, shifting her to one side but still holding her aloft. There were tears in his eyes.

Her dad never cried.

Not even when her mom left.

"You're all I've got, aren't you?" he asked gently.

"I am. But you're all I've got, too."

"And that's enough, isn't it?" he said, his green eyes peering into her own. "That's always been enough."

"It is," she said, putting a hand against his jaw. He hadn't shaved, his whiskers prickling her skin. "We'll only ever need each other."

They were familiar words. Words her dad used to say to her to comfort her after her mom had left. She could tell he recognized them. "You're pretty bright for someone so young."

She tried smiling at him, somehow managing to pull one off. "Hey, you just said I wasn't little anymore."

"I said you weren't a *little girl*. You're always going to be a Tater Tot."

"Next to you, Hulk Hogan would be a Tater Tot."

He smiled back. That was good, she thought. "You better get going," she said. "Cece and Blain might get mad that their new driver is missing in action."

"Yeah. You're probably right," he said, setting her down. "Cover for me, would you? Tell them I've had a touch of the flu."

"Will do," she said with a conspirator's smile.

He turned. She didn't follow. He turned back, still walking. "You coming?"

"Actually, all this talk of going to the bathroom has me thinking I might need to go, too."

"'Kay. I'll see you over there."

She waved. He glanced back once more before heading off to a victory celebration that she wouldn't normally miss, but at the moment she had bigger fish to fry.

Becca Newman.

Lindsey turned on her heel and marched her way through race fans, crew members and the occasional toolbox being pushed toward a hauler, her frequently muttered, "Excuse me," falling on mostly deaf ears.

"Hey, Lindsey," John said when he saw her coming at him. The back of the hauler was lowered to the ground, her feet rattling the ramp she stepped so hard.

"Hey, John," she said. "Becca still inside?"

"She is," John said, giving her a curious look.

"I need to see her," she said, stepping into the glow of the hauler, the interior light casting a glow around the back end of the big rig.

"Go on in," John drawled, sounding more southern than her. "She's in the lounge."

"Thanks."

Inside the hauler a couple more of the guys called out, smiling at her as they stowed transmissions, brake rotors and anything else they might have had out for use that night. Lindsey smiled back, but she kept moving straight ahead. No time for idle chitchat.

She didn't even knock before opening the lounge's door.

"Lindsey," Becca cried.

She'd been crying.

Lindsey fought the urge to roll her eyes. "You. Are an idiot?"

"Excuse me?"

"You heard me."

Becca looked away, and if Lindsey wasn't mistaken, tears were building up on her lashes again. "It's not what you think."

"You love him, don't you," Lindsey said, though it wasn't a question, it was a statement.

Becca lifted her chin, her eyes glittering when she answered, "Yes."

"Then tell him that," Lindsey said, stepping farther into the room.

"You make it sound so simple."

"It *is* simple," Lindsey said, shuffling forward another step. "The two of you are perfect for each other. You both love racing more than life itself. You both have this really annoying habit of telling me what to do. And you both think you're right all the time when, in fact, you're usually wrong. Like now."

But all Becca did was smile a bit, a smile that disappeared as quickly as it'd come.

"I won't put myself through it again," she finally said, looking away.

"Through what?"

"Loving someone. Caring for them. Losing myself a little bit at a time."

"That's ridiculous," Lindsey cried. "You can't force yourself out of love simply because it's the easier choice."

"Oh, yes, you can."

"But that makes no sense. That's like…that's like…being in a car accident and being afraid to drive again."

"Nonetheless, there are people who've done exactly that—never gotten in a car again."

"Oh, yeah, right," Lindsey said, crossing her arms. "Name one."

"Look, Lindsey, I've made my choice. I don't expect you to understand. You're too young to know what it feels like to be left behind."

"No, I'm not," Lindsey said, uncrossing her arms. "You think I didn't cry over the loss of my mother?"

"That was different."

"What was different about it? I had a mom. One who supposedly loved me. And then one day, I woke up and she was gone."

"She chose to leave you."

"And that's supposed to make me feel *better?*" Lindsey asked, suddenly angry. "You think just because your husband's life was taken away that it's different than what happened to me? At least you knew your husband loved you. My mom *chooses* not to love me. She *chooses* not to call me. She *chooses* not to have a darn thing to do with me and if you think I'm supposed to feel better about that because at least she didn't *die,* you're wrong."

"Lindsey—"

"No," Lindsey said, stomping her foot. "Don't try and say something stupid like you know better than me about this stuff. Or how hard it is when someone dies. It's hard on me, too. In fact, it sucks. But you want to know what sucks even more? This whole time I was thinking you were a better person than my mother, but you know what? You're not. At least my mom had the guts to leave me for someone she thought she loved. Yeah, it hurt that she loved that guy more than she loved me. But I still *get* it. I don't get how someone could be afraid to love my dad."

"I never said that. And that's not what this is about."

"Yes, it is. And you don't have to say you're afraid. I *know* that's what you are. But you know what? My daddy is the best man on earth, and if you're too afraid to love him then forget it. You don't deserve him."

Turn Out the Lights...
By Rick Stevenson, Sports Editor

I know I'm not the only one out there saddened by the demise of single car race teams. I've heard from enough of you to know that, like you, I miss the days of one-car teams doing their best to win the year-end championship, but then, I've never made a secret of my old-fashioned sentiments.

I am sad, however, to see Newman Motorsports swallowed up by BI Motorsports.

I truly thought that Becca Newman, as owner of one of the few remaining single car teams, was uniquely poised to survive the multicar conglomerates. I should have known better.

Turns out Becca Newman's struggles have been far greater than anyone thought. Will Black, President and CEO of the often cursed Black, Inc. Motorsports, offered to merge with Newman Motorsports to "help them along," or so we're told. I hear differently.

I'm hearing rumors that BIM actually plans to oust Ms. Newman at its first opportunity, which is possible due to the unique nature of the merge. It's not a partnership, folks. It's an investment of capital funds, and that investment comes with the understanding that BIM will manage the funds—and the business.

One hopes this isn't true, but since I'm not privy to the "legalities" of the deal, I have no way of knowing for sure. But one thing I do know: often what starts as a rumor turns out to be truth—at least in this industry.

PART FOUR

To err is human. But to err against another
human is just plain wrong.
                                    —Anonymous

CHAPTER TWENTY-FOUR

"WHAT DO YOU MEAN I'm fired?" Becca heard herself say, the words seeming to come from the other side of the room.

Will Black, the man who'd styled himself as merely "an investor," gave her a look of false pity, one that completely missed the mark thanks to his beady black eyes. "We're letting you go," he said softly.

"But...you can't do that."

"Actually, he can," Will's attorney said, a thin, balding man with John Lennon glasses and a forehead that would make Frankenstein proud.

"As you know, Mr. Black owns controlling interest in the team. Technically, he can do whatever he wants, including firing you for gross negligence."

"Gross negligence," Becca asked, incredulous. "What are you talking about?"

"You released Adam Drake," Cross answered. "A driver who had enormous potential and whom

Mr. Black had high hopes of grooming to be his team's next star."

"*His* team," Becca said, still looking at Will. "This isn't *his* team," Becca said, standing. Her black, knee-length skirt rode up her thighs, but she didn't care. "This was *my* team. You're lending me money as a partner. As a friend. Not as my boss."

"Becca," Will said softly, "you must admit your decision was a poor one."

She could tell he was trying hard to pretend he felt bad about all this. But she knew better. She saw the spark in his eyes, one that he couldn't quite hide. Self-satisfaction. Greed. It hung on his face like the Grim Reaper's grimace.

"Perhaps, but it's my decision."

"Actually, we feel differently," Cross said.

"Well, that's too bad."

"Ms. Newman, we don't want this to get ugly, but we're prepared to do whatever it takes to enforce our position."

"And how are you going to do that?"

"By having you forcibly removed, if need be," Mr. Cross said. "And then using the courts to enforce our position."

"You can't do that."

"Actually, we can," Cross said. "But feel free to fight us…in a court of law."

"You know I can't afford that."

Mr. Cross shrugged. Will Black looked anywhere but at her.

And the truth hit Becca like a slap in the face.

"You meant to do this from the very beginning, didn't you?" Becca asked. "When you came to me all those weeks ago, this is what you were planning."

"Of course not," he said, sitting up straighter at the same time he tugged his jacket over his stomach. "You know how much I care for you."

"Don't hand me that bull. You don't care about anybody but yourself. The Chase for the year-end championship is almost over. You've got only four races left to get your driver to the top and you'll do it by whatever means possible."

"I don't know what you're talking about."

"Tell me you don't plan on immediately removing and replacing my new Cup driver, and that you didn't plan this all along as a way of giving yourself an edge over the competition once The Chase started."

"Well, that's a given," William said. "I have to do what's best for BI Motorsports."

"And what about what's best for *me?*" she asked.

"This is business, Becca. Nothing more," Will said.

"Oh, yeah? So now that I've been fired, how will I pay you back? That seems like a poor business move."

And then a sudden thought hit her, one that had her reeling. "Wait a second. You're going to start dismantling *all* my teams, aren't you?" She leaned against her desk, voice lowered. "I'll make no money that way. No winners' purses. No souvenir sales. That's what you planned all along, isn't it? Get her to sign over controlling interest of the team and then shut her down."

"Becca—"

"And as an added bonus you'd then have another driver out there to help you win The Chase. Someone who'll run interference if your Cup driver gets in a tight spot. Someone to draft with. Someone to scuff tires. You're all set. You've got the cars already built and the driver set to go, now all you need is to get me out of the way."

"That's not how it is," Mr. Cross said.

"Yes, it is," she said, leaning back and shaking her head, her dark gray suit coat pulling against her shoulders. "I've been in this business long enough to know that's *exactly* how it is. I'm just disgusted with myself that I didn't see it coming. 'I want to help you,'" she mimicked Will Black. "'We'll be a team.'" She curled her lip. "I should have known better. Immoral assholes like you are rampant in the industry."

"Ms. Newman," Mr. Cross said. "There's no reason to start calling anyone names. You have no evidence my client has plans to dismantle your teams—"

"*Names?* If I were calling him *names,* I'd tell him he's the biggest rat-faced liar that ever walked the earth."

"Becca," Will said, sounding aghast. But she didn't buy it. He wasn't surprised. He'd done exactly as she accused. And he was a *bad* actor.

"Don't worry, gentlemen," she said softly, the word "gentlemen" drawled out for effect. "I won't cause a scene. I'll leave quickly and quietly, just like you want, but this isn't over."

"We don't expect you to go," the attorney said. "We're prepared to offer you a job on the administrative side of things."

"Doing what? Typing payroll checks? I don't think so."

"You don't have to leave," Will said again, but he sounded like a teenager trying to convince a parent not to leave him alone for the night.

She leaned across her desk again. "Yes, I do, and you know it. Just like you and I both know the truth about what went down here."

"You can still be involved with the team," Will said. "You're still a part of Newman Motorsports."

"Right," she said, straightening her own suit before taking out her keys. "My lawyers will be in touch."

She slammed the door, getting down the hall on pure anger, anger and the sickening lump in her stomach that made her want to puke.

But one look at Sylvia's face and all her bravado faded.

"Ms. Newman," she said, tears in her eyes.

"You know?"

"It was in Rick Stevenson's column this morning," she explained, her eyes growing red around the edges as she fought back tears. "I didn't think it was true, but then they showed up and I heard you yelling and—"

"It turned out to be true," Becca finished for her.

Sylvia nodded, then got up from her desk saying, "Ms. Newman—"

"No, don't," Becca said, holding out a hand. "There's no need to cry. I'll be back."

"Do you think so?"

"I know so," Becca said.

Only she didn't.

She didn't know that at all, she thought, trying to stifle a quick burst of panic.

"But thanks for the support," she said to Sylvia, giving her a hug.

"I'm here if you need anything," her longtime assistant said.

John, her NASCAR Craftsman Truck Series crew chief, stood behind Sylvia.

"Hey, what's going on here?" she asked. "Y'all act like you'll never see me again."

"Ms. Newman," he said, his blue work shirt stained with grease and other things. "I'm so sorry—"

"Don't be," she said, giving him a gamine smile. "I'm going to fight this, damn it."

"And in the meantime we'll be racing our hearts out for you," he said, coming forward to give her a hug, too. "Until you're back."

He smelled of oil and cleaning solvent, and he probably transferred grease onto her suit, but she didn't care. She hugged him tight.

It was that way her whole way out of the complex. Someone would stop her—Connie; Brian, the truck series spotter who worked on chassis during the day; Chris, the rear-end specialist; and right behind them would be someone else. By the time she made it to the front doors Becca felt dizzy from the effort of holding everything inside because the truth of the matter was, she wasn't at all convinced she could fight this. Will Black was crafty and he knew she didn't have the money to fight him. He *knew* it.

The realization made her want to throw up.

But she was proud of herself, because when she left Newman Motorsports, she left with her head held high.

No one noticed when she broke down inside her car.

CHAPTER TWENTY-FIVE

She decided to sell the house. If she wanted to fight Will, she'd need the money, so she really didn't have a choice. She'd long since sold off every other piece of property she had. Her home was the only thing left, and even that she didn't own free and clear. She'd be lucky to walk away with enough money to hire an attorney and rent an apartment.

And it was her own damn fault.

She'd put herself in this financial position, first by using the money she'd gotten when Randy died to expand the teams, and then when sponsors had proven scarce, mortgaging the properties she owned to see her through. She'd been hedging her bets. Hoping things would turn around. They never had and so now here she was.

Maybe she really was incompetent.

Of course, once word got around, her phone started to ring. Cece and Blain offered to bail her out. But she'd only be getting deeper and deeper into debt. It was time she stopped doing that. And if part of those consequences was walking away from the team until she sorted it all out, so be it.

But her first meeting with her attorney didn't go all that well, for while there was no official "termination" clause in her loan documents, the simple truth was that Will had the money to fight her in court—and she didn't.

So she retreated to her house once more, wondering what to do and if she'd finally lost her race team, a thought that was truly incomprehensible.

She'd had the house on the market less than a week and already there'd been a buyer, someone who wanted to close escrow within thirty days. That was good because she could use the money. Her mortgage was due. Her attorney wanted his retainer. And her first payment to that lying, thieving William Black was due, too, Becca thought, sitting on the bench swing Randy had strung beneath the picturesque branches of a giant maple. The tree's leaves scattered around her, creating a yellow sea. She flicked at some of those leaves with her toe, snuggling deep into her off-white sweater to ward off the evening chill.

Three more weeks, she thought, looking out at the cove that hugged the edge of her property, the pines and oaks and aspens that she loved so much casting shadows on the ground.

God, she would miss this.

"Hello, Becca."

She flinched, but to be honest, she wasn't all that surprised he was here.

"How are you?"

She turned to face Adam. "How do you think I'm doing?"

He looked good. And worried.

She had to turn away.

"Probably not all that good," he said. "At least if the rumors are true."

Becca took a deep breath, steeled herself before turning back to him again. It was hard, but she forced her gaze up.

"Most of the time they are."

"You look tired," he said.

She released an exasperated huff of breath. "I've been packing, getting the house ready—"

Dreaming about you.

"You've been having panic attacks?"

She drew back, surprised by the question for some reason. "How do you know?"

"Cece told me."

She shook her head, glancing out over the cove again. "I'm fine."

"You've been pacing the house at night, unable to sleep, keeping Michelle up—"

Once again she swung back to face him. "She told you that, too?"

He smiled a bit, his own eyes shifting to the cove. She watched as his gaze darted around, the smile turning suddenly sad. "How are you going to leave it all?"

Game over. She was tired of dancing around issues. "I was just asking myself that same question."

He came toward her. Becca tensed, thinking he meant to touch her again, her pulse skittering into high gear at just the thought.

"You don't have to leave," he said, keeping his distance.

She closed her eyes for a second, taking a deep breath—and smelling him. "I'm not going to accept help from Cece and Blain. Nor Lance and Sarah Cooper." Both of whom had called and offered their support.

"There are others who would help, too. You're not without friends in this industry."

He smelled so good. She kept her eyes closed, inhaling his scent, memorizing it.

"I know that, Adam. But I need to do this on my own." She turned, forcing a smile to her face.

"Ironic, isn't it? You get your foot in the door right as I'm forced to make an exit."

"Don't leave."

"I'm trying not to."

"You're going to win this battle."

"Maybe. Maybe not," she said, the swing gently rocking back and forth. "Maybe it's time for me to get out of this business, anyway. Maybe I should have done that a long time ago."

"Don't say that."

But as she said the words, for the first time she wondered if they were true. "Thanks for coming over," she said, trying to change the subject.

"You knew I would."

And still he didn't move nearer. She waited for him to do it, though in truth, she didn't know what she'd do if he did. But he didn't.

"Adam, I'm—" She swallowed, swiped a lock of hair away from her face. The sun had started to go down, a slight breeze kicking up as it always did this time of day. "I'm sorry about…everything."

"I'm not."

Her gaze jerked to his, Becca wondering if this was it. If this was when he'd take her into her arms.

"I'm not sorry for anything that happened. You're a wonderful woman, Becca. I'm just sorry it didn't work out."

Didn't work out. Was that what happened? Was theirs a relationship like so many others out there? The kind that just "didn't work out"? She didn't know. That was part of her conflict. She didn't know what they'd had. Except love. Yes, definitely love. They'd had that and more. *Lindsey.*

"How is Lindsey?"

He smiled, his first genuine smile since she'd seen him standing there above her. "She's fine. Excited about my race this weekend."

Becca could imagine. "You're racing in a Cup race this weekend, aren't you?"

"I'm going to try. Who knows if I'll actually succeed at qualifying. Cup racing is a whole 'nother ball game." A ball game she'd struck herself out of.

"I'm sure you'll do great," she said. A part of her wishing she could be there. But she wouldn't go back. Not until this thing with Will Black was over, for better or worse. "Cece told me you are. It's a pity you can't do any more truck races without ruining your chance for rookie of the year next season."

"Yeah, but next year I'll be able to do a full schedule."

"And probably end up winning that title."

"From your lips to God's ears."

"It'll happen, Adam. You're good."

"Not good enough."

"Sure you are," she said, stuffing her hands in her sleeves. The wind was cold.

"Not good enough for you."

She turned toward him, his words startling her so much she couldn't speak for a moment. "Is that what you think?"

"What am I supposed to think?"

That I'm a coward. That my life fell apart four years ago and I haven't been able to get it back. That I'm afraid of loving you. Afraid that you'll leave me. Like Randy.

"Not that," she said. "Please, Adam, don't think that. You're the best man I've ever met."

"Aside from Randy."

She swallowed again, tears suddenly rimming her eyes. "Aside from Randy," she said, smiling up at him.

He nodded, just once, her words seeming to be what he'd come to hear. "I better get going," he said. "I just came by to—"

She waited, breath held, waited for…

What?

"Came by to see how you were doing."

"I'm fine," she repeated again softly.

No. I'm not. I'm not fine. I've lost everything,

even the house, the house I shared with Randy. I'm not fine.

"Goodbye, Becca."

And why didn't he *see* that?

"Goodbye, Adam."

He turned to her. She thought he might—but, no, he just gave her a quick smile, turning away. She watched him turn to climb back up the knoll, the late evening sun casting an orange glow over his sweater. She almost turned away, but something made her stand there, something that built up inside of her and made her feel—

What?

But then he was gone.

SHE BLOCKED HIM from her mind. She had no choice, because the other option—the one that involved thinking about him every second of every day—wasn't really an option at all.

But the routine of racing clung to her. She knew intuitively that it was Wednesday, and that the NASCAR Craftsman Truck Series haulers would be arriving. On Thursday she knew practice was going on. Friday was the day she dreaded most, particularly that Friday, because she knew Adam would be practicing a NASCAR NEXTEL Cup Series car. And even though she told herself she wouldn't watch, she still kept a TV plugged into the family room wall. Still turned it on, the familiar sound of racing engines humming in the background.

He qualified fifteenth.

She shouldn't have been surprised. While it wasn't the pole, it was still a pretty amazing accomplishment.

And you shouldn't be watching him do it, either.

But she couldn't seem to stop herself. Besides, the not knowing was worse than the watching.

So she watched. She watched him during Saturday's morning practice and she watched him during Happy Hour—the final practice of the weekend. And even though she told herself she didn't care, she found herself listening for mention of Will Black's drivers. That was how she learned how close BI Motorsports was to winning its first championship. She knew then that she would watch the race on Sunday.

What she didn't know was how that one race would change her life.

"YOU READY FOR THIS?" Blain asked as he handed Adam his helmet.

"I'm ready," Adam said, taking the thing from him.

"And just so you know, nobody expects you to

go out there and kick ass. This is your first Cup race and plenty of people are wondering what the hell we're doing here and so you can take it easy. But you should know that Cece and I believe in you, Adam. So go on out there and show them what you've got. Just stay safe."

"I'll be fine," Adam said, popping in his ear-pieces and then pulling on his helmet, the bottom settling near his HANS device.

He'd be fine.

For Becca's sake.

But not because he had something to prove to her. He'd long since proven he could drive, and drive well. No. He owed her what he was about to do.

"Stay safe," Blain radioed again, tapping him on the helmet before closing up the safety net.

Oh, he planned to stay safe. It was Terry Russell that needed to watch out.

Terry Russell. Pilot of the number thirty-three car, and BI Motorsports's star driver. All he had to do was finish the race in fifteenth place or better and the championship was his.

Not if Adam had anything to say about it.

It was dirty pool. Unethical. Blain would miss out on winnings.

Blain would understand.

William Black had stolen Becca's team. Oh, sure, she still owned forty percent of it—in theory. But everyone in racing knew Mr. Black planned to wrest that away from her, too. He'd already started dropping hints about "consolidating" his two teams. Oh, no. Payback was a bitch and this bitch was about to slap Will Black in the face.

"Start 'em up."

He didn't plan to throw the race, he thought as he started his engine, the sound of the crowd audible even over the sudden roar of the motor. Oh, no. He'd just make damn sure Terry finished no better than sixteenth.

"They're rolling off," his spotter said.

Adam tightened his hand around the wheel. Terry's yellow-and-white car sat three rows ahead of him. Son of a bitch had outqualified him. That had pissed him off so bad he'd almost lost his cool yesterday.

He'd calmed down now.

"Go, Dad!"

Lindsey's voice. Adam queued the mic. "This one's for you, buttercup."

"Buttercup?" she said back, sounding like the teenager she would one day be. "Ugh. Don't call me *buttercup*."

"What would you like me to call you?"

"Princess of the Garage will do nicely."

He bit back a laugh. "Yes, Your Highness," he said, turning his head to the side a bit when he passed his pit box. And there she was, Lindsey's red hair visible even from beneath her ball cap.

"I'm proud of you, Dad," she said as he drove by.

"Thanks, Princess of the Garage."

He caught the tail end of her laughter. "Don't do anything I wouldn't do."

Ah, yes. There it was again: proof that his daughter was way too smart for her own good.

"Roger that," he said, his car picking up speed as he shifted through the gears. But he wasn't going to do anything illegal, per se. All he'd do was rattle Terry's chain. Get his goat a bit—if he was given the chance. The rest was in God's hands.

And Adam firmly believed God was on his side.

"Ready to go green," his spotter said a few minutes later.

In the stands, sixty-five thousand people got to their feet and in the infield, people did the same. Adam could see the multicolored masses wave their hands, flags and anything else they happened to have, the effect as colorful as the Las Vegas marquee outside.

"Green flag. Go, go, go."

Adam went, and there was no rush of adrenaline, no burst of sudden fear—just a calm sense of determination.

"Clear high," the spotter said.

Adam hadn't even realized he'd passed somebody. He had his eyes firmly planted on the back end of thirty-three, the yellow-and-white body flashing in and out of traffic. He didn't hear the sound of the wind against the frame of his car. He didn't feel the back end sliding out from under him, his car far looser than he'd like. He didn't notice any of it. All he wanted to do was get to Terry's car. Then they'd see what happened.

It took him less than twenty laps to do it.

His foot lifted off the gas, working the clutch and brake as they went into turns one and two. Should he take him out? Nah. He couldn't do that. Terry Russell might be an arrogant prick who thought he was God's gift to team owners, but Adam didn't want to risk his life. No. What was needed was a good old-fashioned bumping and nudging. The kind that would piss him off and maybe destroy his concentration. Adam hoped.

So he closed in on his opponent, bringing his nose right up against his back end.

It was at that point that Adam realized he had a pretty good car.

"Damn," he found himself saying to whomever was listening. "This is kind of fun."

"You're hotter than oil on a Victoria's Secret model," his crew chief said.

"Well, someone better tell this boy to get out of the way."

He took his car closer to Terry's back end, drafting him for a bit and then drifting to the right so the guy could see him.

"Hi," Adam said, lifting his hand, but he didn't open his mic. "Do you know me? I'm the guy who used to date the woman your boss screwed over. I know that's not your fault, but I'm still pissed as hell and so I'm sorry for what I'm about to do."

Adam swung back up the track as they entered a turn, his head feeling as if it weighed a couple hundred pounds as he fought the Gs. His tires wanted to move right, and Adam had to jerk the wheel repeatedly to keep it behind the thirty-three.

Okay, so maybe he was a little tight. He could deal with that.

They shot out of the turn. Adam waited until they were just about through it before tapping Terry's bumper.

Terry's ass end broke loose.

Adam grinned. But the boy held on to it. That was okay because Adam was certain he'd caught his attention, and that he was pissed off real good. And Will Black. He hoped Black was up in his suite jumping around like Yosemite Sam.

He let his car get closer once again, drifting up the track to the right and taking the air of the thirty-three's spoiler.

Terry almost lost control again.

Cool, Adam thought. This might be easier than he thought. And actually, Terry was playing right into his hands. He didn't want to get out of the way and so Adam was perfectly within his rights to do whatever he could to get him to move. But the truth was he had a better car than Terry's and if he had truly wanted to pass, he could have.

But he kept seeing the look on Becca's face as she sat beneath that maple tree.

He backed off once again, but not before seeing the middle finger Terry waved at him. Oh, yeah, Adam could just hear it now.

That damn rookie came up behind me and drove me straight into the wall. I'm a championship contender. What the hell is he thinking?

I'm thinking of Becca Newman.

He drifted even farther back. But only for half

a lap. He waited for the perfect moment before making a run on him—right as they entered turn three. They were the only two cars around, the front runners having long since pulled away, the nearest pack of cars ten car-lengths back. Perfect.

"Howdy," Adam said as he ducked down low, alongside the white-and-yellow car in less than two seconds. Two more seconds and he was nearly in front of him. Five seconds later and he heard the word *Clear*.

Time to move in front of him.

He let his car drift up the track, smoothly positioning himself in front of the thirty-three's nose. But once there, he checked up a bit, not much, but enough that Terry would have to slow down, too.

"Get a good look," he told him. "This is the last time you'll see my ass end."

Because he was done messing with the guy. His anger had faded. The rush of racing had soothed his inner demons. He was still pissed as hell at Mr. William Black, but he wouldn't take it out on his driver anymore.

He put his foot into it.

Terry Russell stayed with him.

That was interesting. Maybe he'd lit a fire under the guy's butt.

It became obvious that's exactly what he'd

done because as they approached turn one, Terry came right back at him, Adam's spotter calmly reporting he was still there, Terry thrusting his nose into Adam's rear bumper right as they entered the turn.

Adam felt his car begin to turn.

"Oh, you—" He fought it. Hand clenched, heart pounding, he fought for control, his backside fishtailing wildly, Terry blowing on by the right as they left turn two.

Tit for tat.

Score one off the little guy.

Mashing down the accelerator, Adam aimed for the thirty-three's back bumper. But he didn't have a good run on him thanks to nearly spinning out.

"You okay?"

"Fine," Adam clipped out. "But that guy's going down." Because even though Adam had started it, he didn't like being passed. Not now. Not ever.

"We've received a warning from NASCAR to take it easy. That's Terry Russell you're battling with and he's poised to win the championship."

"I know exactly who he is," Adam said, his eyes narrowed as he fought to catch up. "*And* who his owner is," he emphasized. "If that's not reason enough *not* to take it easy on him, I don't know what is."

"Adam," his crew chief said gravely, "don't do anything stupid."

He pressed the mic button on the steering wheel and said, "I'm just gonna race him, Rob. That's all."

"I know. I know. But keep your nose clean."

Five laps ago he might have said, "Roger," to that comment, but that was before Russell tried to put him into the wall again, and the way he did it— not just checking up slightly as Adam had done earlier, but majorly stomping on the brake. Adam had nearly gone into the wall to avoid hitting him.

His hands tightened on the steering wheel, his eyes fixed on the yellow-and-white car. He willed himself to get closer, battling a car that was turning awful tight as the laps wore on.

"The twenty-one's coming," his spotter said.

Lance Cooper. In the back of his mind, Adam registered his teammate's presence, but at the moment he was too intent on catching the thirty-three to worry about it.

Another lap passed. Then another. Until finally, *finally* he caught Terry at the exact spot he'd almost gone into the wall, and this time Adam didn't check up as he entered the turn. This time he let his nose smash into Terry's bumper.

Terry almost lost it.

"Payback's a bitch," Adam said as this time, he took the inside line.

But the guy managed to hold on to it. *Impressive,* Adam thought as they were suddenly side by side, the Plexiglas duct on Adam's left side whistling angrily as air from Terry's car hit the edges of it.

"Outside," his spotter said calmly.

He fought to stay ahead.

"Still outside."

Terry ducked his car down low. Adam heard metal grind against metal. He cursed, tried to duck right. Too tight. They collided again.

"Still outside."

I know that! Adam wanted to yell, but he was too damn busy trying to keep his car on the track. He moved down lower. The sound of screeching metal stopped just as they entered turn three.

And then Terry was gone.

"What happened?" But he hadn't queued his mic and so it was a rhetorical question. He looked in his mirror just in time to see Terry hit the wall, Lance Cooper's front end right about where Terry's back end used to be.

"Did I do that?" Adam asked.

A second later his spotter said, "Yellow flag."

"Did I do that?" Adam asked again.

"Negative," his crew chief said. "Lance Cooper sent him into the wall."

CHAPTER TWENTY-SIX

THEY'D TAKEN TERRY OUT.

Becca stared at the TV screen, watching the replay of the wreck over and over again.

"That's a real pity," the announcers were saying. "Terry Russell needed to finish fifteenth or better in order to clinch the championship. Now he'll be lucky to finish at all."

They'd taken Terry out.

Or had they? Adam had been racing Terry Russell pretty hard, but he hadn't done anything wrong until Russell had tried to send him into the wall. And Lance might have just gotten a good run on Terry, hit him in the back bumper by accident.

Yeah, right.

Damn it. She wished she were at the track. Wished she were listening in. She'd know for sure then if what she'd just seen was payback.

"Let's watch it again," one of the announcers said.

Becca leaned closer to the TV, the sole piece of furniture left in the nearly vacant house. There was Adam, ducking down low. And here came Lance.

Boom.

"That looked intentional," one of the commentators said.

"Yeah, and we're getting word now of some radio chatter that might confirm this was more than hard racing. Have we got that audio?"

"We've received a warning from NASCAR to take it easy. That's Terry Russell you're battling with and he's poised to win the championship."

"I know exactly who he is. And who his owner is. If that's not reason enough not to take it easy on him, I don't know what is."

She clapped her hands to her face.

"My word," the announcer said. "That makes it sound as if Adam Drake was on a mission."

"Maybe he was," said another announcer. "For those of you in the audience that don't know, Adam Drake used to work for Becca Newman, owner of Newman Motorsports. Newman Motorsports was just taken over by BI Motorsports in what industry insiders call NASCAR's first hostile takeover of another race team. It would appear Adam Drake took that takeover personally. Maybe even went after Terry Russell in retribution."

"And we're receiving word now that NASCAR wants to talk to Mr. Drake after the race," said the first announcer.

Oh, jeez. That couldn't be good. They'd come down on Adam hard if they thought he'd taken Terry out on purpose.

But the fact remained that he *hadn't* taken him out. Lance Cooper had.

Lance, who loved her like a sister.

Becca stood up, going to her living room window. Her feet echoed in the empty room, the TV still playing in the background.

If that's not reason enough not *to take it easy...*

She kept hearing the words. And the inflections behind them. *If that's not reason enough,* he'd said, a wealth of emotion put into those five simple words.

She covered her face with her hands.

"You gonna sit here in this big empty house and watch that race all day?"

She turned. Michelle stood there, the housekeeper refusing to leave her side even though Becca couldn't afford to pay her now. "No, actually. Tell the movers to come and get it." She smiled tremulously. "I've got someone to see."

"NASCAR WANTS TO SEE YOU," Rob said after dropping the safety net.

"I know," Adam answered, wiggling out of the

car. He was covered in sweat, Miami's humid air actually feeling cool against his head.

"Not bad for a rookie," someone said.

Adam looked. Lance Cooper walked toward him, his blond head sweaty, his orange firesuit hard to miss even with all the people milling around pit road.

"Twelfth place," he said. "I'm impressed."

"Don't be. I had a good car. Probably should have won it."

"Yeah, but you had some damage," Lance said, eyes twinkling. "Thanks to our friend Terry Russell."

"Yeah. Thanks for saving my ass," Adam said, holding out his hand.

"My pleasure."

They shook hands, both of them exchanging a secret smile because Adam knew by now that Lance had taken Russell out on purpose. Lance apparently confessed all to his crew chief who, in turn, had told Rob. Of course they were all sworn to secrecy.

Becca Newman had been avenged.

"You're headed to the NASCAR trailer, too, I hear."

Lance nodded just as his wife tackled him with a hug—which, given that she was pregnant, was quite a sight. "You did it," she cried excitedly. "You took the championship away from BI Motorsports!"

"Shh," Lance warned, looking down at Sarah with tender impatience mixed with love. "It was one of them racing deals, remember?"

"Oh, yeah, right," she said, long, reddish brown hair bobbing as she nodded. "I'll get the lingo down sooner or later."

"I know you will," Lance said, bending and kissing her.

Adam had to look away.

"You ready?" Lance asked, looking over at him.

"Ready," Adam answered and Rob and the boys began to push his car back toward postrace inspection.

"Off to get your wrists slapped, huh?" Sarah said. "You know, I used to be a kindergarten teacher and so I might be pretty good at wrist slapping. You think maybe NASCAR will let me do it to you?"

"I don't know," Lance said. "But that might be kind of fun. If they say no, maybe we can do it later."

The both chuckled as, in the grandstand, the crowd started to cheer and Adam knew they were crowning the new champion. One day maybe he'd be there. For now he was happy with a twelfth-place finish.

Had Becca seen?

He doubted it. Right now she was probably locked in that house of hers, staring at pictures of Randy as she packed.

He shook his head, telling himself he should just move on, but unable to do so. Because even though she might stare at pictures of her dead husband, Adam still loved Becca Newman.

He would always love Becca Newman.

BUT IN REALITY, Becca wasn't staring at a picture of Randy. She was staring at his grave.

"Hey there," she said softly.

It was the same thing she said to him every time she visited, Becca standing in the exact same spot—exactly in front of the gray marble headstone. It was a beautiful day. The kind of day that came after heavy rain. Crystal blue skies and a clear horizon, the trees around the twenty-acre park washed clean by the heavy drops.

And as she always did when she came to visit, she closed her eyes, tipped her head back, trying to see if she could "hear" Randy as she stood there. But, of course, she never could.

The pain of his loss washed over her yet again.

She opened her eyes and stared at the headstone with his name and date of death chiseled into the surface. That was all the headstone said. No outline of a race car. No verse of scripture. At the time of his death, she'd stopped believing in God. She'd directed all her anger toward the heavens and by the time she saw reason, it was too late.

"Bet you're glad I didn't get the headstone that played music, though, huh?"

But her smile faded as she stood there, the wet grass oozing moisture through the leather soles of suede half boots.

"I've come to say goodbye, Randy," she confessed, and though she tried to hold them back, a tear still managed to escape the confines of her lashes. "I didn't mean to fall in love with Adam, I really didn't," she confessed, her voice clogged with tears. "It just sort of happened. I turned around one day and there he was."

She inhaled sharply, tipping her head back and looking up at the sky. A breeze kicked up and she tucked her hands beneath the lapel of her brown, suede jacket. "I fought it, Randy," she told the sky. "You know I did. I didn't want to love anybody else but you. I only ever wanted to love you. From the moment we met in high school, right up until the day you died, you were it for me."

The tears fell faster now, the moisture on her face chilled by the breeze. "But I can't do it anymore," she said softly. "I can't go it alone. God knows I tried," she said with a self-deprecating laugh. "And look at what a mess I've made of things. Your team's in William Black's hands and I've lost just about everything we owned."

She closed her eyes again, her heart pounding in a way that usually meant one of those anxiety attacks was coming on. But instead of fighting against the panic, she embraced it. Welcomed it. Told it she wasn't afraid of it anymore.

She had Adam.

"I love him," she said, her nails digging into her palms. "I love him and I need him. All that hogwash about not wanting to lose myself was just that. Hogwash. I was just afraid. But I'm not anymore. He needs me and his little girl needs me. Lindsey. That's her name. And she's the most wonderful little girl. You would have loved her."

She felt peace.

It stole across her suddenly, calming her, soothing her pulse like the touch of a mother's hand—a feeling, rather than spoken words

I understand.

"I miss you," she said through a throat gone thick. "I'll always miss you. But it's time for me to move on. I realized that while watching Adam race. All this time I've been afraid of letting go. Afraid that if I lost the memory of you, I'd lose everything. But you know what, I've already lost everything and that's all right. It's really, truly all right. I'm going to be okay. You're not here by my side anymore, but I'm going to be okay, with or without our race team. And *that's* what I came here to say."

The deep breath she took helped to fortify her shoulders, helped her to stand up straighter as she moved her gaze to the gravestone once again. "I love you, Randy. There's a spot in my heart that will never stop loving you. But there's room in my heart for another man. And for a little girl. I hope you understand."

I do.

And this time it truly sounded as if someone had spoken. The words were so clear in her head, so undeniably Randy's voice that she almost turned. But there was no one around, and it was time now, she knew.

"Goodbye."

Time to go home, she thought as she turned away. Home to Adam and Lindsey.

CHAPTER TWENTY-SEVEN

LINDSEY ALWAYS HATED that her birthday was in November.

Every year it was the same old story. "I would have gotten you more, but Christmas is right around the corner."

That's what her dad always said. And even though she knew that the real reason why she didn't get a lot of presents was because her dad couldn't afford them, it still bugged her. Not because she didn't get a lot of gifts. That wasn't it at all. It was just that Christmas always stole her thunder.

But not this year.

Oh, no, she thought, pulling on the swanky new jeans that her dad had bought her the day before, fancy flowers and swirl patterns sewn around the cuff. Today was going to be special, because for the first time in her life she was going to have a birthday party at her house.

Got it?

Her *house*.

Her dad had bought the beautiful three-bedroom home less than a month ago, compliments of the pay raise given to him by the Sanderses. For the first time in their lives they weren't hurting for money. They had a new car out in the driveway and there were a bunch of new friends coming over from her new school—friends who didn't make her life hell like Frances Pritchert. Even Brandy was coming from Tennessee. Lindsey couldn't wait to show off her new things.

"You coming down anytime soon?" her dad asked from the doorway.

Lindsey shrieked, holding the new shirt she'd been about to slip over her head in front of her. "Da-ad. I'm getting dressed."

"Then why'd you leave the door open?"

"I thought you were outside getting things ready."

"Well, obviously I'm not."

"Duh," she said, clutching the shirt with one hand and trying to shoo him away with the other. "Leave me alone."

"I'm not leaving."

"You have to."

"Not until I give you something."

"Oh, yeah?" she asked, visually searching for a clue as to what it was. She didn't see anything, which meant it might be money. Cool.

"I'll turn around so you can finish dressing."

"Thanks," she said, tugging the super cute new shirt over her head. It was totally awesome with its flared sleeves and tie-dyed pattern on the front. "Okay, done," she said, flicking her hair over her shoulders.

"I think I'm having a sixties flashback."

"Dad. You weren't even alive in the sixties."

"No, but I know how they dressed."

She snorted. "Right. Like you know anything about fashion."

"You might be surprised," he said.

Lindsey was happy. The feeling stole over her suddenly, probably because she was standing in her very own room decorated exactly like Raven's bedroom on TV, right down to the bright orange-and-blue beanbags, a room that was in their very own house—no more having to hear the neighbors, *thank you, Lord*—and her dad looked happy, happy for the first time since that loser Becca Newman had thrown him over.

"Come here," her dad said.

Lindsey crossed the room and sank into his arms. Happy. That's what she was. And that's what her dad was, too, even if sadness did steal across his face from time to time.

"I love you, Dad."

"I love you, too," he said softly, then gently drew back. She watched as he fished something from his pocket. It wasn't money, darn it, but it looked to be—

"A lug nut?" Her brows lifted to her hairline.

"Not just any lug nut," he said. "This here is one very special, gen-u-ine, bonafide lug nut from my very first Craftsman Truck Series race."

"Neat," Lindsey said, trying hard to sound enthusiastic.

"I even bought you a gold chain to dangle it from. I bet your new friends will think it's pretty cool."

"I bet," Lindsey said, mentally putting a finger down her throat.

"Of course, if it's not your cup of tea, you might like this better." He reached to his left, grabbing something hidden by the wall to the side of the door. A painting, she thought. Great.

He turned it around.

Lindsey gasped, her hands going to her cheeks.

"Oh, Dad."

Matted beneath a black frame were pictures. She and her dad at the track when she was six. She and her dad working on a car together. A picture she'd taken when she was seven and pretending to be a model posed atop one of his race cars, and the best picture of all: the two of them in Victory Lane, her arms wrapped around him, a grin on both their faces as they looked into the camera.

"Daddy," she said again, softly this time, her lips pushing out as she fought not to cry.

"I couldn't have done it without you, kiddo."

"Yes, you could have," she said, wiping away tears. Darn it. She was going to cry off the mascara she'd snuck onto her lashes.

"No, I couldn't have," he said, setting the picture down and pulling her into his arms. "And I want to thank you *so* much. You're the best daughter a dad could ever ask for."

"Thanks," she said on a sniff.

"Of course, if you don't like that, I also have a hundred dollars to give you."

She drew back, eyes wide. "You do?"

"Is that mascara you're wearing?"

"Nope," she said, ducking out of his arms. "Thanks for the picture, Dad. I'll hang it in my room."

She headed for the stairs, only to draw up short when she saw *her* standing at the bottom.

Becca Newman.

"Hi, guys," she said softly.

Lindsey could tell her dad had seen her, too, even though he stood behind her. A glance back revealed that she was right. He drew himself up, seeming to grow taller in just a split second.

She turned back to Becca saying, "What are you doing here?"

"Actually," Becca said, "I came to see both of you."

And Lindsey's heart leaped, because there was a look in Becca's eyes, a look that made Lindsey think—

"But if this is a bad time…"

"No, no," Lindsey said, doing a complete reversal of opinion because she was certain, well, *almost* certain that Becca was here to patch things up with her dad. "We're just getting ready for my birthday party. But we've still got a few minutes before people start to arrive."

"Is that why the door was open?" Becca asked. "I thought someone had forgotten to close it, but it's your birthday?"

"Yup," Lindsey said, suddenly grinning from ear to ear. She had a feeling she was about to receive the best birthday present of all. "You can come if you want."

"Lindsey," her dad warned.

Lindsey glanced up at him. He looked tense. And upset. As if he didn't want Becca around anymore.

What a bunch of bull.

He was still in love with her, Lindsey thought, her hopes soaring. She could see it in his face. He might be glowering down at his former boss, but Lindsey wasn't fooled.

"I'm going outside to check the decorations," she said, bounding down the stairs two at a time. "You can talk to my dad alone."

"But, Lindsey—"

"See ya," Lindsey said, heading toward the back of the house and the sliding glass doors, which she quickly disappeared through.

"But I wanted her to hear this, too," Becca said, glancing up at Adam who still stood at the top of the stairs.

"Hear what?" he asked.

And Becca knew. She knew the time had come to lay it all on the line. She swallowed, took a deep breath, realizing that it was now or never.

"I wanted her to hear how much I love you," she said, clenching her fingers against their trembling. "How much I love you both."

And still he stood there.

"And how sorry I am that I hurt you. That I was too much of a coward to take the love you offered." She had to look away, couldn't keep staring up at him when all he did was stare right back. "I was a fool for asking you to give up racing for me. It was a moment of madness. My only way of trying to control something that couldn't be controlled. That's been my problem all along. I wanted to control you. Out of fear. Fear of letting go," she admitted. "Fear of losing control of my heart when what I should have done was simply give it to you."

She met his gaze again, her eyes rimming with tears. "But I couldn't control it, Adam. I couldn't control my feelings. And so here I stand, still in love with you, only now I'm terrified I'm too late. Terrified that I've driven you away."

At last…at last he came down the steps, slowly, Becca's heart beating faster with every step.

"You shouldn't be afraid," he said stopping right in front of her.

"I shouldn't?"

"No."

He stopped in front of her, arms hanging by his side. She waited, breath held, waited for sign, a look, anything to tell her that she hadn't blown it.

"I love you, Becca."

"Adam," she said, her eyes closing at the same time he drew her into his arms.

"I love you," he said softly. "I never stopped loving you. And I never will."

"Oh, thank God," she said on a sob.

He held her, he held her tight—maybe too tight, but she didn't care. She drew back, his face blurry from between her tears. "I'm so sorry."

"Don't be."

"I can't help myself."

"Then I guess I'll have to think of a way for you to make it up to me."

"I guess you will."

"Yes!" they heard someone murmur. "Yes, yes, yes!"

And when they turned, both Adam and Becca laughed because Lindsey was doing a dance out on the back patio, where she'd apparently been eavesdropping.

"I knew it," they heard her say. "I just knew this would be the best birthday ever."

And you know what? It was.

EPILOGUE

I<small>T WAS THE MURMUR</small> of a voice that woke Becca up, the blissful peace of sleep interrupted by the sound of—Adam?

Darn it, she thought, opening an eye.

"And so the beautiful lady told the prince that he could come to work for her in her castle."

Becca huffed. She turned her head the other direction.

And there they were.

In the corner of their spacious bedroom, a night-light cast a soft glow onto his face and their baby boy's.

"And when the prince went to work in the kind lady's castle he discovered that he'd fallen in love with her." One of his fingers stroked the side of the baby's face, their son looking up at him as if he understood every word. "But when the prince tried to kiss the fair maiden, she wouldn't let him." Adam widened his eyes, leaning toward a bundle swathed in a light blue blanket that rested in the crook of his arm, making a scary face. "Obviously, she hadn't been reading her book of fairy tales."

"Obviously the prince didn't know how to kiss the fair maiden properly," Becca said, sitting up.

Adam's head jerked up, a look of surprise on his face, one that was followed by a grimace of chagrin. "I was trying not to wake you."

"You forget that new moms have the hearing of a bat." She slipped out of bed, one of her thin white sleeves falling off her shoulder. She fixed it absently and went to stand by her husband.

Husband.

After all these months she still couldn't believe it. Nor that she was a mother, Becca thought, staring down at her son. Kevin Joseph Nicholas Drake had been born sometime between the final practice at Richmond and the Saturday night race—which Adam had won—much to everyone's delight. Especially Lindsey's. Becca's stepdaughter didn't know which pleased her more: having a new baby brother or being in Victory Lane again because— as she'd told Becca—she just *knew* the girls from her old school were watching and she hoped they were kicking themselves for being so mean to her.

Becca hoped they had miserable lives for being so mean to her.

"He seemed to like my story," Adam said softly, one of his fingers gently stroking Kevin's face. It amazed her that a man who controlled three thousand pounds of race car on the weekends could handle a child so gently, so tenderly.

"Really?" she asked. "I think he looks a little bored."

"Nah, he's not bored," Adam said with a gentle voice. "He's happy," and his face softened even more. "Just like me."

Their gazes caught and held, Becca's heart doing that strange little thump that it always did whenever Adam looked at her like that.

"I'm happy, too," she said.

"As happy as the day I won rookie of the year?"

"Well, maybe not that happy."

He smiled.

"Will you two be quiet?" came a voice from down the hall.

The both looked toward their bedroom door, as if Lindsey might be standing at the entrance. But of course she wasn't.

"I have a biology test first thing in the morning."

"Then get to sleep," Adam called, Kevin's eyes widening at the sudden noise.

"Yeah, yeah, yeah," they heard down the hall.

Becca smiled inwardly. Her stepdaughter was a handful, but she wouldn't have her any other way.

She glanced back at father and son. Kevin looked about ready to cry, but Adam moved his face right down next to his again, giving him a smile that Becca knew Kevin couldn't see—he was still too young to make out anything more than colors—but that he seemed to understand nonetheless. He gurgled something to his father, his head nesting into the crook of Adam's arm.

Becca's world felt complete. During that moment of time a peace filled her like none she'd felt before. No, not even the day Adam had stood up on the awards ceremony podium and accepted his award for not only Rookie of the Year, but the year-end NASCAR Craftsman Truck Series championship. He hadn't done it for Newman Motorsports, but he'd used the money he'd won to pay back her loan, much to Will Black's chagrin. Her team belonged to her once again, and she had the hottest driver in the business piloting her NASCAR NEXTEL Cup Series car—Adam Drake.

"You forgot to tell him the end of the story," she reminded him.

"I wasn't going to tell him the end, I was going to show him."

"What do you mean?"

He reached a hand up, hooking it behind her neck and drawing her down. Becca closed her eyes, their lips connecting so softly, so tenderly that it brought tears to her eyes.

"Like that," he said a long while later.

"That's a good way to end a story," she said, drawing back a bit to meet the gaze of the man who had changed her life. Who had given her more happiness than she'd ever thought possible. And that had taught her to love again.

"Hmm," he said, the look in his eyes mimicking her own. "Maybe you have been reading your book of fairy tales after all."

"And maybe I'm living one," she said with a soft smile.

"Maybe we both are," he said equally gently.

"People," came a voice down the hall again. "Biology test."

Adam and Becca giggled, and then kissed again, then giggled some more as down the hall, in her *That's So Raven* room, Lindsey smiled.

They were impossible, she thought, snuggling into her covers, a smile on her face.

And they were the best parents in the world.

Well, *most* of the time, anyway.

AUTHOR'S NOTE

As many of you might know, *The Variety Show* I wrote about is based on a real life "talent search" sponsored by Roush Racing. Obviously, I took the liberty of changing a few things (to fit within the confines of my plot), but I tried to offer a realistic and accurate view of what goes on behind the scenes. Any errors are strictly my own.

I hope you enjoyed *ON THE EDGE*, as it is my sincerest pleasure to bring readers stories set in the garages of NASCAR. If you'd like to discover more about my books, drop on by my Web site. I love to give away monthly prizes. And, yes, that is a shameless bribe.

www.pamelabritton.com

All my best,
Pamela

pamela britton

77098	IN THE GROOVE	___ $6.99 U.S.	___ $8.50 CAN.
77035	DANGEROUS CURVES	___ $6.50 U.S.	___ $7.99 CAN.

(limited quantities available)

TOTAL AMOUNT $ _____
POSTAGE & HANDLING $ _____
($1.00 FOR 1 BOOK, 50¢ for each additional)
APPLICABLE TAXES* $ _____
TOTAL PAYABLE $ _____

(check or money order—please do not send cash)

To order, complete this form and send it, along with a check or money order for the total above, payable to HQN Books, to: **In the U.S.:** 3010 Walden Avenue, P.O. Box 9077, Buffalo, NY 14269-9077; **In Canada:** P.O. Box 636, Fort Erie, Ontario, L2A 5X3.

Name: _____
Address: _____ City: _____
State/Prov.: _____ Zip/Postal Code: _____
Account Number (if applicable): _____

075 CSAS

*New York residents remit applicable sales taxes.
*Canadian residents remit applicable GST and provincial taxes.

HQN™

We *are* romance™

www.HQNBooks.com

PHPB0906BL